D1491152

RELATIVE STRANGER

Also by Stewart Lewis

Rockstarlet: A Novel

STEWART LEWIS

a novel

RELATIVE STRANGER

alyson books
NEW YORK

© 2008 BY STEWART LEWIS

MANUFACTURED IN THE UNITED STATES OF AMERICA

THIS TRADE PAPERBACK ORIGINAL IS PUBLISHED BY ALYSON BOOKS
245 WEST 17TH STREET, NEW YORK, NY 10011

DISTRIBUTION IN THE UNITED KINGDOM BY
TURNAROUND PUBLISHER SERVICES LTD.
UNIT 3, OLYMPIA TRADING ESTATE, COBURG ROAD
WOOD GREEN, LONDON N22 6TZ ENGLAND

FIRST EDITION: JULY 2008

08 09 10 11 12 a 10 9 8 7 6 5 4 3 2 1

ISBN-10 1-59350-068-8
ISBN-13 978-1-59350-068-9

LIBRARY OF CONGRESS CATALOGING-IN-PUBLICATION DATA ARE ON FILE.

COVER DESIGN BY VICTOR MINGOVITS

this is for Roman

*"We must be willing to get rid of the life we planned,
so as to have the life that is waiting for us."*
—*Joseph Campbell*

part one

strangers

1

LIFE HAS A WAY OF tricking you. You wake up, you begin your daily rituals, you laugh, you work, you dream, you cry. Then as you crawl into bed at night, you pause for a moment and wonder if that's all there is. No major setbacks, no catastrophes, just the normal course of hours passing into days, weeks, years. Perhaps, secretly, you wish for something cataclysmic to shake up your life, to shatter the familiar earth you walk on.

But in truth you never know what awaits you around the corner. You could suddenly discover that the drama you thought was safely confined to the stage is sitting beside you in the audience—smirking.

———

GARRET REACHED HIS ARM out of the crack in the tanning capsule. He blindly groped around the little table beside him, knocking his pack of Exports and his silver Rolex onto the floor before finding his ringing cell phone.

"Yes?" he said, trying his best to sound as if he were in the middle of something important.

"It's me. Bad moment?"

He could picture Alan on the other end, probably in that ill-fitting tweed sports coat of his. "Not for you, dear. What's up?"

"Our leading lady has arrived," he said, in an ironic and slightly nasal tone. "With an entourage, no less. And get this—she was wearing a fanny pack."

"No."

"It gets worse. It was pea green."

"I suppose it's better than hot pink," Garret said, wondering briefly if it was safe to use a cell phone in a tanning booth.

"Not by much. When's your flight?"

"Two. Listen, I . . ."

"Make sure you bring a sweater. I checked online and London's cold and damp."

"You're my director, Alan, not my mother."

"And I hope that sexy little phone of yours works over there, 'cause we have a show opening on a little street called Broadway in less than a month, and I can feel Mitchell watching over us. What kind of producer goes abroad when his show is about to open?"

"The organized kind who has everything well in hand and complete faith in his director to cover for him while he's gone."

A buzzer went off, and the blue electric warmth that had been bathing Garret's skin faded. He pushed the bed open and stepped out of its giant mouth, stretching his sinewy body.

"What's that sound?" Alan asked. "I thought you said you had meetings all morning?"

"Alan? You there? I think I'm losing you."

———

DRESSED HEAD to toe in Prada and swathed in obscenely priced moisturizer, Garret exited the tanning salon, carrying his black garment bag and a briefcase. He walked across Bleecker Street while trash, leaves, and urbanites of all ethnicities bustled around him. He felt like a small piece of a giant machine, weaving his way, perpetuating a cycle.

He stopped to watch a young couple reluctantly kiss good-bye, noticing the birth of romance in their faces—such a real sense of love that he could almost see them twenty years from now, sharing the afternoon on a porch in the country, the same look in their eyes. It made him a little sick.

As he turned north he saw an old woman struggling to get an immense bag of laundry up her last step. Instinctually, he dropped his bags and ran up to help. Her white hair wisped around her dark face, which appeared to be caving in, despite a brightness in her eyes worthy of a starlet.

"What have you got in here, Stonehenge?" Garret asked, hoisting the bag.

"Oh, how charming, you're British?"

"Born and raised," Garret said proudly. Though there were millions of British people in New York, his accent still favored him.

"I knew a British sailor once, a real pistol he was . . ."

Garret checked to see if his bag was still on the sidewalk.

"I'll bet. All sorted then?"

". . . but a real gentleman like yourself. Yes, thank you so much."

"No problem at all, really. Cheers."

Garret retrieved his bags and walked into the pedestrian flow of Sixth Avenue—seamlessly back into the machine. He wondered what purpose, if any, his part really served. He was financially successful, healthy, and very "together," as Americans put it. But he felt like he was moving horizontally through life, avoiding the past and seeing the future, but not having the courage to really step into it. He knew that eventually there would be nowhere to go except forward, and he was counting on some sort of incident, a catalyst that would push him through.

He cut down a side street and gazed up at the windows of

the buildings, dotted with plant boxes from which ripe flowers stood proud in the midday sun. Spring in New York City held an air of the unexpected, all this life bursting into a place where there was so much to begin with. He walked fearlessly but could still sense something following him—a buried secret, an unforgiving memory. And the images he came upon strangely correlated to his life: the dirty man with the basketball wearing the scowl of his father; the kid on the stoop grinning toward the sky and placing his arms out exactly as Mitchell would have done.

A passing mail lady gave him a sharp, apprehensive look, as if he had something to hide. He held out his hands: *Look, no cookie jar.*

The city meant a different thing to everyone. For Garret it was a theatrical playground of sex and money and games. The jungle gyms were sleek lounges and loft apartments where shirts were ruffled and deals were made. He had come here after college with nothing but a modern suit and a good hair-cut, and now he had everything, but it still wasn't enough.

He dropped one of those fancy new one-dollar coins in the upturned hat of a frail violin player and briefly wondered whether he had packed some Xanax for the flight, or if those were even allowed. Didn't he hear liquids were outlawed now? *Pretty soon you'll have to fly naked*, he thought, hailing a cab while smirking at the image of a plane full of naked tourists reaching into the overhead bins.

2

LUCY WALKER MOVED with loose, reckless steps, carrying an airline ticket in her teeth and a large metallic-black duffel bag over her shoulder. Her pink hair seemed to glow in the afternoon light, making her into some kind of punk angel. She bent to pick up a hat that blew off a stranger's head on the other side of the crosswalk, ran up, and handed it to him.

The man seemed pleasantly surprised by her goodwill, instead of expecting it, as some New Yorkers did.

"Ah, thank you," he said.

"Cashmere, right?"

The man's face softened. "Italian, in fact."

"Good color with your skin tone," Lucy said, adjusting her nose ring.

He blushed and awkwardly said, "Right." As he walked away with a noticeable bounce in his step, she smiled at his back and blew a piece of hair out of her face.

People tried to hold Lucy's gaze as they walked by, but she didn't notice. Lucy was pretty in anything—a dress, pajamas, wet, tired, tattooed, covered in mud. It was normal that people stared. She was magnetic.

She slipped on her retro sunglasses and continued down the street, her silver vinyl pants making a squeaking noise as she took the subway stairs two at a time.

An old one-armed man with pale skin and a few strands of hair sat across from her on the A train to JFK, mumbling to

7

himself. He was wearing a huge, thick, red sweater even though it was almost June. He appeared calm until he noticed Lucy's eyes on him, and his arms started to shake as he rattled the plastic bags that obscured his feet. His terrified eyes bulged out of their sockets, piercing whatever he looked at. *This is how my mother is going to end up*, Lucy thought, placing her iPod headphones into her ear, eyeing him to the music of Imogen Heap. *What the hell is going on?* His plastic bags were filled with old dolls, some bald or missing an eye, faded from pink to brown. He looked as if the world was out to get him and his dolls, and he was trying so hard to survive, to keep them safe. He spent the entire ride rearranging them, and by the time the train arrived at JFK, the dolls were back in their original positions. *Hide and seek.*

She waited for her mother at the gate while taking small bites of an apple. The massive planes outside the glass windows looked like overgrown mechanical birds slowly cruising the tarmac. She loved to fly, to be suspended above the earth and the clouds, to not think about boarding school, which lately had been tedious and melodramatic. She did love her design class—and Alex, when he wasn't stoned and stupid. She couldn't wait to pop the bubble she'd been in for four years and breathe the air of the real world, come to the city and start a life. High school was so passé.

When she saw her mom, she had a sharp feeling that something had changed between them, but what? She looked hungover and anxious.

Lucy started counting the days until graduation in her head. *Soon I will be free.*

She knew her mother meant well, but there were things between them—heavy, broken things that were beyond repair.

Lucy had begun to feel that she had eclipsed her mother in emotional maturity, or at least common sense.

Lucy hugged her and smelled that cheap soap she used, along with coffee and a hint of gin. Was she drinking in the morning now? They waited to check in at the gate in silence. When Lucy finished her apple, she threw it over a child's head into a nearby garbage can.

"Two points," Lucy said.

Her mother rolled her eyes and moved Lucy back into the line. But that was the problem. Lucy was no longer going to be defined by lines. She was going to sprout to life like those foam fish you drop in water, and take up way more space than she appeared capable of.

Her mother was mad at her; she could tell by the lack of eye contact. But Lucy had an arsenal of memories that would always allow her to get out of jail free. The embarrassment over her drunkenness at parents weekend, the missed piano recitals, the overall pathetic attempt to raise a child. She looked up at her mother and realized that underneath the troubled, weathering veneer was a beautiful woman.

She rested her head on her mother's arm and felt it tense a little. She moved away, then her mother pulled her back close. She didn't want to be cuddled, but she also didn't want to be rude and resist, so she just sighed and started twirling a piece of her hair.

They got to the counter and the woman with pancake foundation and too much lipstick spent a few moments with their IDs and said, "I have some good news and some bad news."

3

AS GARRET ENTERED the first-class cabin of United flight 612 to Heathrow, he noticed the flight attendant had a fixed expression of contempt—a perpetual smirk. Her nametag said "Jo."

Garret surveyed the cabin. He was slightly irked himself, partly because his new Blackberry was acting up (he had already replaced the thing once) and partly because the overhead compartments were not only full, they were overloaded. He stood there, stewing in a heavy silence, his mouth slightly pursed as though the last thing he had eaten was bitter, unsavory. Even with his sour expression, Garret was sexy. He was sexy in ripped jeans, in couture, at 6 a.m. after drinking all night, at a funeral. As a matter of fact, he liked to score dates at funerals, his logic being that grieving people were gripped by a vulnerability only sex with strangers could—if momentarily—solve. But he could hunt his prey anywhere.

"Excuse me," he said rather impatiently to Jo, "have you got a space for this?"

"Are you in first class?"

He tried not to smile. "What do you . . . think?"

"I don't make presumptions," she said, shifting her weight.

She's good, Garret thought, and decided to play along.

"I see. Well, young lady, could you perhaps *presume* to sort a place for my carry-on?"

A few passengers turned their heads. With a wave of her dark chocolate hand, Jo cut off another passenger and turned to Garret.

"Sir? You need to bring it down a notch so I can work with you here, all right?" Then, under her breath, "I'm not your sky-slave, honey."

Garret brushed off his lapel as if her tone had generated dust.

Jo grabbed his garment bag and expertly maneuvered it into the closet at the front of the cabin.

"Not only effective, but efficient," Garret said with a smile. "And, I might add, hostility is the first sign of affection."

"Give me your ticket stub," she said.

He obliged. A few other passengers stared at him as he settled in, but he paid them no mind. He was back to his Blackberry. He was determined to figure the stupid thing out, and became so engrossed that he didn't notice the girl with pink hair, a nose ring, and talking pants take the window seat next to him.

———

AFTER TAKEOFF, Garret could see Jo smiling to herself as she prepared the drink cart. Though clearly perturbed, she seemed interested enough to sneak glances his way. After the plane leveled, she casually walked the few steps over to him.

"Settled in, are we?" she asked politely.

"I suppose."

She wiped some lint off the top of the seat and casually asked, "Are we going to London to see a lady friend?"

"Indeed," Garret replied sweetly, "and her name is Trevor."

Jo widened her gaze and straightened her United smock. Though keeping a straight face, Garret internally celebrated her discomfort.

"Well," Jo sighed, "you learn something new every day."

In the next seat over, the previously bored Lucy came to life. "That was tight," she said. "Do you really have a boyfriend named Trevor?" Without pausing to let him answer, she went right on, as if someone had dropped a handful of quarters into some hidden slot. "Guess what . . . my best friend Cora? Her brother's gay and he's like, so cool. Very smart, and *very* stylish."

Garret cleared his throat, shifted in his seat.

"Are you like, a designer or an architect or something? Cause there's like, a lot of homo, um, sexual people in those kinds of professions. My uncle was gay, totally. But no one ever talked about it. No one even seemed to know, but I mean, c'mon, his apartment was meticulous and his shoe collection was *beyond*. Not to mention the Sicilian tile and throw pillows. Throw pillows! Hello? Bachelors don't exactly subscribe to *House and Garden*."

Lucy pulled her knees to her chest and tilted her head sideways. Garret smiled a little but was slightly stunned. Even though he had been living in the country for over ten years, he was still amazed at the brashness of some Americans. And this one was practically a child.

"I never did see a boyfriend, though," she went on, "but I know he probably had a hot one. He'd always take off to Paris or Madrid, and I would picture what they would look like, their bodies wrapped together in some hotel bed, the window open, laughing together from their guts, stopping to stare. . . ."

Lucy took a deep breath and looked right at Garret. "Not on the edge of a dream, but in a dream—like the movies, but real life. Lovers that are boundless and sometimes tragic but alive, you know? Alive."

Garret nodded. *Who is this girl?*

She seemed to have an insatiable appetite for life, and he felt like she might consume him. He braced himself in his chair and contemplated her words. Something about her passion was infectious.

"I'm sorry," she said. "I go to boarding school, which is so tedious and monochromatic. . . . It's like a bubble. It's just nice to talk to someone who's colorful."

"I'm actually wearing all black," Garret joked.

Lucy looked down at her wrists, where a dozen silver bracelets jingled. She started fiddling with them, and when the seat belt sign dinged off she turned to Garret abruptly, another coin kicking in.

"Are you a top or a bottom?"

Garret held up his hand. "Whoa, hold on a bit here. What am I, your bloody school project? Let's find out how gays live?"

Lucy hardly heard him and continued.

"Cora's brother's a bottom and he says it doubles your pleasure, like the gum. I personally would be a top cause I'm a total control freak. I guess if I were a lesbian, I'd be the one with the strap-on. There are girls in my school that are like dykes-for-a-day when Melissa Etheridge comes to town. It's so lame."

Garret had never understood that expression, lame. It didn't make sense. Americans just made up definitions for words.

"Well, you're certainly not lacking in opinions," he said. His heart had picked up. He had always felt nervous around children, but this one seemed to be able to challenge him intellectually, which he certainly was not used to.

"Yeah, what's wrong with that?" Lucy asked.

"Well, normally I don't have inappropriate conversations with total strangers, never mind children."

The inflated moment had burst and he needed to get his bearings, so he got up to go to the bathroom. Inside the tiny space, it smelled of almond soap and gasoline. He looked at himself in the mirror and furrowed his brow, seeing himself somehow differently, at a new angle. He thought again of the couple he had watched on the street. Did he want that? Is that why it sickened him? Could Trevor be that person to him?

He washed his hands, a ritual he did at least five or six times a day, perhaps as overcompensation for all his sexual encounters, one of which he had experienced earlier that day. He licked his finger, flattened out an unruly eyebrow hair, and checked his pores.

When Garret returned to his seat, he found Lucy looking at him expectantly, waiting for an answer, and Garret realized how beautiful she was. Her extreme hair color and nose piercing had hidden it before. Now her hair was back and he could really see her eyes, like a pair of spotlights illuminating everything she looked at.

He stayed silent and she kept staring at him.

"So, what'll it be? Pitcher or catcher?"

Garret could feel sweat forming at the base of his neck.

"Well, Miss Curious, you seem to have the answers already."

Lucy leaned close enough that Garret could smell the raw sweetness of her young breath. "I bet you're a pitcher."

Garret noticed an eavesdropping middle-aged couple react with poorly concealed horror from 4a and 4b and felt strangely elated, mischievous. One of the things he loved about moving to the States was that he didn't have to be so *proper* all the time, especially since as a child in England he had constantly been under the watchful eye of his stern, ever so proper father. And something about this girl was liberating.

"That remains to be seen," Garret said. "But positioning aside, I have learned that it is best to be fearless. Those are the moments that can be absolutely brilliant. Sex is about letting go."

Jo came back with some hot towels. Lucy grabbed them both and said, "Here, let's do each other!"

Lucy covered Garret's face with the steaming cloth as if she were taming a wild animal. Garret reciprocated the gesture to her, but with careful apprehension, as if manipulating a bomb.

"That was so erotic," Lucy said.

Garret chuckled. "Exactly what I was thinking."

"My mom doesn't think things are erotic; her idea of pleasure is double coupon day at the Shop 'n Save. She's extremely uninformed as well. She thought *Will and Grace* was on the religious channel."

Garret saw the woman behind them crack a mini-smile.

"She tries, though. I'm just bitter cause she won't let me get my tongue pierced."

"Why on earth would you want to do a dreadful thing like that?" Garret asked, touching his own fingers to his tongue.

"For sex, dummy."

"Oh, I see."

"It's like, the ultimate oral tool."

Garret remembered a guy he had dated who had one. He had thought it a bit cumbersome.

"So you must be uncut, right, cause you're like, Euro?" Lucy asked.

Garret shook his head. *Third degree from a teenager. This is extraordinary.*

"What, I'm serious, uncut, right?" Lucy prodded.

"Must you be so base?"

Lucy drew back into herself briefly, jangled her bracelets, and then gave him a just-tell-me-cause-I'm-cute look.

"Actually, I'm British, although I have Italian in me, and no, I'm not answering that question."

A few minutes later, more coins kicked in and she turned to him as if they were suddenly best friends.

"Okay, here's what I want, on top of a career, of course. A European man, with a six-pack stomach and hazel eyes. He will be rich but humble, and with great style. Not some turtleneck-sweater-and-khaki-wearing Proust fanatic from Nantucket, somebody who works with his hands, a sculptor maybe . . . or an antique restorer, what do you think?"

Garret opened his mouth to reply, but the coin dropping was steady and constant. She used her hands to dance around the words.

"Get this. We'll live in a breathtaking villa and cook with olive oil and red wine from the grapes and olives in our back yard. . . ." She let out a musical sigh and touched Garret's arm. "Let me tell you a secret. I once licked Hershey's Syrup off this girl's nipples. It was truth or dare and I got triple-dared."

"Hmm, I wasn't aware there was such a thing," Garret said.

"Well, it was anticlimactic. I would be open to being gay, but lesbians are too butch. Except the lipstick ones. Is your boy-friend cute? I bet he's a super snack, like, ten years younger than you—"

"Eleven," Garret shot in.

"Eleven, with full lips and high cheeks, probably perfect skin, a flawless torso, and some endearing imperfection like a little birthmark on his bubble butt. Oooh," she said, closing her eyes, "I'd love to watch."

Garret smiled and said, "The birthmark is on his shoulder."

Lucy let out a noise that sounded like a cross between a sigh and a moan. Apparently the coins ran out for the moment. The plane ascended and as Lucy got up to go to the bathroom, she fell into his lap. Normally, he would have been mortified, but for some reason he just laughed, hugged her a little, and helped her back up.

As she walked down the aisle he saw her steal an ice cube off the stewardess's tray and pop it in her mouth.

Yes, there is certainly something about this girl.

He noticed a journal sticking out of her bag and was tempted to pick it up and read it. Instead, he just held it for a minute, ran his tanned, slender fingers over the cover, and then placed it back in its original position.

4

THE LITTLE PACKETS containing their "meals-in-the-sky" sat in disheveled heaps on their trays. Garret opened another tiny whiskey bottle, the ice crackling as he poured it into the glass. He had always thought it such a pleasant sound, even as a boy watching his father pour his nightly two inches of scotch. He noticed Lucy's empty mini-Cabernet bottles. *Where was I when I was seventeen? Certainly not on a plane by myself drinking wine.*

"Where are your parents?" he asked her, as if it were an afterthought.

"My mom is in the back; they oversold the plane and bumped me up here. Since I have never flown first, she let me take it."

"Welcome to the big time."

"Thanks. So what does he do, your hottie?"

Hottie, Garret thought. *That he is.* But he feared Trevor was going to be akin to the rest of his liaisons—mere confections, sweet and filling for a minute but lacking sustenance. His longest relationship had been three months.

"He's a visual artist, has an opening this weekend."

"Of course, darling," she replied in a pseudo-English accent.

"I keep a flat in London, but he's taken a temporary flat in Brighton, you know where that is? Sort of England's equivalent of San Francisco."

"Cool. Are there like, leather bars and blatant public sex?"

Perhaps it was the whiskey, but Garret was beginning to admire her candor.

"Not exactly. We are talking about England, darling, and although the aforementioned activities may take place, it is entirely more tasteful and discreet than in San Fran."

"Tell me about it; our country's psycho. Killing sprees in schools, terrorism, KKK, crack babies. That's why I want to move to France. . . ."

"There are no crack babies in France?"

"I don't think so."

Garret laughed. "You're young. You have courage, and a good dose of conviction. I say, realize your dream and go there. Even if you have to waitress for years, or clean motel rooms, go there. Be in the dream as you said, not on the edge of it."

"You remembered."

"Of course," Garret said with a thin smile. "I produce plays, and, well, I tend to notice interesting dialogue."

They looked at each other acutely, as if trying to see deeper in, then turned forward in silence, their lips slightly open, a soft gaze in their eyes.

"My only problem now is my mother. She has major issues."

"What about your dad?"

"I never had one, and she never told me why, and after a while I just stopped asking. I might try and find him myself next year." Lucy peered out the window for a minute and then continued. "She was real pretty as a girl. I have this picture of her, when she was my age, and it's the most favorite thing I own." She made a humming noise and scratched at her head, making her bracelets clink. "She's always loved and supported me aside from being a total lush, and somewhat irresponsible. She won this vacation to London from a radio station and she thinks taking me is going to build some bridge between us. Right. That bridge has already burned."

Garret was in awe of how her thoughts belied her age.

"How so?" he asked.

She gave him a *Do you really want to know?* look.

He gently patted her shoulder. *Yes.*

"Well, she tries to control my life when she can hardly control her own. I have this boyfriend I've seen, on and off, and he's a little older. He's been a senior for like, three years. He rides an old Vespa and is a kick-ass graffiti artist. My mother thinks he's trash, thinks I'm going to get hurt. She wants me to cut it off. So Alex, my boyfriend, was caught in my dorm room at school and I got detention and now she wants me to promise her not to see him again. I mean, hello? It's like, her own issue. Just because she made some bad choices doesn't mean she can't let me live through mine." The bracelet symphony continued as she raised her arms, her hands strangling an imaginary person. "Uggh, projection."

"Sounds like the last girl I dated, in college. Always projecting, as you say." Garret chuckled to hide a burp. "She was the reason I switched to men permanently."

Lucy turned her soft brown spotlights over to him seriously, as if she truly understood.

"But I'm sure she's quite fond of you," Garret told her as he felt his own face soften. "Perhaps more than you know."

As the plane started its descent, they both fell silent.

"So," she said, "you must have the coolest life—a big-time producer with yummy boyfriends, nice clothes."

"Yes, I suppose. But even so, lately I feel like something's missing—that my life has this gaping hole that needs to be filled."

"Well, do you know what the filling is?" she asked.

"Not yet. But I think it has something to do with the L word."

"You're a lesbian?" Lucy joked.

"No. Love."

"Yes, love."

Garret thought about Alan, his pear-shaped, slightly neurotic, and immediately lovable best friend and colleague. *He's the only person I truly love besides Mum. Myself? Well, I certainly hope so. Perhaps not enough . . .*

As they exited the plane, Garret was reluctant to say goodbye. Something in the way his breath caught, an awkwardness filling the space between them. *Should I hug her?*

"If you get lost or something, my flat is right across from the South Kensington Tube stop, on the Circle Line, OK? Big red door."

"OK, thanks," she kidded, "see you in ten minutes." She turned around, and Garret curled his lips at the sight of her bouncy steps walking out of his life.

Though he could not approach them from where he was, Garret saw Lucy's mother greeting her and stopped to stare. There was something recognizable about her. Her stance, the hair. *An actress?*

When Trevor approached him, Garret quivered.

"You look like you've just seen a ghost," Trevor said, his perfectly styled blond hair expertly halving each of his big blue eyes.

"No, but a very peculiar young lady."

5

LUCY FELT lightheaded as she turned away, the airport's bustling sounds and movements becoming a silent blur around her. There was a strange drop in her stomach, like the day she first kissed a boy on the train tracks. *Will I ever see him again?*

The sight of her mom snapped her out if it. Joyce was not a mother one could imagine running through a field—maybe with her elbows on a bar, telling strangers what she could have been. She put her hand on Lucy's shoulder as they walked to the train.

Lucy noticed her mother's free arm waving loosely, the hand shaking slightly.

"So, where are we staying?" Lucy asked.

"At this supposedly charming old hotel. West End."

It made Lucy cringe when her mom expertly gulped down two pills dry after they got in the cab, but she quickly escaped into the world going by out the window. She loved the sense of age, how the buildings were more stone than glass and contrasted sharply with the verdant trees that lined them. The cabbie was listening to a soccer game.

"They call it football here," Lucy said.

Her mother smiled. "I know."

The hotel had a ruby red interior and a large yellow chandelier. As her mom checked in, Lucy touched the large plants that lined the lobby to see if they were real.

"Well, I don't know about you, but I could use a nap and a shower," Joyce said as they rode in the small elevator with fake chestnut walls.

In her room, Lucy ran her fingers over the gilded mirror and checked the firmness of the mattress. She ripped off the bed cover and fluffed the pillows while running a bath. This was cool. She was in England.

———————

THAT NIGHT LUCY and her mother sat in the quaint hotel restaurant while the handsome waiter with a thick accent (was it French?) informed them of the evening's specials. Lucy was still feeling an unknown elation and was compelled to flirt with him, ignoring her mother's disapproving eyes.

"Would you care for a beverage of some sort?"

"Yes, I'd like a glass of merlot," Lucy said, pronouncing it perfectly.

Her mother put up her hand. "She means a cola, please, and I'll have a gin and tonic."

The waiter walked away, making a cat noise under his breath.

"Thanks," Lucy said, as if the word had teeth.

"Lucy, you're seventeen years old; you cannot just order wine whenever you please."

"Mom, it's Europe. Can't you just cut me a little slack?"

"I'd say I've cut you a lot of slack, little lady, especially since you're now entertaining boys in your dorm room. I understand if you don't want to go to college right away, but Lucy, what is it you see in Alex?"

"Are we really starting this?"

"He's a dead-end street. And your behavior—do you know

how that makes me look? That is a very prestigious boarding school and I'm proud you're able to go there."

Lucy had the urge to splash her water in her mother's face. "Since when do you care about prestige? It's my brains that got me in, anyway. Certainly not your money. We know about that shortage. That's why I'm on a scholarship."

She didn't want it to go this way, but when her anger built to a sharp point it needed to be inserted somewhere.

"And you wonder why I'm driven to drink," Joyce said. "How could I have created such a monster?"

Lucy stopped eating her piece of bread for a second and stared at her lap. She knew there was more coming.

"Is this how you treat your own mother, who is taking you on vacation in London?"

Lucy looked up with soft eyes. Repair time.

"Look, it wasn't right to break the rules. But it's not like Alex and I were smoking crack or anything. He's really just a friend. Can't you see that? It's about companionship." Lucy pointed at the bottle of pills next to her mother's water glass. "Oh, I forgot, you wouldn't know about that because *those* are your companions."

Before her mother could rebut, the waiter delivered the drinks, and Lucy said, "Wow, soda! How charming and original."

———

THEY POKED AT their food in a leaden silence. Lucy looked up at her mother, who seemed very far away. She was sorry for her last remark. She loved her mother but was tired of taking care of her when she was drunk, which she had done as long as she could remember. One time when she was eleven, she had actually driven her mother's car home.

More minutes went by, until Lucy said, "Look outside your blurry bubble, Mom. I'm just someone who is growing up, and sometimes I've felt alone in the process, you know what I mean?"

"Of course I do, it's just—"

"You were the one who raised me, although at times it was vice versa. . . ." She paused, got a little choked up.

"There's something not right with that boy. I just have a bad feeling," Joyce said before inhaling her drink. "You know, I was a kid once. Like yourself. I fell in love, but I was careless and distracted, lost. You were my new life, my way out. I disappeared and started over. I would hate to see—"

"Well, I'm glad I could be part of your movie-of-the-week moment." Lucy placed her napkin over her food and got up, walked to the bathroom. She stared at herself in the mirror.

I just want to start a new life. Maybe she's right about Alex, but she's one to talk. She's really picked some winners over the years.

———

WHEN LUCY returned, her mother was slumped over the table, her head on her arm, the tiny white pills spilled out on the black tablecloth. She stopped and stared blankly, and something in her died: the courage to help her mother, the strength to wake her up, the will to even care. Her eyes brimmed with tears as she grabbed her bag and ran toward the exit. She saw the concerned face of the cute waiter in the reflection of the glass door as she pushed it open, bursting onto the street.

I can't do this anymore. She has to grow up so I can.

A disheveled bum approached her, sloppy and begging, trying to lean on her to keep his body upright.

"Get off me," Lucy said, running faster.

She felt disembodied, wandering around the sex shop alleys of the West End that lured people with neon lights and the promise of release. Tears streaked her face like tiny rivers, drying fast in the night air. She was moving quickly, not sure where she was headed, until she finally stopped near Covent Garden and looked up at an old church. She suddenly wished she knew how to pray, and wondered if it even worked if you did. She turned around and saw the sign for the Tube's Circle Line, and something told her to get on. She walked down the long stairway, jumped the turnstile, and waited for the train.

I can't do it anymore. I'm graduating. I have my own life to worry about.

The train came, and she got on and sat down. It soothed her. It felt good just to be moving somewhere. Away.

6

ON THE EXPRESS train to Brighton, Trevor turned his baby blues to Garret and spoke in a flat tone. "So, tonight is Bruce and Liam's party."

Those wretched queens, Garret thought. He was woozy from the plane ride, but clearheaded enough to have a realization while studying Trevor's pleasant profile: *I don't even really know you.*

"How could I forget," Garret replied.

Trevor smirked and flipped through his *Hello* magazine while nursing a pomegranate juice through a straw. His lips were dark red from the drink, making him look slightly evil in the dusky light.

Trevor was gorgeous, and although Garret was old enough to know it wasn't all about the beauty, he often turned defenseless when it was around.

As the train carved through the industrial area near the airport and into the countryside, Garret thought about the girl on the flight. How her words and confidence seemed to flow as effortlessly as the green hills outside the window. How she said the word *love*, a word that seemed exquisite but untouchable—a wispy cloud on the horizon or a body of water seen from a plane. For him it had all been lust up to now.

Garret snoozed until they arrived, and seemed to gain a renewed vigor as they exited the train and walked along the Brighton pier.

All of a sudden, four drag queens sauntered down the boardwalk next to them, all dressed as Jackie O. They were highly animated and histrionic. One of them winked at Garret, while another pinched Trevor's ass. A small crowd started to follow them, whispering under their breath.

"Clearly they're going to the same party we are," Garret said.

"You think?" Trevor replied.

"It's my fourth year, believe it or not."

It was an affair that had grown in both affluence and attendance yearly.

"It's very Pink Pound," Trevor said.

Garret hoped Trevor didn't think of him as part of the Pink Pound. Yes, a group of male homosexuals basically ruled the world of finance in London, but most of them were a sight for sore eyes—desperately in need of a treadmill and a salad.

Garret heard two of the Jackie O's say, in unison, "Scandal," and another sighed emphatically and said, "Poor thing." Were they referring to him?

The last one, who clearly didn't have Jackie O's figure, fanned herself and added, "*Quel dommage.*"

Two old ladies stared and pointed at the procession. One of them said, "Look, Jackie O!" The other one said, "Jackie O, O, O, OH!"

Trevor laughed, but when Garret went to put his arm around him, he tightened his shoulders.

"What's wrong, dear?" Garret asked.

"Nothing. Just, let's go."

Garret felt his cell phone buzz in his pocket. A text from Alan:

Okay, there is more than one fanny pack. What does she have in them, trail mix? Style police not in contract. Anyway, don't eat that deep-fried wonder bread they try to serve you for breakfast. Kill, I mean kiss, Trevor for me. Call me every five.

Garret smiled. *That's what Mitchell used to say.* And with a quick sinking in his stomach, he flashed to Mitchell's face, turning with the refrigerator door, the calmness in his eyes, his moist lips. The indelible image that had been seared into Garret's brain—an image at once beautiful and terrible, laced with guilt and always haunting.

"Hang here," Trevor said, going into a store to get cigarettes.

Garret sent Alan a text back:

Well, fanny pack girl is going to bring our box office home, so I don't care if she's got crack in there. Going to a party. I scheduled another PR meeting for when the show comes to the West End. Toodles.

Trevor came back and they made their way to the party. They were led through the large wooden door by a butler who was waiting outside.

Garret immediately saw the host couple, a caricature of husband and wife: Bruce, a forty-something ex-pat from L.A., wearing an iridescent, clingy T-shirt and a frilly scarf while reclining in a giant, raspberry-colored chair lined with pillows; Liam, British as British gets in his seersucker suit and handkerchief, sternly sitting on a tiny wooden apparatus that resembled a footstool. They were chatting with several of the early guests, who were all nicely dressed, marginally attractive, but very successful men. Bruce was flamboyant and gesturing freely, while Liam was stoic and unemotional.

Bruce greeted Trevor with a look of motherly love, then Garret with a look of thinly veiled pity.

Before Garret could even realize what was transpiring, Trevor ran off with Bruce, and he was left alone. He overheard a portly man talking to Liam about a play he had produced in New York, and then saw a cute younger man in the corner on a cell phone. He debated which way to go and did a small dance, finally deciding to approach the young man.

"Aren't you Garret Millward?" the boy asked as he hung up.

"If you want me to be," Garret replied, a little too suavely.

The boy's phone rang again and Garret turned away and wandered down the hall where abstract paintings loomed as giant, colorful messes—much like a lot of these people's lives, including his own. At the end of the hall he peered into the slightly open bathroom door.

Bruce was dipping his long pinkie nail into a small bag of white powder, raising it to Trevor's nostril.

Well, starting early, Garret thought. Although he occasionally indulged, cocaine was not his thing.

"Girl, you in trouble," Bruce said to Trevor. "I am so sure you showed up with him. Damian's here, you know. You are so bad!"

Damian?

Trevor looked at himself in the mirror and giggled, wetting his finger to smooth out his bangs. Bruce gave himself a pinkie-full and went on, "You can't be working him like that."

Garret scooted away before they came out, bumping into the aging, eccentric socialite known as Dr. Posh.

"Oh, how are we, dear thing?" Dr. Posh said as they pressed their cheeks together on both sides. "You mustn't fret, darling, there is not enough time for that. After all, it is the start of a glorious summer. Pray come down to the beach house in Cornwall—it's fab, darling, simply marvelous."

"What do you mean I mustn't—"

"Did you know Dee Dee and Miss Thing are here as Jackie O? They are totally phenomenal. Four of them! So chic. Damian!"

Dr. Posh ran off, leaving Garret bewildered. He watched Dr. Posh whispering to Damian, a full-lipped, cinnamon-skinned young man with black hair and green eyes. He grabbed a cocktail off a butler's tray, downed it, and put the glass back. *If the joke is on me, I might as well be drunk.*

Later, the Jackie O's did a runway show up and down the living room. Garret saw Damian covertly signal for Trevor to follow him, and they stole down the stairs into Liam's famous wine cellar.

Garret followed and cracked the door, looking down to see Trevor kissing Damian hard on the lips, the dusty pinot bottles stacked all around them. He burst the door open and walked down the stairs.

"That's tops, Trevor, that really is," Garret said.

The two of them jumped away from each other. Damian looked at Garret as if he wanted him to join in, and Garret was suddenly revolted by all of it.

"Go on, don't mind me. Suck away," Garret said quietly, and turned back up the stairs.

Back in the main room he swilled another drink and stewed over what he had seen. For some reason, he thought about his father. Maybe the geezer had a point. While the whole gay thing might not be wrong, right now it was quite tiresome.

The Jackie O's began to sing show tunes.

When Trevor came out, Garret impulsively grabbed him and they left the party together, meandering down the Brighton Pier. The water hissed over the tiny rocks and the reflections from the Ferris wheel lights wavered like a giant fading sun on the sea. They walked in silence until Garret said, "Trevor, I need you to be straight with—"

"Sssshhh, get in," Trevor replied, referring to an abandoned shopping cart on the pier. Garret smiled and climbed in. As it slowly began to rain, Trevor pushed Garret swiftly in the cart. They were swerving, howling, laughing, until the cart banged on its side, and Garret fell out. The laughter settled, and a sober silence grew. They stared at each other, knowing what was next. Garret felt a sudden rage heat his insides, and he grabbed Trevor and pushed him against the rail of the pier. The rain came down harder and the wind fiercely whipped their skin. Garret stared into Trevor's eyes and said, "Say it. . . . Say it. . . . SAY 'I LOVE YOU, GARRET.' SAY IT," he screamed. "SAY IT!!" He was acting like the stupid fags he despised, but he didn't care. He was angry and felt like a fool to have been manipulated by someone half his age.

Trevor didn't say anything. He only stared as Garret loosened his grip, backed away, and then turned into the dark.

Garret sat down on a bench in slight shock. The air got colder and colder.

Eventually, he got up and walked to the station and boarded the last express train to London. For a while he just let his body warm up and stared at the blackness whizzing by. As the train reached the city, Garret realized that although he was quite keen on Trevor and very hurt and humiliated, he had not been yelling at Trevor on the pier. He had been yelling at his father.

He wiped at his eyes as he departed the train and made his way onto the Circle Line Tube, which was particularly loud and rattling. His body had thawed and felt almost weightless. His mind was numb, but his heart was empty.

He turned and noticed a girl at the far end of the car, face in her hands, quietly sobbing. He caught sight of her nails, jet-black, and from the sound of her bracelets knew right away it was the girl from the plane.

He shuddered and slowly got up, crossed over to where she was sitting, and gently crouched next to her. For a few moments he just watched her, clutching her own face, slowly rocking. Then he said, "You know, it's not very becoming of a lady to cry in public. . . . I was going to wait until I was at least in my foyer."

Lucy looked up in amazement. "Oh my god, it's you."

"In the flesh," Garret said.

She started to speak slowly, with short quick breaths in between the words. "My mother . . . she's a mess and . . . I've been taking care of her, but I can't anymore. She passed out in the restaurant and . . . I ran . . . I just ran . . . I . . ."

After a moment, he pulled her to his chest and for a long time, they stayed like that, not quite strangers in a tight embrace, while the train hurled them through the dark tunnels of London's Underground.

"I didn't even get your name."

"Lucy," she said, softly.

"Garret," he replied, even softer.

7

GARRET AND LUCY sat side by side in the all-night fish-and-chip shop as if they'd known one another all along. Lucy dumped the brown sauce on her fries and Garret salted his. They were both content in the silence, still processing the fluke of running into each other.

After they finished, Garret said, "Trevor broke up with me."

Lucy looked at him with genuine concern.

"The funny thing is I'm deadened to it. It's more than that. It's not Trevor, it's me. I've been chasing all these young men, burning through them as fast as the money I'm spending on them. I suspect it's related to this major aversion I have toward my father, or him toward me."

"Sounds like a shrink's wet dream."

"It's a long story," Garret said.

"It's a long night," Lucy replied.

"Well, first, we're going to make sure your mother's sorted."

They left the chip shop and walked to Piccadilly. Garret loved London when it was deserted—all the regal architecture seemed better suited to calm than chaos. They found a lone taxi and rode to the hotel.

When they arrived, Lucy asked the bellman if he had seen her mother go up.

"The lady who had a bit of a kip in the restaurant?" the bell-man asked.

"Yes."

"She's OK," he said. "The waiter helped her to her room."

Garret felt giddy in the elevator. He was going to a teenage girl's hotel room. He held back a giggle as they tiptoed past her mother's room to Lucy's, where she plopped down on the bed and said, "OK, now tell me."

Garret caught a glimpse of himself in the mirror and tried to imagine his face without the unruly eyebrows of his father.

"There was this one day, in November, about twelve years ago . . ." he began.

Lucy took each sock off with the use of her big toes.

"And . . ."

"And it was the last time I spoke to my father."

Lucy turned toward him. "At least you had one."

Garret sat down by the window, rolled his cigarette case in his hands.

"True enough, I suppose. Never thought of it that way. Anyway, it was the day I told him that I was . . . gay." Garret opened the case and flipped an unlit cigarette through his fingers. "We were up north, on the cliffs near where I grew up. There was a slight rain and heaps of fog—I couldn't see inches from my face."

"What did he say? When you told him," Lucy wanted to know.

"Two words. 'Good heavens.'"

Lucy snorted.

"It's not funny, really. I mean it is, but it's not. There was this look in his eye that I had never seen, one of total and utter disgust, that still troubles my dreams."

"What about your mother?"

"We're sorted. We talk all the time. I'm going to see her tomorrow. We have to meet at my aunt's house though. Can you imagine?"

"Jeez. Didn't they get the memo? . . . Gay is the new black," Lucy said.

"Right. Anyway, I started to chase boys because I knew my father would disapprove, but also because I'm sexually insatiable. The thrill is in the catch."

"So, you're a player."

Garret let out a little smile and said, "You could say that."

They heard some people walking in the hallway, slurring their words. Garret flashed to the scene on the pier. He should have seen it coming.

"So, what about Trevor?" Lucy asked, as if she could hear his thoughts.

"I foolishly thought it could be different with him. He let me come all the way here to tell me, well, *show* me really—everyone seemed to know except me, the big joke was on Garret."

"That sucks."

"Yes, it certainly does. Lucy, I'm incredibly knackered and I really want to smoke this fag, and if the minibar's closed, I'm afraid—"

Garret noticed Lucy's face deflate with sadness. He walked over and knelt by the bed, removed a stray piece of hair that was balanced on her nose.

"Listen," he said, producing a silver business card from his wallet, "why don't you call me when you return home. You're only an hour from New York, right?"

"Less. Can I come visit?"

"I don't see why not." Garret kissed her on the cheek. "Good luck with your mum."

"Good luck with your dad," she said, rattling his arm.

"I'm afraid it's beyond that, but coming from such a sweet girl like yourself, it makes me hopeful."

Garret made his way to the door, then turned around for one more look. Lucy was still on the bed in the soft light, staring at the ceiling. She seemed awake and dreaming—perhaps of her impending adult life, away from her mother, away from herself. She held the business card above her head as if it was some sort of portal, a secret power.

"There is a reason I met you," she said, knowing he was still in the room.

Garret nodded and gently closed the door.

When he arrived at his flat he went right to bed and slept like a baby, waking with much less of a hangover then he expected. Must have been the chips. He noticed a single silver bracelet on his wrist—one of Lucy's—and smiled. *When had she put that on?* He flashed to her look in the hotel room when he first said he was leaving—so innocently fraught.

He showered, gathered his things, and got ready for his journey up north to see his mother.

The train ride was painless, and Garret spoke to Alan on his Blackberry. He was his usual frantic yet somehow charming self. He told Garret that his little orange cat, Tramp, had gone to the vet and was diagnosed with a benign tumor that would cost four hundred dollars to remove.

"I told Tramp to get used to it—the tumor's not going anywhere," Alan said.

Garret laughed quietly. Alan could tell something was up and asked what was wrong.

"He dumped me, Alan. And everyone knew. Can you believe it?"

"Actually, I can. Are we seeing a pattern here? Not of people dumping you, but I have to believe you would have been on to the next—"

"He was different," Garret protested feebly.

"What? Better hair gel? Another inch on his pecker?"

Garret despised Alan's smugness at that moment. After a short silence, Alan changed the subject. "What was the ratio at the party?"

"One in five," Garret said with a hint of a smile.

Ever since they first met, Alan and Garret had rated parties as to how many cute guys there were.

"I'm sure you gave it a curve," Alan said.

Out the window, the English hills stretched freely, covered by lush patches of fog and dotted with cows and goats. The train raced through it all, unflinching.

"I'm so sorry you got dumped, honey." Alan was earnestly apologetic, but Garret could tell he was relieved. Alan had never liked Trevor. In fact, in the ten years they had been best friends, Alan hadn't really liked any of Garret's boy toys.

"Well, it's not even losing him; it's the way he went about it. The whole party was looking at me knowingly, and he had this other boyfriend already, some Damian chap. It was all perfectly horrid."

Garret could hear Alan being interrupted by the stage manager telling him the cast was ready for him.

"Well, honey, not to worry about those tired queens, they're just looking for the next soap opera snack to feast on. We're starting the run-through."

"All right, I'll be home late tomorrow night."

"I'm holding my breath," Alan said.

Garret hung up as the train approached the small stop where he was to meet his mother.

By the stone ticket booth, Mrs. Dorothy Millward waited, in tweed with an umbrella by her side, thin and aging but elegant and proud.

Garret always loved seeing his mother in her own element, outside the rigid, almost despotic rule of his father. As a boy, he used to sneak in and watch the ladies' weekly card game, his father off hunting or drinking in the pub. He remembered her being so confident, so in charge, and all the ladies looking up to her as their leader. He'd secretly look on with unabashed admiration when she would tell a story that would melt the whole room or give some advice that was hard to hear but appreciated. That was the part of his mother he cared to remember—not the cowering, passive, delicate woman she was around his father.

They hugged, and she tried to take his bag.

"No, Mum, please, I've got it."

"You look so handsome, dear."

"You don't look so bad yourself, Mum."

They drove to Garret's aunt's house in relative silence, Dorothy catching glances of her son and occasionally touching his leg with her hand. As they approached the quaint house, Garret put his own hand on top of hers. She noticed the bracelet.

"What is this, dear? You were never one for jewelry."

"It actually belongs to a . . . a friend," Garret said.

"Well, you do look like you've got some sort of secret."

They arrived and settled in. Dorothy put out Garret's favorite cookies and they munched in between sips of tea. Garret felt the world and his worries go away, sitting with the woman who loved him more than anyone and had raised him with such well-intentioned care. The play, his father, Trevor, Mitchell, it all vanished into the air around him. What was left was simply a mother and a son, the love between them a braided rope that could pull barges.

After a while, Dorothy spoke.

"You know, it would be nice if you found someone, I don't know, closer to your own age perhaps. Thought about settling down?"

Garret remembered Alan's not-so-subtle remarks in the same vein.

Perhaps they're right.

"Yes, maybe so. I've got to get this next play off the ground first."

His mother's face became stern and her eyes focused. "And I will not have this silence between you and your father go on much longer. It's killing me, and although he would never admit it, it's killing him too."

I doubt it, Garret thought.

Dorothy topped off his tea with the kettle.

"I'm not sure if that will happen," Garret said. "Remember, I'm a 'disgrace' to the family."

"Well, I've been working on him, slowly."

"A brave lady you are."

Dorothy smiled and brushed her hand across Garret's face. "You could be of any persuasion in the world and I would love you for all my days."

———

THAT NIGHT, they ate pub fare at the local—a dimly lit, wood-paneled room with dark green cushions lining the benches. Dorothy actually drank two pints, and they laughed about his father's face when he caught Garret in one of Dorothy's dresses.

"What's extraordinary is that out of all my dresses, you picked the one that was Chanel," Dorothy said.

"Of course, Mum, did you think I'd pick some dreary number from a bargain shop?"

Their laughter settled and Dorothy discreetly wiped away a tear from her left eye.

"Look at you, Garret. How could he not be proud?"

"Well, Mum, I've been asking myself that same question for quite a while now."

———

GARRET SLEPT soundly that night, considering he was in his cousin's saggy bed, surrounded by old and smelly stuffed animals.

The next day, as she put Garret back on the train, Dorothy said, "Don't worry dear, I've got an idea. Call me when you land safely."

"Will do. I love you, Mum."

On the train, Garret stared out the window in pleasant contemplation, fiddling with the bracelet on his wrist.

8

AFTER SOME SHOPPING, Lucy and Joyce ate lunch in a crowded London restaurant across the street from the hotel. Lucy noticed the darkness around her mother's eyes as she stared into space, stirring her coffee with an unsteady hand. She was trying to be sympathetic, but inside she was thinking, *I'm almost free.*

"Was there someone in your room last night?" her mother asked, snapping back to reality.

"Yeah. A serial rapist."

"Lucy, I'm serious."

She flashed to Garret's mysterious dark eyes, his high cheekbones sloping down to his prominent lips. "The guy I met on the plane. I saw him on the Tube. We just talked. He's gay, remember?"

"Yes, I do, actually."

"Good, at least there are a few brain cells left."

The waitress cleared their plates and raised an eyebrow.

"I'm not perfect, Lucy."

Lucy remembered when Joyce used to pick her up in fifth grade every Wednesday when school got out early, and they'd go to the movies and pour peanut M&M's into their popcorn. It was their regular "date." She had looked forward to those dates more than anything, until the one day Joyce never came, and Lucy had to walk the two miles home. When she got there, she found her mother passed out in the backyard, her dress open, exposing one of her milky breasts. Her first thought was, *Oh my god, she's dead*, but then a large man with a mustache came out of the kitchen door with a blender and two glasses as if nothing was wrong. There were no more movie dates after that.

Lucy put down her napkin and placed her hand on her mother's wrist, stopping her mid-sip. "Nobody's perfect. But you have to help yourself."

Joyce took a sip of her coffee, then said flatly, "I know."

They spent the rest of the day sightseeing, but Lucy studied the people more than the sights. Londoners wore the coolest clothes, stuff you could never pull off anywhere else. That evening they went to a play about a dysfunctional family and Joyce kept laughing at weird times, which annoyed Lucy. The star of the play, a man pushing fifty but quarterback handsome, was in the lobby when they were done. Joyce gave him a hug and was beside herself. Lucy just tried to get her out of there. They got ice cream and sat under the awning of a sex shop while it rained. Lucy was nervous, especially because her mom was standing next to a giant picture of a black cock.

That night in bed, Lucy could hear her mother singing in her room next door. It was an old song she used to sing, but the words changed every time she sang it. Lucy put Garret's business card on the bedside table with her bracelets, then turned toward the wall and traced her hands over the olive trees on the wallpaper, allowing herself a smile.

———

THE NEXT DAY they took a train to the airport, and Lucy leaned against her mother, who looked out the window day-dreaming. Before their plane landed in New York, the captain informed them they were in a holding pattern, which was how Garret had described the way he was feeling—in limbo, caught. She tried to hear his voice, smell him on her shirt. She tried to sketch his hands, but they ended up looking too bony. Her mother woke up sweating when the plane touched down, and Lucy gave her some water and a napkin she had saved for her. Everyone onboard looked tired and the plane smelled ripe. She was so relieved when she finally got home and into her bed.

IN THE MORNING she went back to school for exams, and when she ran into her advisor (whom she'd been avoiding), he asked her about college. She simply said, "I have something else in mind." She didn't know what that was, but she could feel it. New York City was something to everybody, and for Lucy it was a gravitational pull. A place she hardly knew anything about but already loved.

At graduation she got drunk and slept with Alex. She knew it was a pity fuck, but she also felt it was a rite of passage, a way to bookend her high school years. Afterward, he told her he was eighteen, not seventeen. Why would you lie about one year? High school was tired.

THE NEXT TWO weeks felt like a year, but finally the day came when Garret agreed to meet her for lunch. She dressed in her favorite jeans and a vintage motorcycle T-shirt she found at a thrift store. They met at a café in the West Village where two bulldogs lounged on a floor of mismatched tiles.

He kissed her on both cheeks when they met, and Lucy blushed. They sat awkwardly for a moment, not accustomed to being together in such a planned context.

"So how's your mum?" Garret asked when the waiter brought their drinks.

"Same. Her exterior is intact, but you can tell there is something lurking underneath. Like one minute she's just going to crack," Lucy said.

"You just basically described everyone on the planet."

"Well, there are degrees. How was your mom?" Lucy asked.

"She's grand. She has some plan and thinks my pop and I are going to reconcile. I'm doubtful."

Lucy started to feel more comfortable. She sipped her soda and put the glass down a little too hard. "Well, I graduated!" she announced.

"Yes, congratulations, that's superb!"

"I drank bad tequila and mercy-fucked my boyfriend. Now I just have to figure out what I'm going to do."

"One step at a time."

"That should be my mom's motto."

Garret smiled and tousled her hair, which was now back to her normal auburn color. "I like the hair. Suits you better."

"Thanks," Lucy replied, trying to play down the compliment.

AFTER LUNCH, Lucy felt light on her feet as Garret led her around the corner and up his brownstone steps, through the door, and down a long hallway to his gleaming, spotless apartment. The decor was super-modern, the furniture masculine and stark. Everything was done in soft, muted colors, like a clean slate on which to add color. Lucy was in awe as she plopped her bag on the steel-framed couch.

"Wow. This place is flawless."

"Glad you approve," Garret said proudly.

She walked around slowly and took it all in, then peeked into the kitchen, which aside from a large, comfy yellow chair, looked like a display model that had never been used. Garret's phone buzzed and he swiftly answered. While he talked she ran her hands over the polished surfaces, opened the fridge. Pellegrino bottles, neatly lined up in two rows. Some fancy-looking cheese. Champagne. Pinot grigio. Dark chocolate.

Garret hung up the phone and hip-checked her aside, grabbed some Pellegrino and poured them each a glass. Lucy didn't care for the bubbles but drank it anyway.

"Who was that?"

"Sheila, our costume designer."

They sat down on the couch and Garrett pointed at the sketchbook that was sticking out of her bag. He reached for it, but she grabbed it first, flipped it open to the right page, and then placed it in his lap, showing him sketches of her hat designs.

"It's my glorified housewife collection," she said.

Garret's jaw loosened as he slowly turned the pages. "These are proper designs. Where did you learn to do this?"

"One of my art teachers is a milliner. She was my mentor. She said I should get them looked at."

Garret took another phone call and this time, while he listened, he carried her book with him, still looking through it. Lucy could almost feel herself levitating above the floor. When he hung up, he ran his hand lightly over her favorite rendering, a vintage red hat she'd added some modern lines to.

"That hat says courage, but also excess."

Garret looked at her skeptically, as if she were reading a script. He turned the page and stopped at a wispy white hat with exploding feathers.

"That one is grace."

Garret's phone buzzed again, but he ignored it.

"Lucy, these are up to par with some of the renderings of our top costume designers."

She tried to look cool but felt hot and wobbly.

"Well, I may just have an idea. I could ring Heather Bridges."

Lucy shook her head to make sure she heard correctly. "What? You know Heather Bridges? She's like, a fashion goddess!!"

"I can't promise anything, but we'll see."

Lucy felt like a stunned insect. Her peripheral vision got blurry and the tips of her fingers tingled. *A possible meeting with Heather Bridges? Oh my god!*

"Listen, I'm thrilled you came, but I've got to go meet up with Alan, and you've got a train to catch. Call me tomorrow?"

Garret guided Lucy out the door and kissed her on both cheeks.

———

AS LUCY NAVIGATED the tree-lined street, she turned back a couple of times and stared at Garret's building.

Did that just happen?

Suddenly, the world looked different.

Maybe if I get a job here, I could get an apartment too. New York City brimmed with possibility. She noticed everything: trees growing through concrete, kids standing in crooked lines, smoking on stairways. Groomed men in square-cut suits holding shiny briefcases. Everything appeared rich and vivid, and everyone seemed deep in their own story. She couldn't wait for hers to begin, and even though she had always thought the saying was trite, now she knew what it meant: *Today is the first day of the rest of my life.*

9

EVEN THOUGH HE could afford taxis, Alan preferred the subway. He enjoyed the loud rumble, and it made him feel a part of the city, purposeful and alive. To Alan, New York was about actors—even the ones that weren't on the stage. Everyone had an act, a plot stirring, a scheme brewing, from the guy selling stolen paperbacks and hairdryers to the mogul making billion-dollar deals over steak lunches, served by the busboy from Queens who could turn out to be a rap star making just as much. That was the beauty of it. Opportunity.

When Alan stood up at his stop, a young woman handed him his *Times*, which he was about to leave behind. She smiled like this sort of thing happened every day.

"I should just tie everything around my neck," Alan said.

Above ground, he walked among the hipsters who seemed to have replaced the intellectuals in his neighborhood. When did being a model with jeans halfway down your ass make you cool? What happened to the real hipsters, the artists that started a revolution instead of maxing out the black card at Diesel? That's why Alan loved the theater: it was an art form that still had its own, more authentic glamour, not just anorexia and heroin chic.

As Alan entered his apartment, a large poster of Gloria Swanson looked down on him with beautiful, haunting eyes. He grabbed some ice cream out of the freezer and started eating it on his bed. His mother called from Long Island, and he debated letting it go to voicemail but picked it up at the last second. She brought up Garret immediately.

"No, Mother, he's with some girl. He met her on the plane."

Alan stroked his cat, Tramp, who was now on antibiotics for the tumor.

"Seventeen, I think. Listen, I don't feel like talking; I've been yelling at my cast all day. I'd say call me, but I know you will, incessantly. Bye."

His cat looked at him as if to say, *You are pathetic.*

"Oh, Tramp, you know nothing of love; you're just a spoiled feline princess with tumor issues."

He got up and went to his tiny kitchen for some water. A true New Yorker could maneuver expertly in small spaces. The intercom buzzed.

"Go away," Alan said into it.

"It's me," he heard Garret say.

Alan discarded the ice cream and fixed his hair. He buzzed him up, and they sat in the living room sipping coffee. Alan noticed something different about Garret but couldn't pinpoint it. He wanted to find out about the girl but didn't want to seem pushy, so he filled Garret in on what was happening with the play. In turn, Garret told Alan about the meeting he had before he flew back.

"Major potential for our West End run."

"I'm sure you charmed the fuck out of them," Alan said.

"They were concerned as to why we were opening so late in the season, and I explained our theory about avoiding Tony fever, although you and I know it's because we had to wait for Miss Fanny Pack to finish her movie."

"We'll make it work," Alan added.

Garret picked up a black-and-white framed photograph of

Alan in his dancing days. The lighting was complimentary, the shadows carving out his muscled torso.

"You were a looker," Garret said.

"Yeah, well, the key word is 'were.'"

"Well, we cannot all be young forever."

Alan looked at the sexy scar on Garret's chin, his clear eyes and smooth skin.

"Yes, but some of us age more gracefully. You haven't changed a bit. Except for that hair in your ear."

Garret got a panicked look on his face and felt around his ear.

"Ha! Got ya."

"Listen, Alan, there's something I want to ask you. You know the girl I told you about?"

"Yes."

"I know we have unions for this sort of thing, but do you think you could find a job for her, some sort of costume apprenticeship? She's quite capable . . . a great head on her shoulders."

"Doesn't she live upstate?" Alan asked.

"She could commute, I suppose."

"Garret, she's only sixteen, isn't she?"

"Seventeen, and she's designed a hat collection!"

Garret was doing his head twitch, which meant his mind was lost in some ideal future he was creating.

"What has gotten into you? Since when are you feeling altruistic toward teenage girls?"

"I don't know, Alan. There is something about her. I haven't quite got a grasp on it yet, but there is certainly something."

"I'll see what I can do."

Alan refilled their coffee cups and told Garret he could smoke by the window if he wanted.

"By the way, how is Miss Fanny Pack?" Garret asked.

Alan sighed dramatically. "I have to say, she is remarkable. A strange woman, but she can act her tits off. During the farewell scene last night at rehearsal she moved me to complete tears."

"Alan, you cry at commercials on TV," Garret said.

"Only when they say cotton is the fabric of our lives."

"My point exactly."

When Garret left, Alan retrieved the ice cream from the trash and started to finish it. He looked at the picture Garret had referred to—the day he was cast in a European tour of *Cats*. He could get that body back if he wanted to.

Tramp begged for some ice cream and Alan let her lick the spoon.

"Dairy whore," he said, dropping the box on the kitchen floor. He walked to the window to secretly watch Garret turn the corner, then picked up the picture he had referred to and slowly shook his head.

10

LUCY FELT TINY on the streets of midtown. The endless billboards of moving lights, the smell of burned peanuts, the puzzle pieces of sky through the spaces between the looming buildings—it all mixed together in a smash to the senses. She wanted to put it all in a blender and drink it up.

When she had gotten the call from Garret about helping out with the costumes, she screamed, "Yes!" before he could even finish the sentence. Her mother had given her a piercing look when she hung up the phone. Lucy told her that this was her chance to really learn something, in the real world. On the train in, she felt this incredible sense of power, that nothing could stop her, that her world was unfolding so fast she had to run to catch up with it.

The early June air whisked past her face, carrying with it the threat of the sweaty summer days just around the corner. When she arrived at the stage door, a security guard let her in and showed her to the fifth row, where Alan sat with various stage managers and script supervisors.

She looked around for Garret. A flustered Alan gave her a *now you* look, but took the time to introduce himself and tell her to "hang tight."

She sat down and waited patiently. She noticed Alan's confidence in talking to his colleagues, and in turn how they all looked up to him. She felt so lucky to be there, marveling at the huge theater, the plush red seats, the dust hanging in the air below the rehearsal lights, the actors sitting Indian-style eating fruit and baguettes. But where was Garret? He was supposed to introduce her to the costumer she was apprenticing with for the next couple of weeks. Lucy was so giddy with anticipation that she had to press her hands against her thighs to stop her legs from bouncing.

"Excuse me," she politely interrupted Alan, "is Garret—"

"He's probably shagging some delivery boy. Don't you know him yet? Never on time, and entirely unpredictable. Who knows why he's such a good producer."

"It's his smile," said one of the stage managers.

Alan shot him a look that could put out flames and said, "Or not."

Lucy laughed. Even though Alan had this way of berating people when he talked, he was inexplicably pleasant. She knew he didn't like her, or the idea of her, but that would have to change.

"OK, people," Alan said with a twist of his hands, "snack break is over, it's blocking time, and you better be off book!"

Lucy watched the rehearsal with wide eyes. The actors seemed so comfortable, so fluid with each other, blurring the lines between performance and real life.

After a scene in which two characters kissed, Alan threw his hands up in the air. "Is that how you kiss your shrink? Come on, people. This is forbidden. Put some passion, some chutzpah into it!!"

During a scene change she noticed Alan furiously jotting down notes. She peeked over his shoulder and saw that he wasn't writing notes at all, but a single word, over and over, pressing so hard that the paper was frayed. She had to bend her neck farther to read what the word was: *Garret*.

Alan noticed her snooping and closed the script in his lap.

The cover page read, *Don't Wake the Angels*, a new play by Ryan Daniel.

"So what's it about?" Lucy asked him.

"A crazy lady," he said.

"Sorry, I'm not here to intrude. I am just so glad to be out of boarding school."

"Well, I could think of worse places," Alan said, eyeing her suspiciously.

"My school was limiting," Lucy mused, as if it were something that happened to her years before. "Too many small minds."

Alan gave her another peculiar look. The lead actress was doing some weird stretches with her face.

"Why is she crazy?" Lucy wanted to know.

"Well, as you can see, one half of the stage is her perfect family, and the other half is her shrink—she goes back and forth. Her shrink tells her that her family died in a fire, so we don't know if it's all in her head or not."

"Sounds heavy."

"Welcome to life."

Alan opened his script again, running his finger over the lines to find his place.

"I like watching you work," Lucy said. "You're very, I don't know . . . real."

Alan laughed. "Sometimes I wonder if they even hear what I'm saying."

"I think they do," Lucy said.

"Well, you seem to be sure of a lot of things for such a young girl," Alan said, biting into a banana.

"I just know that I want things to change. I feel like I've been living in a cave."

"Yeah," Alan said while chewing, "high school can be so oppressive."

Lucy hated it when adults spoke in that satirical tone, as if she didn't know they were being facetious. When would they realize she was as smart as they were? She decided to follow his lead.

"You'll understand someday," she said, followed by a hair flip and a leg cross.

Alan chuckled and called for the scene to start.

Lucy distracted herself by fiddling with her bracelets. *Where is he?*

Alan stopped the scene shortly after to show them the blocking. He was so passionate, so serious, that Lucy became mesmerized. The mere thought of her being part of this play made her heart rate quicken. She looked again at Alan's script and once again saw the doodle of the person she felt so fortunate to have met: *Garret.*

11

GARRET COULD HEAR Alan yelling downstairs. He was up in one of the abandoned dressing rooms at the theater, getting a brilliant blow job from one of the stage tech interns. The young man had eyed Garret and commented on how handsome he looked in a suit, to which Garret replied, "You have a minute?" and led him up the freight elevator, where they kissed until Garret was almost breaking through his pants. Now, the guy was worshiping it like it was his first lollipop. Garret let his head fall back. *Should I let it go in his mouth? No, definitely not.*

Garret was professional in every way, but the lines were smudged when it came to sex and getting off. He smiled and tipped his head back even farther.

After a few minutes, Garret pulled out of the boy's mouth and released onto his own taut, tanned stomach. The intern smiled up at Garret, stood up, and showed Garret his own erection, which exploded with barely a yank.

Those were the days. He must be not even twenty.

Garret grabbed his handkerchief and wiped his stomach, then the floor. He suddenly remembered Lucy was coming to meet him.

Bollocks.

The kid zipped up his jeans and Garret adjusted his belt.

"What's your name?" Garret asked.

"Joshua."

"I'm Gar—"

"Garret Millward, duh," Joshua said. "Listen, would you like to get some dinner some time?" Joshua was sheepish, shifting his weight.

"Quite possibly," Garret said, and handed him his card. "Now you might want to get back to work before they start to worry."

Joshua scooted out, but not before Garret pinched his butt. As he headed down himself, he caught his reflection in an old stage mirror and styled his hair.

Ever since he had arrived in America, Garret had been amazed at the abundance and ease of anonymous sexual liaisons—something he never would have imagined doing in England. Americans were so free that way, and he loved it. He retained his veneer of dignity and class, but underneath lived a layer of decadent impurity. But all that would change. Or would it? He took the steps two at a time.

———

WHEN GARRET entered the theater and saw Lucy sitting alone behind Alan, he stopped briefly to catch his breath. In the sea of empty red seats, Lucy was a beacon of unmistakable beauty.

"Hey there, princess. Sorry I'm late."

"Hi!"

Alan turned around and whispered, "Could you two take it outside? This is a rehearsal, in case you hadn't noticed."

"What bug crawled into your apple?" Garret whispered.

Lucy giggled.

"Listen Garret, this show goes up in two weeks, in case, oh yeah, that's right, you're the producer, you should know that."

"Alan, I'm going to leave you alone to work your brilliance. I'll show Lucy to Sheila's lair."

Garret led her beneath the stage to a large room they were using as a makeshift costume area. Lucy gazed around with zeal at the old costumes and the history that seemed to ooze out of the walls. There was a woman under a single lamp at an old wooden table, sewing a hem on a dress. Garret introduced Lucy very formally, considering he had just received a blow job from a stage tech.

As Garret watched, Sheila showed Lucy how to sew a hem. It was obvious that Lucy already knew how and was humoring her. Garret smiled, and turned to leave.

AFTER THE RUN-THROUGH, Garret found Lucy and led her back into the theater.

"We're going to the park," he whispered to Alan as they walked by.

"Well, please, toke one for me," Alan said.

Lucy giggled again as Garret motioned for her to follow. When they got onto Forty-fifth Street, Lucy put her hand on Garret's shoulder and said, "Newsflash. He likes you."

"Well, he has an odd way of showing it."

Lucy motioned toward a hotdog stand and grabbed Garret's arm. "C'mon, I'm famished. Let's get one."

Garret looked at the food in the cart as if it was some foreign, hazardous substance. "You are not really going to eat—"

"Oh, please, it's a hotdog. Get over it."

Lucy put everything on two dogs and Garret apprehensively took a bite while they walked.

"Hmm," he said, "it's actually quite good."

They made it up to Central Park and Lucy led him over to a bench in the shade.

"Listen, Cora sent me a text, and she and some of my other friends are meeting in this secret place downtown. You wanna come?"

He looked at her spotlight eyes, so pure and insatiable. He had always been adventurous, but being around Lucy reinforced the fact. "Well, I suppose so."

On their way out of the park, Lucy grabbed Garret's hand. "What is it," she asked as they descended the subway stairs, "about Alan? There was something else. I could tell."

"Really?" Garret feigned ignorance.

"Yes, do tell," Lucy ordered him.

Garret didn't say anything until the train came and they got into the last car, shared only by a large sleeping woman.

"Okay, Alan 101. We met about a decade ago during the opening of *Jesus Christ Superstar*. He was a dancer, and very fit, and I was what you would call a 'production assistant,' which clearly didn't amount to more than looking pretty and following the director around, whom Alan was dating at the time. And since I know you'll ask, yes, Alan and I did in fact fornicate on one discreet occasion when we were very young, but Alan was always with . . ."

Some kids got on the train, screeching with adolescent energy.

"Mitchell," Garret whispered.

When they got off at their stop, Lucy tagged Garret and ran out really fast. People stared, as if Lucy had stolen something and Garret was chasing after her, which quite possibly was the case.

They rounded the corner onto the avenue and walked on the shady side. They stopped at a Don't Walk sign and suddenly people were thick around them. The sign turned and they joined the flow of pedestrians.

"Why did you whisper when you said 'Mitchell'?" Lucy asked.

Garret didn't answer, just neatly wiped his eye with his thumb.

They cut down a Tribeca side street, industrial and deserted, where an old green car that a mobster could have driven in the 1950s was parked. Underneath it, steam was rising from a hole in the street, making the car look like it was riding a cloud. When they passed, they saw an old droopy dog in the driver's seat.

"To me, this is New York. It's like a painting," Garret said, putting his fingers up and framing the scene. "Everywhere you look, there is a story."

"That dog looks so old and peaceful, almost like he's a spirit," Lucy said.

They walked through Chinatown, where orange lanterns were strung across lampposts and the smell of dried fish and incense permeated the air. Sometimes just being in the city was all-consuming—it was hard to think about anything else.

After a while she gently took his hand and started humming.

"How peculiar," Garret said to himself as he followed Lucy down a long alley, "she can do something else besides talk."

"Easy, killer, I heard that."

They hopped over a small fence and walked alongside what looked like an old motel, the numbers on the doors rusty and incomplete. They turned the corner and there it was, like some kind of urban oasis: an empty, abandoned pool where her friends were hanging out. Lucy ran ahead, went down the ladder into the deep end, and hugged Cora, a smaller, darker version of herself.

Garret carefully climbed down the ladder, trying not to scuff his shoes.

Lucy introduced Garret proudly, showing him off as if he were her boyfriend. "Isn't he fabulous!"

"Yum," Cora said. "Fritos go with lunch."

Garret was confused. "What?"

"She means you're a snack. A hottie," Lucy clarified.

"Right. I could be her father!" Garret said.

There he was, dressed in a crisp black suit even though it was seventy degrees, between Lucy and her disheveled, punkish friends, who were smoking and playing hand-held video games. One kid, with spiky black hair and a small mangy dog, offered Garret a puff on a joint. He thought about it, then took it between his manicured fingers, and drew in a hit.

Garret looked around. *How bizarre. We are in an empty pool. This place will probably all be gone in a month. Condos for yuppies.*

Lucy and Cora got up and went off to a deli to get Cokes, and this tough-looking Asian girl sitting next to him asked what his problem was.

"Hmm?" Garret didn't hear her correctly.

"What's the problem?" the girl said again. "You were furrowing your brow just then."

"Oh, well, if you really must know, Alan, my partner, well, my working partner, is a bit cross with me, but it's the same bloody cycle, he gets stressed and takes it out on me. And I think he's jealous of Lucy, which is ridiculous."

"Not really, just means he likes you," the girl said.

Garret started to feel lightheaded and the tips of his fingers tingled. "I can't remember the last time I smoked marijuana, and when I did, it certainly wasn't light out."

"It's 4:20 somewhere," the girl said.

"It makes you very giddy. I forgot about that."

A red-haired kid put a Prince CD in a portable player. "Purple Rain" blared out of the box, echoing off the pool's dirty blue walls. Lucy and Cora came back down and sat by Garret. From above, they must have looked like some sort of tribe in a secret huddle, the man in the three-piece suit its leader. Someone turned the music down and there was a group lull.

"You know, I quite like Prince," Garret said, "but I just never understood the sex appeal. To me he's a bit like a dwarf dipped in pubic hair."

Lucy's friends remained silent, and then everyone started to laugh.

The spiky-haired kid said, "That's tight."

Garret looked puzzled.

"It means he likes your analogy," Lucy whispered to him.

"Right," Garret said, "I'm down with that."

"This guy's dope," another kid said.

"No, I'm afraid I'm not a drug dealer," Garret warned.

They all laughed again and abruptly fell silent. A bird swooped down and landed right next to them, stared at each person with clear, inquisitive eyes, then closed them and flew away.

"An angel," Lucy said.

———

THAT NIGHT THEY returned to Garret's place after eating Italian food, feeling sated but exhausted.

Garret listened to his messages: Alan, sounding tense but lighthearted, his mother, sounding excitable and warm, and an unknown male voice asking to page him in a soft, sex-fueled tone.

"Is that one of your tricks?" Lucy asked.

"Do you even know what that word means?"

"Duh."

During their dinner, Lucy had subtly hinted that it would be easier for her to spend the night since she had to be at the theater in the morning, and after the second glass of wine Garret obliged. Lucy called her mother and told her, and now here she was, wearing one of Garret's old T-shirts and curled up on his couch. He wanted to memorialize the moment, as she looked so pretty and at ease—a portrait of a happy girl.

"Well, I'm heading off for some beauty sleep, and I suggest you do the same. There are towels in the hall bathroom."

"My friends really liked you."

"Well," Garret said, doing the little shake of his head he got from his mother, "I liked them as well. They were dope, as you say."

IN THE MORNING, Garret left a note for Lucy to lock the door behind her and went for his morning run, seven on the dot, his favorite time of the day—alone with his thoughts, the forward rhythm of his legs, the sweat down his temples, the sounds of the city waking up. The stumps of old dock posts stuck out of the Hudson River like a small army reaching for the new sun. The air was damp and tepid. Summer was coming; this would be one of the last times he would run outside.

He felt a peculiar but not unpleasant feeling in his stomach, and imagined it was similar to the feeling you get when you fall in love.

12

LUCY OPENED HER EYES slowly and focused on the splash of bright red in the modern framed painting on the wall next to the bed. *I'm in Garret's house.*

She got up and walked sleepily to the kitchen, drank some orange juice out of the carton, and called her mother as promised. She seemed hung over and worried.

"Yes, I'm OK. He's gay, Mother, G-A-Y. Not a threat. He said I could stay here on the nights when I have to be here late."

Lucy sank into the big yellow chair in the breakfast nook and sighed.

"OK, I'll be on the 6:10."

She hung up and walked from room to room, feeling the rush of being alone in a new place. She didn't want to go back to Westchester. She imagined this was a normal day in her life, that she lived in that very apartment. She took her time getting ready, listening to Death Cab for Cutie on her iPod while she hard-boiled some eggs.

During her day at the theater, she tried to be as diligent as possible, and Sheila seemed impressed. At lunch, she brought Alan a bagel, and he reluctantly accepted, as if she might have poisoned it. Garret was in meetings all day.

THAT AFTERNOON Lucy took the train upstate, and her mother was late to arrive. When she finally did, she pointed at Lucy's hair. "It's your normal color now."

"Yeah, hello? You were there when I washed it out," Lucy said. *Is she already going senile?*

"Well, I like it. It looks better than the pink. Much better."

"Thanks. Mom, are you alright?"

"Yes," she said, and Lucy tried hard to believe her. She had always tried to believe her, but it was like dropping a letter off the top of a building and hoping it would land in someone's hand. A letter in her mother's handwriting that said: *Help.*

The two of them talked about the internship on the way home, and Lucy bragged about her sewing expertise.

"See, I did something right," Joyce said. "Taught you to sew."

When they got home, their usual routine began: Joyce mixing drinks and talking to her friends on the phone, Lucy upstairs listening to music and working on her designs. A while later they met in the pale yellow kitchen cluttered with day-old coffee cups and empty wine bottles. Joyce tried to hug her, and Lucy pulled away, but eventually came back to embrace her. The kitchen, a mess of memories, lay still around them.

———

DURING THE NEXT few days commuting into the city to work on the play, Lucy fell into a rhythm and felt herself drifting away from everything she had once known so well: her mom, Alex, her other school friends. She felt like one of those trees she saw growing out of the cement, pushing away her roots, and reaching toward the sky—a bright, better place. She didn't even want to go to the pool, though Cora kept sending her text messages.

That Thursday night her mother actually cooked, and after the meal they washed the dishes together. Lucy had been trying to find a way to ask for the money her mother had been saving for her because she wanted to move into the city permanently. She knew it wasn't enough, but she wanted to have it in her possession, a seed that could grow. She decided to just barge right in.

"Hey, Mom, do you have, um, the money that we talked about?"

"Yes, but I can only give you some of it now."

Something inside Lucy's belly snapped—a rubber band of pent-up emotion—and she dropped the plate she was holding. "You spent my money?"

Joyce didn't respond, just started picking up the plate pieces.

"What did you spend it on, Tanqueray?" Lucy wanted to know.

Joyce threw the pieces in the trash and slapped her daughter across the face. Tears rushed into her eyes. "You don't like me anymore!" She reached into a drawer and handed Lucy one hundred dollars with a trembling hand.

"Forget it," Lucy said, slapping the money to the floor and running up to her room.

Lucy couldn't remember her mother ever hitting her. Shaking her hard or slapping her hand, yes, but never her face and with such force. Her cheek stung as she stared at the stains on the ceiling. She decided to ask Garret about getting her mother some help.

THE FOLLOWING evening after rehearsal, Garret took Lucy to a dinner party at the home of Christian Horne, a British publicist and socialite who was semi-responsible for discovering the Beatles. He frowned at Garret when they entered and said, "I see we've found a wayward girl. And a sweet one at that. I'm afraid, however, that she'll be the only one. Not to say that many of the gentlemen you'll meet tonight wouldn't look stunning in a dress. Please, come this way."

The place took up the entire floor of the building and overlooked Central Park from the west. The dining room sat twenty. Lucy was completely astonished, and relieved that she wore her good shoes. She was underdressed by far in her cotton top and crumpled skirt, but the red heels worked; she could tell by the reactions of some of the men, who like Garret, were meticulously dressed and stunning. The food was served on elaborate platters and the champagne was smooth as butter. Lucy sat across from Garret, between Richard and Ramone, a bickering couple who looked identical. She supposed Christian figured she'd be a good buffer. But she felt uncomfortable sitting opposite Garret. Since the table was the size of a large car, he seemed so far away.

Garret tried to covertly show her how to leave the fork in her left hand. She didn't understand. Garret mouthed the words, "Don't switch," and she said, "Oh!"

Christian noticed and sniggered.

A young man named Stefan, who seemed slightly unnerved, sat next to Garret. *Probably an old trick of his*, Lucy thought. He asked Garret to come with him to Splash bar after the dinner, and Garret looked over at Lucy, who was trying desperately to eat like a lady but still felt like a girl, and said, "Not tonight, I'm afraid."

At that moment Lucy felt like she was at the very center of the planet.

"You broke up with Trevor, right?" she heard Stefan say.

"Yes, I like the sound of that," Garret replied.

"So, who is it then? C'mon, you're never alone."

"Depends on how you define alone."

ON THE WAY HOME in the cab, they were content in the silence until Lucy said, "I saw that Stefan guy all over you."

"Yeah, so?"

"You like him?"

"Not really. Already had him," Garret said.

"That apartment was *to die*. Christian was really funny. Was he really John and Yoko's best man?"

"Yes. But more important, he was their friend."

The cabbie sped up and swerved around a double-parked truck. Someone honked at him and he didn't even look.

"What do you think is more important, friends or family?" Lucy asked.

"I think, my darling," Garret said, touching the tip of her nose, "that they are one and the same."

LUCY GOT A CRAZY idea in her head while sitting at Garret's home computer the next day. After writing down some of the locations of AA meetings near her mom's town, she ordered paint, a brush, and a drop cloth from an online hardware store, using her mom's credit card.

Thirty minutes later, a delivery boy showed up at the door while Lucy was opening a bottle of wine. He was punk rock cute, and he dipped his head closer as if he were trying to smell her. He dropped the stuff inside the door and handed her a card, "That's my number if you need anything else."

Lucy looked at him coyly and said, "Anything?"

He smiled and looked at his watch. "My next delivery's not for half an hour."

"Well, I guess you could stay for a little."

Lucy's heart started to pick up the pace. She hadn't seen Alex in forever and the thought of kissing someone new teased her in the bottom of her belly.

Paint Boy sat down and Lucy stared at him. He looked tough on the outside, but she could tell he was actually shy.

"Can I kiss you?" she asked.

"I don't know." He turned red.

"Kissing," Lucy said while straddling him in the chair, "is more intimate than fucking."

She ran her lips by the soft part of his neck under his ear and then kissed him. He tasted like peanuts. She closed her eyes and thought, *I can do anything.*

She got up and skipped over to the stereo, put a Moby CD on, and prepared the materials. They started to paint a wall in Garret's living room bright orange while sharing a coffee mug of wine.

"Does the person who lives here know you're doing this?" Paint Boy asked.

"Not exactly."

"You're crazy," he said, eyes widening.

Lucy smiled as the color spread over the previously grayish wall. She started dancing around with the paintbrush in one hand.

"Orange is the new black," she said.

When Paint Boy had to leave, he whispered, "Now that we kissed, maybe next time we can . . ."

"Get back to work," she said.

He kissed her this time, and she wanted to rip his clothes off, but she knew better.

She ran back into the living room and started painting and dancing again, feeling reckless and free. In her reverie she accidentally knocked over a picture frame, which snapped apart and revealed ten pictures layered behind Trevor, the picture on top. Lucy was amazed by all the young, cute men—one of them Stefan, the guy from the party.

"Don Juan," Lucy said. "Holy shit."

She quickly reassembled the frame and put it back. She looked up at the wall. It was halfway done.

13

GARRET WALKED briskly down a cobblestone street in the meatpacking district and caught the eye of a messenger on a bicycle whose shirt was cut off at the shoulders, revealing muscled and moist skin covering a beautiful pair of arms. The young man looked back, didn't smile, but turned the corner into an alley. Garret followed him into the shadows, then emerged from the darkness but couldn't see anyone, until the guy came up from behind and tapped his shoulder, kissing him as he turned.

The messenger's hands worked their way into Garret's jeans and his head dipped back. This was the drug. What some would call an addiction—and it was much more sexy that they hadn't spoken a single word to each other. It was some sort of primal, beastly connection.

But the "escape" he usually felt was now something different. Garret had begun, during these encounters, to see pictures in his head. Flashes of fuzzy memories in sepia tones, and that day he could actually hear the voices and sounds. The cliffs in England, the roar of the shore, his father telling him to stop crying and be a man. Mitchell's wise eyes and the creak of the refrigerator door. Alan on the phone saying, *Garret, he's gone.*

A delivery truck with squeaky brakes pulled into the alley and startled them.

"*Merde,*" the messenger said, and hurried off.

WHEN GARRET GOT HOME he fixed himself a glass of water and headed into the living room. When he noticed the wall, he stopped short, aghast.

What?

He saw Lucy running to turn down the stereo.

"What in heaven's name . . . what are you doing?" Garret asked in a high-pitched voice.

"I just thought this room could use a little—"

"Permanent Halloween?" Garret was so shocked he found it hard to fill his lungs with air. "What got into you?"

Lucy just stood there, frozen, as Garret paced around wildly.

"I'll paint it back if—"

"This is my *apartment*, Lucy! Not a bloody playroom. Honestly, who do you think you are? Have you no respect? That is a '91 Bordeaux you're casually drinking! You cannot just come here, into my space, and do whatever you please." He tried to sit down, but his adrenaline got him up again. He walked right up to her. "There's a limit, Lucy. My privacy is important."

Clearly buzzed, Lucy giggled.

"This is hardly a laughing matter, young lady."

"I just like how you say that, 'pri-va-cy,'" she said.

Garret fumed. His blood felt like hot lava surging inside him. *Is this what my father feels like all the time?*

"Don't you see this is not a joke? This is serious. What do you have to say for yourself?" Garret squeezed his glass of water and to avoid it breaking in his hand, he threw it onto the floor, where it shattered.

Lucy silently put down the paintbrush, grabbed her bag, and

slowly left the apartment, leaving Garret stunned, leaning against the partly orange wall.

Am I really crazy for letting Lucy stay here like Alan said? Am I becoming my father? What a horrid thought . . .

After sitting in the post-explosion silence for a bit, he poured himself the last glass of the Bordeaux that was given to him by Mitchell, in 1991, the year it came out—Mitchell had just returned from France and told him it would be *the* year. He was going to drink it with Alan on Mitchell's would-be birthday. *Oh my lord, that's today.*

He took a long slow sip as the shards of the water glass crunched underneath his Italian loafers. He noticed Lucy's sketchbook still on the table. He let out a snicker.

What was she thinking?

He looked through Lucy's designs and finished the wine. He thought of calling Alan but kept putting it off. He dozed on the couch, then eventually got up and did his hygiene routine and put on his silk couture pajamas. As he slid into his crisp white sheets, he told himself Lucy must have gone home or was with that Cora girl.

She'll be fine.

IN THE MORNING, there was still no sign of her, so Garret pressed redial from his landline. Lucy's mother picked up.

"Hello there, Garret here, I'm, well, a mate of your daughter's."

"What?"

"A friend! Well, you know . . . I'm sorry, but did Lucy come home yesterday?"

"No, she was supposed to. Who is this?"

Her mother sounded sedated. He told her he was going to go look for Lucy, and she said, "What happened? What did she do?"

"Nothing," Garret said, "nothing at all."

He hung up and began to slowly pace around. It had started to rain. *Please let her be all right.* He looked at the orange wall again. He stood back to get perspective. Out of instinct, or simply for something to do, he finished painting it.

It looked good. He found himself smiling. Then he heard footsteps and ran to the door. Lucy came in, wet and forlorn. Without speaking, he took her into his arms. For the first time since Mitchell died, Garret started to cry. They sat on the couch. He could tell Lucy was a bit freaked out, so after a minute he calmed down.

"I was so worried," he whispered. "I thought you'd never come back."

"I feel like shit. I am so sorry. I have entitlement issues, I know. That's what my roommate at school said. All my life my mother told me I act without thinking, that I don't have enough self-control, and I guess she's right. I just—"

"Sshh. Where did you go?"

Lucy went over to the wall, noticing he finished it, and touched the dry part with her open hands. "I slept at the pool, I—"

"Lucy!"

"Garret, you were throwing things. It scared me. I can take care—"

"I know you can but please, promise me. Don't leave like that."

"OK, OK."

"And I won't frighten you again. We just need to have rules, boundaries, if you're going to stay over," Garret said, dabbing at his eyes with his shirt collar.

"Of course."

"That wine was a gift from Mitchell. I've been saving it for over a decade."

Garret lit a cigarette and they both stared at the wall in silence.

"I am so sorry," Lucy said slowly.

Garret took a drag and as he blew it out said, "Orange."

Lucy started to smile a little. "It does give the room a little, how do you say, pizzazz?"

"I'll give you pizzazz. But before that, call your mother immediately. She was worried sick."

"Call me crazy, but I find that hard to believe," Lucy said.

"Well, I certainly was."

Garret watched Lucy walk sheepishly over to the phone. In the daylight, the orange wall changed everything. But he liked it.

14

ALAN MARKED AN "X" over another day on the calendar hanging on his door and sighed. Less than two weeks before the opening, and the play was in pretty good shape.

He grabbed his cat from the floor and plopped down on the sofa. Tramp whined and tried to leave.

"I need love, too, Tramp!"

Consuela, his Puerto Rican housekeeper, came to the doorway. "Alan, you should not talk to your cat. It's not healthy." Consuela had come to New York with a backpack and a curling iron. During the day she cleaned the homes of successful gay men, and at night she moonlighted as a dominatrix, punishing the egos of successful married men. All to pay her way through her master's program at Columbia, naturally.

Shit, Alan thought. *It's Thursday.*

"Listen, Consuela, I already have a shrink, so let's just stick to dusting and vacuuming."

"Well," she said while emptying out the freezer, "you did name the cat 'Tramp.'"

"That's true. Kind of cruel, huh?"

"Listen," Consuela said, sitting down next to Alan. "You're going through ice cream like my grandmother, and trust me, you don't want to see what her ass looks like. Two pints a week is enough, Chico, otherwise I'm giving the rest to the homeless."

"Great, now you're not only my maid and my shrink, you're a nutritionist. Did you want to do some Pilates later?"

"Who?"

The phone rang.

"It's your mother; she called twice already."

"Okay, let's add secretary to the list," Alan said.

"Don't stereotype me 'cause I'm a minority."

"So am I, sweet cheeks." Alan smiled and picked up the phone. "Hellew?"

"What is going on with Garret?" asked his mother.

Alan waited until Consuela was completely out of earshot and started to speak.

"Oh, Mother, must you be so shallow, so impure, so gossip-hungry? OK, here's the dirt. The girl is interning with the costumer, and he's getting all paternal, which is a good sign, don't you think?"

"Where is the girl's mother?"

"She's upstate somewhere. I'm beginning to feel insignificant. Lucy has all the power and I'm still a groveling plebeian, a mere serf, I tell you."

Tramp jumped off the bed as if sick of Alan's antics.

"Oh, Alan, don't be so pathetic," his mother said. "It's unbecoming."

Three years ago, in a delusional state, Alan had told his mother that it should have been Garret he was with all along, not Mitchell. It wasn't true; it was only because Mitchell had been working all the time, and Alan was spending so much more time with Garret. He had also been recovering from a drug-filled weekend. Ever since then, his mother would not drop the subject, particularly now that sadly, Mitchell was out of the picture.

"Anyway, I've got that number," she said. "The lawyer we

talked about." Alan could hear in her voice that she'd been crying on the other end. She knew it was Mitchell's birthday. *She's probably cried more than I have*, Alan thought, which made him feel a flash of guilt. "Thanks. Listen, call me later, OK?"

"Fine."

Alan got up and fished around for the ad he saw earlier in the *Village Voice*:

Jump Fitness
Join now
No initiation fee
Two free personal training sessions

That's it, I'm doing it, he thought, and dialed the number. He looked over at his cat for reassurance, but Tramp looked bored in her corner spot by the window.

IT WAS EARLY STILL when Alan met Garret at their local "mixed" lounge, so they went over some notes about the play. Alan became increasingly annoyed as Garret's eyes darted around the place, prowling.

Why do I even think about him that way? Alan wondered. *Probably because he is the only one who really knows me.*

Alan gave up on getting any more work done, chewed on some bar nuts, and offered Garret some.

"Can't. I'm allergic, remember?"

A simple thing Alan had never registered in his brain. Seeing how Garret seemed so at ease, Alan suddenly felt socially inept. Ever since Mitchell died, the only people he interacted with outside of work were his cat, his mother, and Consuela.

Garret continued searching the clientele with a cool and composed look on his face.

"Tell me something," Alan said while chewing the nuts, "do you ever stop?"

"Do you know how many calories those have? It's horrendous," Garret said without looking at him.

"That's not what I asked. And can we not discuss my fat intake? Besides, I joined a gym. The new one above Four-bucks."

"What?"

"That's what I call Starbucks," Alan said.

Garret chuckled. "More like ten bucks now."

"Anyway, you're diverting, as you always do."

"It's a game, Alan, don't you see?" Garret motioned around the bar. "The hunters, and the hunted."

"How tribal," Alan said.

"You know, you should go on the make a bit yourself, wouldn't hurt," Garret suggested.

"I'm not interested in Twinkie club love. I'm old school."

A man, handsome but pushing sixty, walked slowly by and overtly checked out Alan.

"OK, not that old," Alan said.

There was something about Garret's laugh that made Alan feel nostalgic.

"With Mitchell—"

"Mitchell's gone, sweetheart," Garret said. "I know it's only been a year. . . ." Alan could see Garret's face go soft as he put out his cigarette and continued. "We were so close, the three of us. . . ."

"Yes," Alan said, and sipped his drink. "We'd eat ramen and day-old bread from the bakery, talking about how we would change the world, just out of college and clueless."

Alan remembered the ladies who ran the bakery had thought the three of them were so cute they started giving them fresh bread for the price of day-old.

"Tell me, Garret, I want to know, did you sleep with Mitchell other than our threesome when we were kids? Ever?"

Garret wore a sly look that Alan couldn't read.

"No. We just kissed. And you were watching, I believe."

"Oh, such dignity," Alan said.

"Did you ever cheat on Mitchell?" Garret countered.

Alan smiled. "Just with you."

"Yes, but that was in the beginning when things weren't defined. What's going on with the estate?" Garret asked, suddenly concerned.

"You make it sound like I'm an heiress."

"You are. An heir, that is," Garret corrected.

"Well, this heir is under the wrath of Jane, Mitchell's demonic sister."

"Right. Her. Well, you have a right—"

"I know, blah blah blah. I'm just tired of fighting."

Garret went to pay for the check.

"Please be at rehearsal tomorrow," Alan said. "I need . . . I want you there. For me."

"Sure thing, Alan, sure thing. Oh, get this. Lucy painted my wall orange."

The DJ started spinning and a group of loud NYU students entered, oblivious to everyone around them.

"What?" Alan was appalled.

"Yeah. I was bloody furious. But I have to say, I'm sort of keen on it. I also told her she could stay the whole week. I'm not quite sure what has gotten into me."

"You're definitely smoking something," Alan said, as they got up to leave.

Once they were outside, Garret kissed Alan on the cheek the way he always did. Alan was tempted to turn his head at the last second, to really kiss him and see what he'd do, but he couldn't take the possibility of rejection. Not tonight.

15

GARRET CAME HOME to find Lucy asleep on the couch, an issue of *Paper* opened on her stomach. He watched her sleep for a while and then woke her up and led her to the bedroom. After he tucked her in and quietly closed the door, he returned to the couch and took a bite of her half-eaten PopTart.

He picked up the landline and speed-dialed.

"Hello, Mum. Yes, I am sorry, it's the show and all."

"Garret, this has clearly gone on too long. You must speak to him," Dorothy said, her voice crystal clear for being thousands of miles across the Atlantic.

"What will that do?" Garret asked, swallowing his bite of PopTart and wiping the crumbs from his hand.

"Listen, dear, maybe if you met someone he could grow to admire . . ."

"I met a girl, actually," Garret said, looking toward the closed door of the guest room.

"Really?" His mother seemed apprehensive.

"It's not what you think. She's a riddle. She's just a kid." Garret started shutting off all the lights and smiled at the orange wall. "Listen, Mum, I must go to bed."

"Wait, sweetheart, one more thing. When does the play open?"

"The eighteenth. Why do you ask?"

"No reason in particular. I'll speak to you later."

His mum put the phone down but didn't properly hang up,

and Garret could hear the crackle of the fire, could almost smell the English country home he grew up in through the connection. He pictured his father, George, stocky and gray-haired, a dour expression on his face, doing crossword puzzles in between sips of scotch.

"That was your son," he heard her say. "You do have a son, in case you'd forgotten."

His father grunted and said, "I'm not responsible for his sins, dear."

Garret almost hung up, but it was strangely comforting to hear his father's voice, even if the words were cruel.

"Don't 'dear' me. He's your own flesh and blood," Dorothy said.

Since when is Mum talking back to him?

He heard her scoop up her teacup and walk away from the phone. Then she said loudly, "He didn't choose his lifestyle to spite you."

Garret felt a surge of affection for his mother. What would he have done without her? He gently placed the phone back into the receiver.

Even though he was tired, he decided to go back out. The night seemed edgy now; his nerves were frayed. Just beyond the church at Twentieth and Park he could see an almost full moon.

He passed the back door of a place where he used to work when he first came to New York more than a decade earlier, where he sold furniture with an old Chinese man who looked like Buddha and smelled like bouillon cubes. Those days seemed like another lifetime, but he could picture the shop in his head perfectly. The desks stacked up in the front, the lamps in the window, how awkward it was trying to sell furniture in a small rectangular space with high ceilings. How that job had led to the one he had now on account of becoming friendly with the man's daughter, Song, who had long, silky black hair and cleaned theaters in midtown. One day Song had witnessed a director fire his assistant and called Garret at the store to tell him. Her English was sparse and she was secretive about it because her father needed him, but she knew Garret had dreams that didn't involve pushing desk sets. Garrett had made some excuse and bolted all the way to the theater on foot, waited by the stage door thinking, *This is it, this is my chance.* When a handsome, gangly young man came out, he did a double take. "Waiting for someone?"

"Yes, in fact," Garret said. "A chap named Mitchell."

"What for?"

By his smile, Garret knew he had found the right guy. Adorable too. Just then Alan barged out of the door and said to Mitchell, "Found a wayward boy?"

Mitchell then took a call on his cell phone (one of the first ones, just a little smaller than a football), and Garret was left alone with Alan. They just looked at each other. Well, Alan sort of sneered, while Garret tried to look together and collected.

"Look, I heard he fired his assistant?" Garret asked.

"What are you, psychic? That happened minutes ago," Alan said.

"Listen, I'm very keen on. . . ."

Mitchell hung up the phone and said, "I need a drink."

"Or five. Let's go," Alan said.

As they both walked away Garret's hope dwindled, and he stood there like a kid whose kite had gotten stuck in a tree. Then, miraculously, Alan turned his head and yelled, "You coming?"

The kite was back in flight. He was hired around the third drink.

Today, Garret walked up to the very same bar and stood in

front of its large glass doors. A couple came out and lounge music wafted out with cooled air. *What if Alan hadn't turned around that night?*

He went inside the dimly lit club, which had changed names at least three times since, and went downstairs. He got lost in the human pulp of the packed dance floor. The music was excellent—bass-heavy and laced with a soulful female voice. Weeding through the faces, the sea of flitting eyes, Garret started to dance, opening his eyes only occasionally. He spotted a young girl biting at the nipple ring of a Latino go-go boy, and a bald guy dancing with only his head, heaving his skull around on every other beat. Garret turned and suddenly was behind a writhing body in tight pants, bare-chested beneath a leather vest. He impulsively joined him.

Everyone seemed to be taking part in a giant release, a cumulative shedding. The floor thumped as colored lights flashed. The sound filled Garret's body like a blazing current, forcing him to keep moving. They drifted over to a darker corner of the dance floor. *This guy is hot*, Garret decided and kissed his neck, his collarbone, licking a drop of sweat that had formed on his nipple. Garret was so hard that his crotch ached.

But outside in the light of the alley he wasn't as sexy.

The Village People are over, he could hear Alan say.

Still, Garret's cock unfolded out of his pants like a child's toy that was built for surprise. The Village Person took it all inside his mouth right away, which felt warm and cavernous. Garret closed his eyes, the music pumping through the brick wall, muffled bass and the hint of a snare drum.

The guy stopped and looked up at Garret with swollen almond eyes and smiled, then went back down on him.

Suddenly it all seemed wrong. He put himself away and said, "Sorry, mate."

He left the confused Village Person in the alley.

When he got back home he sobbed in the shower. Hearing his father's voice had actually comforted him. Picking up that guy didn't erase anything. He felt impure and angry with himself. He sat down and hugged his knees, letting the hot water run over his head to numb his thoughts.

16

ALAN GOT BACK from his first session at the gym and still had enough energy to start cleaning, even though Consuela just had. He sang along with Blossom Dearie and acted out the songs, using the obligatory cleaning products as props. He was about to belt out the chorus when his buzzer sounded. He hadn't ordered any delivery. Who could it be?

"This better be good," Alan said into the intercom. "Who lurks there?"

He glanced out the window and there was Lucy on the stoop, her bag dangling over her shoulder.

"Your muse. Get over it," she said, holding down the button.

"Oh, I should have known," Alan said.

He buzzed her through, and quickly hid his lunch dishes and lit a candle. He looked at himself in the mirror, freed a lock of hair that was stuck to his forehead.

Why do I care? Ever since Mitchell had gone he'd barely even looked in the mirror.

Lucy entered without knocking, holding a bag of cookies in her hand. "Look!" she said.

"Oh, just what I need, fat-free right? You might as well just tape them to my butt. Get there faster."

Lucy giggled and spun around as if on display.

"And you should watch yourself too, next thing you know you'll be like the ladies at the bus stop who have FUPA."

"What the hell is that?" Lucy asked, stopping mid-spin.

"Fat upper pussy area."

"Gross!" Lucy said, touching her lower belly.

Alan led her to the living room and they each took a cookie and sat on the couch.

"Garret said you need something from me," Lucy said. "What am I doing now, playing the lead?"

Oh that's why she's here. I told him I'd talk to her at the theater. He's probably tricking and needed to get rid of her, the horn dog.

"Well, not exactly. I need you to help the house manager on opening night. His assistant ran off to Lithuania with some nymphet. I have a replacement, but not for the opening."

"Where's Lithuania?" Lucy asked.

"Not in Times Square, peaches. Now listen. All you have to do is to help lead the proper celebs, investors, etc., to their corresponding seat numbers. And get any dirt you can, of course. He'll show you the procedure."

"Maybe I'll get discovered."

"I'm afraid that already happened, honey," Alan said, putting half of his cookie back in the bag.

Lucy looked confused. "What, so first you give me the cold shoulder and now because you need me you're being all nice?"

"Welcome to Hollywood."

"This is New York," Lucy said.

"Whatev. Listen, I would have been nice sooner. . . . I'm just, well, protective, I guess."

"Understandable." Lucy sat back and hurled her bag up onto her lap. "Alan, tell me what you think of these." She took out her sketchbook and showed him her hat designs. "I've been perfecting them since graduation. I want to be a milliner . . . design hats for women," Lucy said proudly.

"You drew these from scratch?"

Wow, starlet looks and talent, too, Alan thought, looking at her, sitting in his home for the first time as if she belonged there.

Lucy looked up and nodded proudly. Alan tried not to look as amazed as he was. "Well, they're . . . hey, you know Garret is friends with—"

"Heather Bridges. He's going to try to get me a meeting."

Alan took a sip of seltzer water and wiped his lip. "Well, moving fast, aren't we?"

"Only way to move," Lucy replied. She swallowed her cookie and lightly punched Alan on his arm. "So, what's stopping you?" she asked.

"From what?"

"Jumping Garret's bones."

Alan chuckled. "I'm not his type."

"He likes you," Lucy said.

"That's the operative word. 'Like.'"

"It's a persuadable like. There's spark."

Alan stopped on a page of Lucy's book. "Hmm, I like this one."

"I know you want him," Lucy said.

"Well, he does pass my requirements for a boyfriend. I just haven't even thought about dating in so long."

"What are your requirements?" Lucy asked.

"The four A's: available, attractive, appropriate, and affluent."

"Hmm. Available?"

"That one's a gray area," Alan said.

Lucy noticed a picture behind Alan on the side table—a younger Garret wearing a top hat and a wide smile. "God, he was even cuter than he is now," she said. Garret's arm was around a slightly older, handsome man with a goatee. She picked up the picture. She didn't have to confirm that it was Mitchell.

"No one will ever fill his shoes, right?" she said softly.

Alan willed himself to stay strong and not collapse in front of a teenager. "Right."

"Well," Lucy announced, "we're having dinner at our place, the three of us, tomorrow. No excuses. I'll slip out early-ish and maybe you can at least try and kiss him."

Alan was charmed. *Does she really think it's that easy?* He looked at Lucy's face, slightly sunburned but alarmingly pretty.

"You're serious, aren't you?" he asked.

"Just come over. I'm making latkes."

"Just what I need, more carbs." Alan handed her the schedule, with her highlighted call time. "Just include a salad, please."

"No prob. And as for the opening—you can count on me, Alan."

"Well, I hear you're doing really well with the costumes."

"Naturally." Lucy grabbed her bag and placed her hand on top of Alan's head. "See you."

Alan sat in the aftermath of Lucy, her bag of cookies spilled out onto the table, her simple words still hovering in his head: *No one could fill his shoes.*

17

AFTER WORKING OUT hard at the gym, Garret walked in the door to his apartment and was pleasantly surprised by the smell of food being prepared—it was a first. Lucy was sautéing like a pro chef and balancing the phone on her shoulder. He stood unnoticed at the kitchen door.

"He's such a bachelor," she said. "These pans have never been used." She twisted in some fresh pepper and took a taste. "No, Mom, I'm fine. I told you. He's a fag, not an axe murderer. The worst thing he could do is make me change outfits."

Lucy walked over and stared out the window as if lulled into a spell.

"He's a friend. He's amazing." She sat down clumsily in the big yellow chair and dangled her legs over the armrest. "He's trying to get me a meeting with Heather Bridges, and you probably don't know who that is cause they don't sell her line at JCPenney." Garrett winced, still in the doorway.

"OK, sorry, that was low. Anyway, I don't care if I'm wiping her ass. I need experience to get my hats off the ground."

Lucy walked back and tasted the sauce again with her finger, then lowered the heat, so it would simmer. She finally noticed Garret standing there and dropped the phone.

"Ah! Shit, Garret, you scared me. I didn't hear. . . ." She giggled and picked up the phone again. "I'm cooking right now, Mom. Yes. I'll be on the noon train, I promise. Bye." She hung up.

"Smells divine," he said.

"How long were you . . . ?" Lucy kissed him on his scruffy cheek and said, "She's not registering the milliner thing. It's like she's on another planet."

"Well, you'll just have to prove it to her, right?"

"That's the plan."

They both sat back down in the breakfast nook, and Garret cracked the window.

"Listen," Lucy said, "I need some backstory. How did Mitchell die?"

"Err. I believe I need a drink first." Garret got up, shook up some Belvedere and ice in his Tiffany shaker, and found the last olive from a jar in the fridge. He took a martini glass out of the freezer and poured, dropping the olive last, like a period at the end of sentence. He took a long gulp, a big breath, and sat back down.

"Mitchell was the biggest producer on Broadway. He knew everyone. Andy Warhol, Mick Jagger, you name it. He was a real mover and shaker, started with nothing and became the toast of the theater scene. He talked his way into Studio 54 one day, when he was nobody, and it all started from there. During *Jesus Christ Superstar*, he was dating Alan, and the three of us became very close. He loved Alan like a pet and was never unfaithful. Well, almost never."

Lucy's eyes turned on their spotlights. Garret took another gulp of his martini and got out a cigarette. It felt good talking about it.

"They were together for over ten years. Eventually Alan became quite a prominent director himself and Mitchell was in deep with some new Andrew Lloyd Weber production deals. They had barely seen each other in months. They were finally going to have a vacation together, in Paris. They had planned it months ahead of time; the both of them were so excited about it. They rushed to the airport to get their flight, and after they got their boarding passes, they were literally running to the gate, and . . ."

The wind picked up and blew some leaves onto the windowsill. Lucy put down the lemon she had been squeezing.

"And he died. Right there in the terminal, in Alan's arms. Heart attack. He was fifty-two."

Lucy closed her eyes. "Jeez."

"And that's not all. That very same morning . . ."

"What?"

Garret had never said it out loud. He desperately wanted to, but something told him it wasn't the time.

"Listen, can we continue this conversation at a later date?"

"Of course," Lucy said, and went right back to cooking. She could sense that Garret was done. He remembered the overly persistent Lucy he had met on the plane, and it was as if he was looking at a different person now. He flipped through his mail to distract himself, and a few minutes later the martini was gone. Lucy came over quietly.

"I got a call from Cora today," she said. "It turns out that Alex, my pseudo-boyfriend, took off for California and didn't even tell me. It's not like I told him I was coming to New York . . . but California? That's like, far."

In that moment Garret wanted to cover her completely, create a barricade around her, make her impervious to the world.

"Well, it sounds like he is a bit unrefined for the new Lucy, wouldn't you say?"

Garret ran his finger across her cheek and started gathering items to set the table.

"How come you're so nice to me?" Lucy asked.

Garret was wondering the same thing himself.

"Hmmm?" Lucy started washing some lettuce.

"I'm not exactly sure, but I think it has to do with feeling useful," Garret said.

Lucy sat up on the counter. "You know, I was thinking about that day at the airport, and how the person in front of us in line had to run to the bathroom with her baby. She would have gotten bumped to first class instead of me."

Garret didn't like to think about those things because once he started it got overwhelming. Every little detail was linked to a coil that influenced his every move. Even though he believed in fate, he preferred to simply take the ride.

"It was always going to happen that way," he said.

Color suddenly rushed into Lucy's face, and she said, "Garret, I wanted to say sorry again, about the wall. That was—"

"The past," Garret interrupted. "Besides, I have to say, it actually suits the place."

The doorbell rang and in strolled a clean-shaven Alan with flowers in his arms.

"Wow," Alan said, noticing the orange wall. "Understated."

Garret and Lucy looked at each other and smiled.

THEY SETTLED into dinner as old jazz doodled out of the stereo and candles gave the room a muted glow.

"I must say, this is quite delicious, Lucy," Garret offered.

"Thanks. It's my famous Romesco sauce. I ditched the potato pancake idea."

"Not only can she cook, the girl can do wonders with headwear," Alan said, gesturing toward the wall. "And now interior design!"

"Maybe I should start a cooking show," Lucy suggested.

"Yeah," Alan said, "call it, 'Out of the box and onto your plate.'"

The phone rang and no one moved to get it. The machine picked up and after Garret's greeting, it beeped. Trevor's voice sounded laced with tears and alcohol.

"Garret, it's me, you there? Listen . . . things didn't work out with Damian. Anyway, call me. . . . I'd love to hear your voice."

An awkward silence ensued.

"Well," Alan said, clearing his throat, "how come he's crawling back?"

"Trevor's a flake," Lucy said. "Garret's over him, anyway."

"Aw, another broken heart to put on the shelf, what is this now, door number 85?" Alan said before taking a large sip of wine.

"Please, let's not talk about my escapades," Garret pleaded.

"The Latin root of that word is escape," Alan said.

Lucy clinked his glass in approval. "Nice one."

Alan did his best imitation of Gloria Swanson. "Words, words, words. You've made a rope of words and strangled this business!"

"*Sunset Boulevard*," Garret said. "Couldn't tell you the year or the actress."

Alan lifted up his arms and said, "But you got one! One out of three is a start."

Garret raised his glass as if toasting himself and sipped.

"OK, I have one," Lucy said, flipping her hair and playing a bitch.

"Are you a 'Heather'? No, I'm a 'Veronica.'"

"I'm afraid the game only works with old movies, dear," Alan said condescendingly, "classics, shall we say."

"*Heathers*," Garret said. "A modern classic."

"Rock on. Two for two." Lucy started to clear the plates and stuck her tongue out at Alan. After she went into the kitchen, Alan asked Garret if he was going to call Trevor back.

"Certainly not," Garret replied firmly. "I don't know Al, I feel different, like something is changing me, something beyond my control. Even things look different. My block, the clouds."

"Take any lithium lately?"

"No, I'm serious Alan. . . ."

Lucy came back in with cookies and sorbet, but only for two.

"You handsome men have some dessert. I'm going to retire. It's hard work being a fabulous teenager. I am exhausted." She winked at Alan, who seemed flushed.

"Right, then, thank you, dear," Garret said.

"*Je vous en prie.*"

"Wow, she knows French too," Alan said. "Maybe it'll be a French cooking show, with a milliner's twist!"

After dessert, Garret and Alan went up to the roof. The city hummed and buzzed around them, the lights from the buildings making illuminated patterns on the sides of the buildings. Garret smoked as Alan stared at the skyscrapers, in between which hung a fingernail of a moon.

"You know, it's strange to say, but you look hot when you smoke," Alan said. "You're like the British version of a Marlboro man."

Garret laughed. "All I need is a horse."

Alan placed his hand on Garret's shoulder, and it felt good to have someone touch him in a nonsexual way. Earlier, when Lucy had leaned on him in the kitchen, he had felt this swell of emotion and could have let her stay there forever.

"I just keep dreaming about him," Alan said.

"Still?" Garret asked.

"You know that part of the show where the angels come out

over the audience? I dream that it's him—all the angels have his face. And then it's as if someone simultaneously cuts all the strings, and they fall. Then I wake up."

They stood, dwarfed by the buildings towering above them. Garret cupped his palm around Alan's cheek. "They will go away. I promise."

18

IN THE MORNING Lucy walked sleepily into the kitchen and downed a glass of milk. Garret had already jogged and was perfectly groomed and dressed. On his way out, he handed her a breakfast bar.

"Here, Alan left this here one time, have it on the train. You better get a move on," he said.

"I can't. It has nuts in it."

"Oh. A girl after my own heart," Garret said, and kissed her hand. After he left, Lucy went over to the window and watched him make his way down the street.

After quickly showering, Lucy locked Garret's apartment and zigzagged up to Grand Central, making her train just in time. As the city turned into suburbia she listened to Snow Patrol and worked on her sketches. When she arrived and got off the train platform, she fiddled with her hair and walked over to a bench where her mom was sitting, feeding a few birds from a bag of bread.

Lucy sat down next to her and looked up. The sky was electric blue with a few wisps of bright white clouds. "Perfect day," Lucy said.

Joyce looked pale in the bright sun and there seemed to be a glow around her head.

"How is Gary?" Joyce asked without looking at her, still feeding the birds.

"Garret. He's great; he's been so nice."

The birds were mindlessly happy and twitching with delight. Her mother seemed mesmerized by them. Lucy took her folder out of her bag and showed her the drawings from her hat collection.

"Look, Mom, just look."

For the first time ever, her mother actually looked at her work. She had seen stuff before, on the walls of Lucy's room and doodles on the corners of pads, but she treated it like wallpaper. Now her eyes showed a different reaction.

"You did these?" she asked.

"Yeah. It's the glorified housewife collection," Lucy said.

"The . . . what?"

Lucy felt a sting of frustration, but instead of lashing out, she told herself to stay calm. At least her mom was trying.

"The demographic. Very Wisteria Lane."

Joyce nodded. When the bread was gone, the birds slowed their movements and stared intently, confused and needing guidance.

"Promise me one thing," Joyce said, folding up the plastic bag and looking hard at her daughter. "Be careful. And when you stay with him, call me. Check in. I'm not some ogre, you know. I happened to be the one that raised you to be this. . . ."

Lucy hammed it up. "Fabulous . . ."

"Fabulous . . . fashion maker," Joyce said while rolling her eyes.

"Designer, Mom. Designer."

"Whatever the hell it is, I deserve some respect."

"OK."

"Movie?" Joyce said, standing up and putting her hand up to shield her eyes from the light.

Lucy flashed to the most pleasant memory of her childhood:

going to movies with her mother on half-Wednesdays. She blocked out the day her mother never showed up.

"Sure."

They started to walk toward Joyce's beat-up Ford.

"You know," Joyce said, as if asking her daughter to pass the butter, "I think I'm going to stop drinking. And I've met this wonderful man. I have a feeling you'd like him."

Please, not another loser, Lucy thought. *Please.*

They approached the car.

"What's his name?" Lucy asked.

They looked at each other over the roof of the car.

"Stanley," Joyce said, preparing for a reaction.

Lucy snickered as they got in the car.

"It's strange, though," Joyce said as they pulled onto the street, "he's this AA type, but he spends all his time in bars."

"What does he drink?"

"Pellegrino."

Lucy thought of the dinner party, and remembered how the color of the bottle had matched Garret's eyes. She had always thought it was such a sophisticated drink, but hated the way it tasted. Sharp and thin, flavorless.

"He says that going to bars reinforces his sobriety," Joyce said.

"Kind of like watching animals in a zoo?"

"Sort of. He has the cutest dimples."

Lucy looked at her mother. Her hair was pulled back and her eyes seemed rested. She looked happy, and pretty, which Lucy had not witnessed in quite a while.

"Mom, are you falling in love?"

Joyce tilted her head a little to the side and said, "Maybe."

Lucy hoped that whatever it was this man was doing to her,

it would last. After the movie, a chick flick that was entertaining but one-dimensional, they had dinner and Joyce ordered ginger ale.

"You're either falling in love or you're on something. C'mon, what is it? Zoloft?"

Joyce smiled. "Nope. Natural high."

"Hmm. Me too," Lucy said.

"Good, you keep it that way. I hear horror stories about girls your age."

The busboy cleared their plates and Lucy knew she had to say something. Cut the chord. Or at least start the fraying process.

"Well, Mom, there is something I want to talk to you about. If this internship works out, I'm going to be moving to New York, and when I'm eighteen you're going to have to, by law, tell me who my father is."

Joyce didn't say anything, but slowly nodded her head.

19

GARRET SPENT the morning in back-to-back meetings, coordinating all the lawyers, investors, and theater administrators with regard to the opening of the play. He felt like a multitasking octopus, each arm doing a different job. That's why he loved working as a producer—tackling unexpected issues, verbally massaging people, having an overall sense of malleability. He could lose himself in the work and not think about his personal life, which seemed like a field of landmines ready to explode with guilt, regret, and longing.

On Seventh Avenue he avoided the seductive eyes of yet another bike messenger (or was it the same one?) and hurried north, weaving among the fashionistas sipping iced lattes and avoiding the trinket-selling street vendors. He finally reached the giant sliding glass doors of the looming, mirrored building. The humid late-June air dissolved into the frigid climate of the heavily air-conditioned lobby. For this last appointment of the day, he was on time.

As he walked to Heather's office on the penthouse floor, Garret got many looks from the various secretaries and interns, male and female alike. Everyone was hypergroomed, trendily dressed and sporting expensive hair, including Garret in his cream-colored linen jacket with matching pants. Though he usually dressed in black, it was a particularly hot day and Garret knew that Heather would appreciate the "old money" look he had going on. Apparently the rest of the office did as well.

He peered around her door. She sat at her desk, looking over specs for what Garret assumed was the fall/winter collection. Heather looked him up and down and sighed as if to say, *Such a waste that you're gay.*

"Alright, handsome, what is it this time?" Heather asked, looking back down at the prints.

"I wanted to ask you a favor," Garret said.

"Shoot."

"I've met this girl . . ."

"Sit," she said, motioning toward a striped gray and white chair. Heather took off her glasses and carefully removed a strand of straightened hair from her eyelash. "Hang on, come again?"

Garret sat down and explained. "She's a kid, really. But real bright, wants to get into the fashion biz, I thought maybe . . ."

"How old is she?"

"Seventeen."

"Babe, this isn't summer camp," Heather said.

"No, I'm afraid you don't understand, she's . . . she's . . . remarkable. She's designed this hat collection. It's very unique, classy."

The phone bleeped.

"Really." Heather seemed mildly intrigued.

Another bleep.

"Listen, I've got to take this, have her call my secretary, the pale one who's probably purging her lunch at present. I'll meet with her next week. Name," she said with a flick of her finger as she put on her headset.

"What?"

Heather's finger, nail painted blood red, flicked again impatiently. "Her name."

"Oh, Lucy. Lucy Walker," Garret said.

She took the call and said, "Heather Bridges . . . hold on a sec."

Garret got up and straightened his suit. "So that's it, you'll see her?" He hadn't thought it would be that easy. It was all because of Mitchell, of course. He had known everyone that was anyone, and was even posthumously pulling strings.

"Unlike half of the playboys within Manhattan's five boroughs, I trust you. You have good instincts. Talk soon, Romeo."

Heather started on her phone call and Garret snuck out.

Normally, at that time in the afternoon he would cruise for a quickie, but the thought went in and out of his head like a butterfly caught in a gust of wind.

GARRET MET ALAN on the corner and they started walking in time together. He noticed something different about him.

"You're glowing, Alan. Did you have a shag?"

"If only. It's called a steam bath. I've been to the gym," Alan said.

"Good for you."

"Yeah, well, we'll see if I keep going."

"All my meetings went off without a hitch. Let me ask you something. You think we're going to pull this show off?" Garret asked.

"You remember last time?"

Their last show had been a hit. The two of them were shot for the cover of *Time Out*.

"Yes, well, that's due to the fact that you're a maniac," Garret said.

"That's why we work so well together. You're the brains and I'm the brawn."

Alan switched his bag from one shoulder to the other and sighed. "Sweetheart, in all seriousness, these last two shows, they're why I get up in the morning. The other night I woke up about three a.m. and started *talking* to him. I actually reached over to his side of the bed. Then I felt this bottomless hole inside me, as if I weren't even made of flesh." Alan looked up at the sky. "Sometimes I just wish I could touch him, just for a second."

When they reached the steps to Alan's apartment Garret embraced his best friend. How many times had he tried to tell him what *really* happened the day Mitchell died? Words caught like leaves in a drain, never quite getting through. But every time it rained their disintegration progressed, and pretty soon there would be nothing left to hold them back.

"See you back at the theater," Garret said.

"Will do."

As Alan started up the stairs, Garret stared at the door and again felt the words, piled against the inside of his heart, pounding to get out.

20

WHEN ALAN CAME home after his fourth workout session, he picked up Tramp and did a little twirl in his kitchen. He was feeling elated, and not quite sure why. It was a clear, breezy summer day, and the city seemed alive with hope. Somehow living on without Mitchell felt more possible, like getting the two outside X's in tic-tac-toe. Maybe there was something or someone out there that would make the row complete.

He put Tramp down and poured himself a seltzer.

The phone rang and he knew it was his mother. *I'm forty-two-years old*, he thought, *I do not need to speak to my mother on a daily basis*. She didn't leave a message, which meant she had nothing important to say.

Alan grabbed the picture next to Mitchell's. It was he and Garret with red and shiny faces in some bar downtown, just after they had met. They had been through so much since then. Plays that flopped, nursing each other through hangovers and various STDs, the alienation of Garret from his father, and most recently the death of Mitchell, after which Garret had been there for Alan from day one, forcing him to eat, bringing him movies. *I was so skinny*, Alan thought. *What happened? I went from not eating a thing to eating everything in sight*.

Alan had never really "dated." It had always been Alan and Mitchell, the perfect match. *My walking dichotomy*, Alan used to call him. Mitchell could fix the refrigerator fan and then whip up an impromptu quiche. He looked great in drag but could hold his own on the basketball court. He would even out-shoot most of the black kids from their old neighborhood. The kids knew he was gay and somehow it bruised their egos more, getting beaten by a queer. Alan had been so proud, cheering him on with unabashed fervor.

He could still picture Mitchell's face in the airport—his last look—like it was yesterday. He was searching for something: a sign in Alan's face, or behind his eyes. He had to find a way to defuse this image, to blur it out of his memory until there was nothing left.

Do memories actually disappear?

In line at the check-in counter about twenty minutes before he died, Mitchell had looked like a guilty child.

"What is it, Mitch?"

"Well. There is something I need to speak to you about."

"Fine, anything." Alan was just so happy to be going away, to have time with him alone and interrupted, away from the theater A-list and their assistants. In fact, Mitchell's office had been warned not to interrupt.

"It's nothing, really," Mitchell said.

"Spit it out, baby."

Mitchell made a noise that sounded like a fake cough. "Well, let's just get to Paris. I'll tell you tonight."

"You're not preggers, are you?"

Mitchell laughed. "Not exactly."

Those were his last two words: *Not exactly.*

They picked up their boarding passes, and the woman behind the counter informed them that they had better hightail it to make it to the gate. They looked at each other, smiled, held hands, and ran. Thinking back Alan realized that their collective *Let's go* was essentially good-bye . . . the last real connection.

When Mitchell collapsed, Alan thought he was joking—he

had always been histrionic. But when his face drained of color, Alan's own heart skipped a couple of beats, then seemed to get slower and faster at the same time.

"Mitch . . . no."

First his searching look, and then his eyes pulsed and instantly went cold.

Alan quivered at the thought as he stroked Tramp's fur. His mind began going through—once again—all the what-ifs and the could-have-beens: *What if the woman at the gate hadn't told them to hurry? What if they had just waited till the next flight? What was it that Mitchell was going to tell me?* These things had gnawed at Alan's brain for the past year like a small animal scraping to survive. And only now was the animal starting to give up. He felt—and hoped—he was reliving it for the last time.

Then there was the issue of the estate.

Alan used to think the money didn't matter, but now he wanted it to spite Mitch's evil sister, Jane. Alan was left half of Mitchell's substantial estate, and Jane was fighting for all of it, even though Alan had been Mitchell's lover for over ten years and Jane had barely even sent them a Christmas card. Two months after he died, Alan had to move out of "their" apartment and Jane had moved in and redecorated. *Strange how she hated homosexuals, yet everything she wore, everything in her home, and basically everything she lived for was all designed by gay men. The hypocrisy is so blatant. What Mitchell wanted to leave me was rightfully mine. Jane will just have to cut back on next season's Chanel bags.*

Alan called his mother back and left a message, inquiring about the lawyer she had connected him with. He had begun the paperwork but he had never followed through. It felt strange fighting for his dead boyfriend's money. But now he was hungry for it.

21

GARRET WAS SITTING on his couch in his boxer briefs flipping through *Departures* magazine, thinking about taking Lucy and Alan on a trip somewhere. His phone rang, and after answering he was startled by his mother's voice. She spoke louder than usual.

"You're father has refilled his scotch and is doing the crosswords. *Herald, Times, Guardian*, all of them. Did you know that I almost bought a dress once because it looked like a crossword puzzle?"

Garret closed the magazine and sat up. "Mum, have you been drinking?"

"I'm coming to your play, with or without him," she said.

"That's great, Mum. Listen, why don't you get some tea."

"Just put some on! Dear, what about the one boy you fancied, the one that I met. Giggled all the time?"

"I'm not seeing him anymore."

"You know we haven't had sex in years," she whispered.

Garret suddenly felt scared. He had never heard his mum talk like this. She sounded very unhinged. He decided to put a kettle on himself, balancing the phone on his shoulder while he walked into the kitchen and flicked on the burner.

"But I remember us in Cornwall, when you were about eight." She let out a sound that reminded Garret of the vocal warm-ups the actors did. "I remember drifting to sleep as the sun was setting. I woke up and saw the two of you down by the shore. You were singing some silly song and the orange sun was glowing behind you. I remember thinking, *Those two will be inseparable.*" She paused and her voice got thinner. "I couldn't have been more wrong, isn't that so?"

"Mum. Why don't you get some rest. We'll talk tomorrow, OK?"

He could hear her sigh and sip what he hoped was tea.

"OK, bye-bye, my dear."

The kettle screamed as he hung up. He knew something was off. His mother barely drank half a glass of sherry. He checked his Blackberry. He was scheduled for another meeting in London before the opening and made a mental note to go up north while he was there and make sure she was all right.

———————

AT HIS GYM, Garret kept thinking of the scene his mother had described. She was right, they had been close, and somewhere in Garret's mind those memories were lodged, although when he tried to conjure them up they were blotchy and unfocused. But he could feel the idea of them. Normally, lifting weights allowed Garret to push away his thoughts, but today he felt vulnerable and strained, as if the opposite effect was happening. He was thick with feelings—real, tangible feelings as heavy as the weights.

In the sauna he avoided the eye of a Latino guy he had once shagged. He was thinking how pleased Lucy was going to be about Heather Bridges.

He showered and dressed quickly, avoiding the Latino guy. He picked up Lucy at the theater and brought her home, sat her down on the sofa, and shushed her when she tried to speak. He was so thrilled that he hesitated, wanting to bottle the feeling, if only for a few seconds. After Lucy pleaded with her bright eyes, he gave in.

"You've got an appointment next week."

Lucy jumped up and ran the length of the apartment; spinning and yelling like a child unable to contain her excitement. For a moment Garret was alarmed, thinking she might break something. But he noticed his own reflection in the window and his smile was so wide he didn't even look like himself. When she ran past him, he grabbed her and pushed her onto the couch.

"Hold on, hold on, it's simply an appointment. You have to do the rest."

Lucy got back up. "Oh my god, I need a drink," she said.

Garret snickered. "Right. Just a smidgen though. Calm the nerves, as it were." He went to the kitchen and returned with an already opened bottle of pinot grigio, poured her a half glass.

"Jesus. Heather Bridges, she's like, my idol."

"Hmm, that reminds me. You are not to say that word, Lucy. In the interview, that is."

"Idol?"

"No, 'like.' You are not, under any circumstances, to say the word 'like,'" Garret warned.

"Why?"

"It compromises the meaning of your words."

Lucy looked confused. "What if I said, 'I would like you to know that . . .'"

"That usage is fine, of course."

". . . you look good in a uniform . . ."

"What?" Garret asked.

". . . and I totally, like, want you."

"She's not a lesbian. And that's another one: 'totally.' Try completely, or thoroughly. Yes, that's good, *thoroughly*."

"OK, so I can't say 'totally' or 'like.' What else?"

She was now genuinely concerned. Garret was touched, but he didn't want to overwhelm her.

"You know what, Goose?"

In reaction to the nickname, Lucy let out a girlish giggle. "Like, what?"

"Your drawings speak volumes."

A silence. Lucy lay down, then abruptly shot back upright, a panicked look on her face.

"What . . ."

"What is it?" Garret asked, startled.

". . . am I going to wear!?"

Garret thought about it. He certainly knew a lot of stylists, but then an idea hit him. "You know, I've got a great deal of my aunt's clothing in this old trunk. I think there are hats too . . . You're so keen on hats, maybe . . ."

"No way."

"Way, darling, Let's have a look."

They ran upstairs to the small storage room off Garret's home office and rummaged through the clothes in his great aunt's trunk.

"She was the most glamorous woman in all my family," Garret recalled. "She was always perfectly accessorized. And she drove a Jaguar."

"Tight," Lucy said.

"But she had style. You can buy glamour, but you can't buy style."

The dresses were a little dated, but Lucy found one that fit, in a blue-gray, that had a classic, modern line to it. Simple and elegant, with a handbag to match. One of the hats looked similar to one in her collection. She grabbed them and said, "Hang on a minute," imitating Garret's accent.

While she was gone, Garret put on a big green scarf and snap-on diamond earrings. He remembered the look on his father's face when he saw his mother making a princess costume for him for the school play. It was his earliest memory, and now that he thought about it, it was the same look he had had on the cliffs that day. Terror, disgust, loathing. The play had been a success. *I was a pretty good princess*, he thought, looking in a mirror and smiling. *Besides, I was five. And it was only because there weren't enough girls in the class. Although I most likely jumped at the opportunity to play opposite the hunky star. . . .*

When Lucy emerged from the bathroom, transformed into a chic woman, Garret stared at her as if she were made of a cloud. He took her into his arms and they danced a makeshift waltz.

"It's such a shame that you're gay," Lucy mused. " I could so fall for you. You're perfect."

"I'm afraid you don't know the half of it, darling. But the dress, now, *that's* perfect."

22

IN BED THAT night, Garret couldn't push Lucy's words out of his head.

You're perfect.

His thoughts drifted back to the day he had gone to see Mitchell's doctor a couple of weeks after he died. He'd made an appointment to be discreet, and asked for the man's confidentiality.

"Sure, of course. What is it?" the doctor had said.

Garret was an emotional wreck. He tried to concentrate on breathing, speaking clearly.

"Do you think, well, let's see, how do I put this . . . ? Would sexual intercourse on the morning of Mitchell's heart attack, would that have had any impact on his condition?"

The doctor shuffled some papers around his desk and spoke in a grave tone.

"Mitchell's heart was not in good shape, and he knew that. He didn't choose to tell anyone. His cholesterol level was very high, he smoked, and he worked all the time but rarely exercised. Even though it wasn't completely apparent by looking at him, this was not a good combination."

"Yes, I know, but—"

"You had sex with Mitchell the morning of his death, is that what you're saying?"

"Yes."

"Well, I can tell you this. Nothing I say or do is going to change what happened, will it?"

"I suppose not. But do you think I should tell Alan?"

"I'm afraid I'm not authorized to answer that. But I'd be happy to recommend someone else to talk to in the meantime."

Garret had taken the shrink's number but never followed up. Now he wished he had.

I must tell him, he thought. *I have to. But how? Well, Alan, your lover cheated on you with me, your best friend, minutes before his heart attack, and it may have contributed to the cause. . . .*

Garret had been living with this sour secret for a year and it was starting to sink deeper into his guilt-laden consciousness. It had rooted itself down far enough that if it didn't come out, he feared it could flaw him forever.

You're perfect.

He turned on the machine that made a soothing water noise by his bed, sipped the last of his tea, and picked up the small, framed picture of Alan and Mitchell, taken days before that morning.

Oh, that dreadful morning. How had it all happened?

The three of them had ended up at Mitchell and Alan's old apartment, after a fundraiser boat cruise around Manhattan. Garret slept in the guest room, and in the morning Alan took an early train to drop Beverly (his miniature poodle at the time, before he got Tramp) with his mother. There was still half a magnum of champagne, so Garret and Mitchell made mimosas and Mitchell cooked his specialty, a buttery egg-in-the-hole.

Why did I do that dance?

After the second mimosa, with the Ecstasy pill from the night before still in his system, Garret started doing this dance with the guest robe he was wearing—Alan's old one. He could almost still feel the warm softness of it against his skin. The robe eventually came off one shoulder, then another, and Mitchell started to kiss Garret's neck and touch his nipples with the back of his hand, then his fingers. Garret was so hard and at attention—it was power. Mitchell was a powerful man.

Why didn't we stop?

A trail of two robes and two ties led to the bedroom, and after entering Garret, Mitchell stopped for a minute and just stared.

"You are so fucking sexy," Mitchell whispered.

"What are we doing?"

"Making history," Mitchell said.

The last words Garret heard out of his mouth.

Making history.

Garret got into the shower afterward and when he got out, Mitchell was gone. He tried to tidy up the house so as to not leave any signs. Consuela scared him to a scream when she came out of the den.

"Little jumpy this morning?"

"Oh, lord. You've frightened me, is all."

Consuela looked at Garret's body with the towel wrapped around him and couldn't help but make a noise.

"What?" Garret asked.

"Nothing, I'll be out of your way."

Garret went to his office that day and could barely think or talk. Everyone kept asking if he was OK. He finally just took off and roamed around Central Park, telling himself that it was fine. Mitchell had cheated before, hadn't he? It would be a moment that came and went.

It was shortly after that Garret's phone rang.

"Hello."

"It's Alan." The voice was cold and dripping with emotion. "Mitchell's gone."

———

AFTER HE FINALLY got to sleep, Garret dreamed that Mitchell was fucking him, onstage, and Alan was directing them. All the tricks and boyfriends he had ever been with were lined up behind Mitchell, waiting for their turn.

Alan was doing his badgering thing, saying, "I'm not buying it! I'm not buying it! Harder!! Fuck him, for Christ's sake!!!"

Garret was crying and when he looked up it wasn't Mitchell anymore, it was himself. He was being fucked by himself.

He ran out of the theater and into the street and looked up at the billboards in Times Square, which all featured pictures of Mitchell, holding the champagne and wearing the robe. He went into a subway car and Consuela was there, across from him, smirking and laughing at him. He tried to reach the back of the train and when he did he jumped into the darkness, which pulled him further and further in, until he was floating in a sky—or was it water?—and his father was singing to him, the same song his mother had referenced, and he woke up with actual tears in his eyes.

23

WEARING THE ENSEMBLE courtesy of Garret's aunt, Lucy stepped into the tallest building in the garment district. Well-manicured, perfectly dressed girls bustled around, drinking frothy cappuccinos and looking gracefully hungover. Lucy walked with purpose and several of them glanced her way as she passed.

This is where it all begins.

A skinny Asian girl escorted her into Heather's office. It was all she could do not to let out the scream that was boiling inside her. She bit her tongue and tried to breathe, peeking around the corner of the office door before entering.

Heather Bridges had a glow about her. Post-facial? She seemed hyper-hygienic and super-sterilized. She flicked at a speck on her tailored black suit and carefully nursed what smelled like chai. She pushed some photos aside as Lucy crept in.

"Well, look what we have here. A little flapper chic?" Her eyes focused on the handbag. "Is that Givenchy? I must say it works. Oh, um, Linda?"

"Lucy. Lucy Walker."

"Lucy, yes, Lucy."

"I like your outfit, too."

Shit, is that the right usage of like?

"Why, thank you." Heather took the compliment head on, staring hard and unflinchingly at Lucy.

To cover up the "like" thing, Lucy added, "Sensible yet sexy."

"Flattery will get you everywhere," Heather said, gazing back at the photos on her desk and rearranging them. She looked up at Lucy quizzically, and then lowered her eyes back to the photos.

Lucy was starting to sweat underneath her dress, even though the air-conditioning was cranked. *Stay calm*, she thought, *deep breath*. It took courage she didn't even know she had, but Lucy lifted her designs out of her bag and put them on the desk, right over the photos Heather was examining.

This confidence, this primal need to do something with her life, took over inside her, and she spoke clearly.

"Listen, I'm going to level with you. I have no fashion experience other than assisting the costumer on Garret's current production, but I love to draw and I'm quick. I've designed this hat collection that I want to someday get backing for. In the meantime I'll do anything, well almost anything, to immerse myself in the fashion world. Heather, I so admire this *empire* you've built here and I would be honored to be a part of it, however . . ."

"Minuscule?"

". . . minuscule that part may be."

Heather glanced at the drawings with barely concealed interest. "The janitor quit, actually . . ."

Lucy felt her face get hot.

"Kidding, Linda, kidding," Heather said.

"Lucy."

Heather flipped through and slowed at a few of them. Those moments were like drops of fuel that ignited a fire in Lucy's belly.

"Whatever your name is, these renderings are notable, some

of the lines, the shading. You've got promise, but it won't get you anywhere without drive."

"I can drive!" Lucy said.

Oh my god. I can drive? What am I going to do now, show her my license?

The phone bleeped again, her lifeline. Heather picked it up.

"Yes, it's Heather. Tomorrow's fine. Eggplant, yes. Right."

She hung up.

"Right, well, I'll give you a shot. As long as you work hard and show improvement, you'll rise in the ranks, if slowly. But in the meantime, tell the English lover-boy to teach you how to make a cappuccino. We'll start you next Monday, 9 a.m. sharp. Report to Gina, got it?"

Now Lucy really wanted to scream. She tried to physically channel Garret, pictured him in her head. *Chill, collect yourself.*

"Great! Thank you so much, Heather . . ."

"Welcome aboard. Listen, you take care of that Garret, you hear?"

Lucy stopped at the door, regained her composure, and turned around.

"Of course."

Lucy didn't notice anyone when she left. She made a beeline for the elevator and finally reached the street, where she released the scream she had been holding in.

A couple ran over to her.

"Are you OK?" the woman asked, genuinely concerned.

Lucy laughed and stretched her arms up. "Yes, actually, I couldn't be better, sorry."

I work for Heather Bridges now? Holy shit!

As she walked, she felt different, as if she had made some rite of passage. She was unbelievably lucky, and that was a good feeling. Maybe all those years of helping her mother and having no father were going to pay off. She would never in a million years have thought that the chance encounter of meeting Garret on that plane could translate into this. She walked faster. It was unnaturally breezy for early July, and she let her hair down. She started making a list in her head of all the people she was going to tell about her new job.

Heather fucking Bridges.

Oh. My. God.

24

AS GARRET AND ALAN walked toward the theater, Garret was busy having a conversation with himself in his head.

Today? No, not today. Then when? After the play. Yes, after the play. I can't wait much longer. There isn't going to be an easy way. I just have to say it.

"What's up?" Alan asked, genuinely concerned. "Are we brooding? You're not your usual chatty self."

"I had this really vivid dream. I was . . . I was fucking myself."

"How perfect!" Alan said.

Garret knew he was joking, but it stung him—it seemed to be a terrible thing to say. "Well, I couldn't sleep."

"What do you mean, you sleep like a—"

"Well, actually, it's not that. There's something I need to—"

Garret's phone buzzed. It was a text from Lucy:

COME HOME NOW

Was something wrong?

He showed it to Alan, who said, "Go. It's a boring meeting. I'll handle it."

They stood, squared off on the sidewalk, other pedestrians moving through them as if they were permanent fixtures. Garret couldn't do it.

"Right."

"And smile," Alan added, "you look better that way."

They parted and Garret found himself cursing under his breath.

HIS GUILT-RIDDEN mood quickly receded when he found Lucy hopping around his apartment like some sort of deranged cricket.

"I take it the meeting went well?"

Lucy stopped hopping and took a seat, let out a deep breath.

"I didn't say *like*."

"That's my girl."

"I start next Monday," she said casually, accenting the news with a swift hair flip.

Garret felt a surge of pride well up like a balloon inside him. He stood up and rubbed his hands together. "That is wonderful news."

FROM HIS LIVING ROOM, Lucy sent text messages to everyone she knew. Garret got an e-mail from his mother, who had recently learned to use a computer. The type was really big.

> Dear!
> Not sure what got into him, but your father watched some show about sex being healthy for aging men. Hurrah for modern television! It is strange, but I feel closer to him—I realize it is the only way he can express tenderness.
> I told him that hating people for being homosexual was *so*

out of style. They even have churches that allow gays! I feel like the tightly woven architecture that makes him up is finally starting to loosen at the seams, soften up and give. He used to be so kindhearted. . . .

Garret could picture his mother writing the words at the old wooden table with her toast points next to her new but unadorned laptop, the afternoon sun casting rectangles of light on the room, the steam rising from her teacup, and the occasional sound of ice clinking in his father's whiskey glass.

I told him I'm going to New York to see you and he didn't look up, started to write in another word on his bloody crossword, which I proceeded to throw in the fire. After a bit of a row, he said he would see you. Isn't that great?
Love,
MUM

Garret shut down the computer and gazed out the window. He supposed he should be happy, but he was confused. *What if I don't want to see him?*

He went into the kitchen and put on some tea. He couldn't process his mother's information just yet. He was still thinking of a way to tell Alan about Mitchell. When the pot boiled he poured two cups and brought one in for Lucy, placing the mug in front of her and tousling her hair. He looked at his watch and realized he had a conference call.

"Holler if you need me," he said.

"OK."

As he went into his study, he looked back at her once more. She seemed so comfortable in his house, as if her whole life had naturally led to that moment.

THE CALL WAS TO PITCH some German investors on the UK run of their current production. Garret loved this part—he was so passionate about it that he was able to transcend the heavy things weighing on his mind. He expressed his confidence in Alan and the cast and used personal touches —things he had remembered from meeting them before. Whether it was business or pleasure, that's all people really wanted in the world—personal connection. He asked about one gentleman's wine cellar (Did he install the special coolers?) and about the other's child (Still a star swimmer?) and he could hear a softness infused into their responses, which said, *He remembered.*

As a boy, Garret went with his father each year to pick up a ham for their holiday dinner. Before, his father would stop off at a special chocolatier and pick up some caramels for the man who sold the ham. It was a small gesture that went a long way, as eventually the man never charged for the ham. Aside from enjoying the trip to the candy shop (Garret would get his own treat as well), he never understood the importance of the ritual. Now, thinking back on it, it clicked. His father always did little things for people. Cigars for the postman, buying pints for the bartenders. Garret supposed, in his own way, his father was a charming man. A thought hit him like a friendly nudge to the stomach: *I am more like my father than I think.*

"You still there?"

"Yes," Garret said, "I was just having a little nap."

The Germans laughed.

"Now, I'd like to go over some of the details regarding the

London cast and how that ties in with some extensive promotion we have planned . . ."

He was on a roll. He used his hands to accentuate his words even though he was on the phone. He had a sense that in addition to the German investors, everything else would work out. It had to.

25

LUCY HAD NEVER really liked tea before, but she was starting to understand the appeal. Along with the sound of Garret's voice behind the closed door of his office, it soothed her.

When Alan entered the apartment softly humming a jazz standard and carrying a giant stuffed bunny, Lucy smiled.

Alan placed the large furry rabbit in her lap.

"It's so cute. You shouldn't have," Lucy said.

"I knew you'd land it."

"I'm freaking. My mother's on her way. She sounded sober, which is good."

Alan stepped over to Garret's wet bar and poured some vodka over ice. "At least someone is. For me it's detox, retox, rinse, and repeat."

Lucy heard the distinctive sound of the thick, clear liquid breaking down the ice and said, "That's a sound I always associated with my mother, and I hope that will change."

"Now it will be the sound of horrific coffee dripping and sizzling embers of endless cigarettes," Alan said.

Lucy hugged the pink bunny while Alan sipped his drink and hummed. They watched the Weather Channel with no sound. The word *humid* flashed across the screen in a cheesy font of fire.

After Alan finished his drink, she turned to him and said, "What was Mitchell like?"

Alan leaned his head back and looked up at the ceiling, exhaled, and then looked at Lucy and smiled. "He could walk into a room and everyone's eyes would gravitate toward him. He never wore socks. He made me laugh."

"You know, if Garret wasn't gay, I would be in love with him."

"WTMI," Alan said.

"No, I'm serious Alan. I feel like he gets me in a way that no one else has. And I feel so, I don't know, at *home* around him."

The doorbell rang. Lucy kissed the top of Alan's head and slowly made her way to the door, looking into the peephole. She opened the door and Joyce took her into her arms before Lucy could speak.

"You got a job? I couldn't have imagined . . ." Joyce sighed. "Wow. This is quite the place."

Alan appeared by Lucy's side. "Well, hi and bye," he said, shaking Joyce's hand and then putting down his drink. "I'm Alan. I'll leave you two alone." He turned to Lucy. "Congratulations. And make sure you feed the bunny."

Alan left and Joyce started gathering Lucy's things.

"Mom, I'm going to be working for Heather Bridges. Can you even deal?"

Joyce looked at her with what seemed like a mixture of weariness and pride. "That's unbelievable." She cupped her hand around Lucy's cheek and said, "I'm still sober. Stanley's helping me."

Lucy couldn't really trust her mother. She knew how long it had been. She had witnessed the gradual descent of Joyce Walker. It had started out with some wine every night, then pills, then hard alcohol, then mixtures and concoctions. But she did look clear-eyed and focused, and she smelled like soap. She couldn't remember the last time her mother hadn't smelled like gin. But this was supposed to be Lucy's moment, which was why her response was unconvincing.

"That's great news, Mom."

Lucy handed her one of the invitations to the preview of Garret and Alan's play, *Don't Wake the Angels*.

"Can I bring Stanley?"

"Of course."

Lucy didn't want to go anywhere.

"Mom, I can just stay—"

"No, I'm sorry, young lady, but you are coming with me," Joyce said firmly.

"You know how thin those walls are," Lucy protested. "I'm not listening to you and Mr. Pellegrino."

"Stanley." Joyce grabbed Lucy's bag. "Shoes?"

"Hang on, I have to say good-bye to Garret."

She walked to his office door and cupped her ear against it. By the sound of his voice, the call seemed to be getting more intense.

"Write him a note," Joyce ordered. "I want to try and beat the traffic."

On his monogrammed pad in the kitchen, Lucy wrote:

Mom came.
Going upstate with her. Call my cell.
Love, Lucy
P.S. You rock my world.

26

THE STREETS WERE bustling with girls in halter tops and guys wearing "mandles." Garret never understood men in sandals—it worked in, say, the Bahamas, but not in the West Village. He sent Alan a text while walking down Greenwich Avenue.

Missed you, and the mom.
The Germans are in.
Going to Therapy (the bar)
Meet me?

Garret got a cab to take him to Hell's Kitchen. He sat at the upstairs bar chatting with the bartender, Chad, with whom he once had a one-night stand. During the conversation, several of the young patrons tried to catch Garret's eye, but he didn't notice. Chad recognized something was off, since he'd previously admired Garret's gift for scoring.

"Wow," Chad said. "This must be serious. That guy over there is beyond hot. Fresh meat from Connecticut."

Garret chuckled. "I'm almost forty, Chad . . . It has to stop somewhere."

"Not me," Chad replied. "I'm going to be cruising the showers in my old-age home."

Garret laughed and was reminded of Alan. The reason he was so scared to tell him about Mitchell was the fear that Alan might disown him. Not only as a business partner—that he could take—but, more important, as a friend.

He paid for his drink with his usual overly large tip but instead of walking home, found himself pulled east to Alan's apartment. He was sure Alan was there and never got the text. He was a bit technologically inept.

As he walked, he could feel his blood surging through his body. Tonight was the night. The secret could no longer live inside him.

Though Garret still had keys to Alan's place, he knocked quietly.

"Hark, who goes there?" he heard Alan say.

"Size magnet." It was an old name Alan used to call him, after Garret had dated a Finnish guy named Helmut who was extremely endowed.

Alan opened the door, looked at him funny, and said, "I haven't heard that in years."

Garret was not used to being this uncomfortable—especially in front of Alan—so he stepped over to Alan's makeshift bar and poured them each a scotch. Garret knew he could sense something was up and wasn't completely surprised when Alan outright called him on it.

"What is it, Garret? Did you find God? Buddha? Madonna?"

"No, Alan." He sipped his drink, waited for Alan to do the same.

"Scientology?"

Garret swallowed and braced himself. "Do you remember the night before Mitchell died?"

Alan's face deflated. "Like the back of my hand. The boat, the Ecstasy, the diner. I can still smell the onion rings."

Garret smiled. It was always about the food with Alan.

"Well, do you remember the morning after?"

Alan looked up at Garret with a seriousness that said, *No, don't even tell me.* He was intuitively sensing where the conversation was heading. He put down his drink rather loudly. "Yes. You slept over and I headed to Scarsdale early to drop off the dog."

Garret didn't have to actually say it. He looked down at the floor.

Alan's face iced over. "Get out."

"We had champagne, Alan—"

"Get. Out." Alan slowly moved over to the door and opened it.

Garret stayed where he was. "I wanted to tell you every day since—"

"So you wait till the anniversary of his death, right before the opening of our play? Please, just get the fuck out of my apartment now."

Garret put his own drink down as his father's face flashed into his mind. He squinted and shook his head to try to erase the image.

"It didn't mean anything," Garret said as he walked out into the hallway.

"Isn't that what they always say? Good-bye, Garret."

The door shut before Garret could say it.

"I'm sorry."

———

ON THE WAY HOME Garret felt an enormous sense of relief, as if someone had peeled off the clouded layer of his brain, letting his thoughts clear. He knew it would be hard, but he had done the right thing. *He will calm down,* he told himself, *it will settle in.*

He stopped at the deli and the Korean woman who was used

to Garret buying Exports and Pellegrino gave him a strange look when he slid the PopTarts on to the counter. It was the same look Chad had given him. It said, *What is happening to you?*

When he quietly entered his apartment, he noticed Lucy's forgotten sketchbook slightly obscured by a pillow, with a picture sticking out of one of the pages. *This must be the picture of her mum she was talking about.* He held the picture out in front of him and his jaw slowly released until it was completely slack.

Garret took the picture of Lucy's mother into the library, where his scrapbooks from college sat next to his theater books and literature classics. He took one out from his third year, found a page with a picture of him with a girl, that same girl.

His mouth fell into an oval shape until two words came out.

"Good heavens."

27

THE NEXT DAY was a blur. Garret's mind was a swirl of so many emotions and thoughts that they all canceled each other out and he was left blank, numb. He pretended, as best he could, that it was a normal day. He avoided both Alan and Lucy at rehearsal and wandered the streets until after dark. Lucy was asleep when he got home. He had been sitting next to a bottle of vodka in the kitchen for hours when Lucy sleepily stumbled in for water.

"I told him," he said gravely.

"What," she said while filling her glass, "that you loved him?"

"About Mitchell."

Garret's face felt like it was going to crack and crumble.

"You never got to tell me, remember?" she said.

"I slept with him the morning he died." Now it felt easy to say. Now it was out in the world, and people had to make way for the space it took up.

Lucy leaned against the cabinet as if the words physically pushed her. He couldn't even sort out who she might be, what this all might mean.

"Oh," was all she said.

"I told Alan and he told me to get out of his house. He's in shock mode."

"Well, I have to say, so am I."

"I'm not sure, Lucy. He did give me a look I hadn't seen before. It was frightening."

Lucy reached out to touch Garret's forearm.

"The worst part is over," she said. "It was killing you, right? Nothing is going to bring Mitchell back."

She walked away and Garret followed her back into the guestroom. They lay on the bed looking at the ceiling, everything suddenly silent and still. Garret slipped off his loafers and peeled off each sock with the toe of the opposite foot. He tilted up and saw their four bare feet, lined up next to each other at the foot of the bed. Garret's feet were larger, but their shape was almost identical to hers.

Her second toe bends in just like mine.

He turned sideways. Next to the bed hung a framed black-and-white photograph of Garret as a boy, on the beach, standing with his stone-faced father towering above him.

This cannot be.

He turned back around, kissed her hair, and got up to leave.

"What?" Lucy could sense he was freaked out.

"No, it's nothing, I just . . . I'm just knackered is all," he said, unconvincingly. "I . . . I just need some rest. I'll be fine, surely. You sleep. I'll see you in the morning."

Garret lay down in his own room and stared, in panic and disbelief, at the light fixture above his bed. He slowly drew in air to fill up his lungs. He swallowed a sleeping pill and concentrated on breathing.

I will sort this all out, but not now. Sleep now.

IN THE MORNING Garret left early and quietly, and walked all the way to Central Park, his mind racing.

Joyce. The bird I was dating in college who disappeared. The whimsy of her, and the openness. Just like Lucy.

As people on bikes, on rollerblades, in cabs and on phones went about their day, Garret sat quietly on a bench, the eye of the hurricane. A single tear dropped down his face, leaving a tiny line to dry in the sun.

He got up and started to walk. He bumped into people and didn't even notice.

Nothing will ever be the same.

WHEN HE FINALLY made it back to his apartment, Lucy was gone. He got out his Blackberry and looked up the number of the only college buddy he still kept in contact with.

"Hi, it's Garret here."

He sipped from his coffee cup, not even realizing it was cold.

"Yes, I know, it's been ages. Listen, do you remember Joyce, yes, the one . . . yes, did you ever keep in touch with her?"

He was pacing around the kitchen now. He looked down at his own shaking hands.

"She did? Good lord. It's . . . it's . . ."

Garret dropped the phone on the floor.

". . . a miracle."

28

GARRET SAW JOYCE waiting patiently at a booth in the restaurant where they had planned to meet. She looked troubled, but relief washed over her face as she recognized him.

"My god, you look the same," she said.

"Hello," Garret said. He could still remember the night they had met. She was wearing a white dress, and she had accidentally cut her finger. Garret had not only fixed up her wound but had gotten the bloodstain out of her dress.

"Have you even aged?" she asked.

"Yes, I have. Considerably." They stared at each other. "She is mine, isn't she?"

"Ours," Joyce clarified.

Garret sat down as a waiter brought them water. He wanted to throw something or scream at her. Though feeling a rush of elation, he knew he had been robbed.

"I have to know one thing," Joyce said. "Did you know it was her?"

"Indeed, the first thing I thought was, *This is my daughter.* Of course not. Although looking back, there were many signs. I even saw you, from afar, in the airport, but couldn't place you." Garret sipped his water and dabbed at his chin with the napkin.

"In London?"

"Yes."

"No one put you up to this?" Joyce inquired, looking around the restaurant as if they were being watched.

"Yes, actually, it's all going to be on *Oprah*."

That got a smile out of her.

"Listen," she said, "I owe you an apology. I should have at least let you know. I just didn't . . . think you'd care."

Garret felt anger enlarge his chest, but it was kept at bay by an equal amount of gratitude. He couldn't go back; it was a master plan.

"I cared before I even knew she was mine," he said.

Joyce twirled her straw in her iced tea. "Is she furious with me?"

"She doesn't know yet . . . and if you don't mind, I'd like to tell her."

Joyce looked at Garret, her face twisted up with confusion. "Be my guest, but don't think you can just walk in and take over where I left off."

Garret instinctively picked up a butter knife. "You never gave me a choice! Bloody hell." He wanted to grab her by the throat. *I am not my father. I am a father.*

He ordered a cocktail and said, "Make it a double."

"You left me, remember?" Joyce said.

"I certainly did not—"

"Well, you had secret showers with what's his name, Ralph—"

"Robbie Sparks. Listen—"

"No, *you* listen. What the hell was I supposed to do? You broke my heart. I never even liked that school. I wanted a way out. Getting pregnant solved it, for then at least. I fucked up. Royally, and I'm sorry."

Her genuine honesty softened Garret. His drink arrived and he took a long, slow sip. *If I forgive her, then maybe Alan will forgive me.*

"This will be hard on her," he said.

"Shit, Garret, what about me? My seventeen-year-old drops me for my gay college boyfriend!"

She had a point. The busboy placed bread on the table while trying to conceal his surprise. Garret cleared his throat, and the kid scurried away.

"I happen to be her biological father." Garret liked how that sounded. *Biological.* "I hear that you are with someone now?"

"Yes." Joyce sipped her iced tea. "I've started to see someone named Stanley. Nice guy, terrible name. What about you?"

Garret lowered his head. "I've ... I've ... sort of been around the block a bit."

"Well, well."

"But," he straightened his tie and stared at his glass, "I think I'm coming home."

Joyce looked at him the same way she did when he handed her the clean white dress. A look of affection, with a hint of confusion.

"I feel like there is something changing me beyond my control," Garret said, the cocktail already warming his blood, starting to make his head swim. "Well, I've got a lot of thinking to do. This is a lot to take." Garret swilled the rest of his drink, put a twenty on their table, and stood up. "I'm sure I'll be seeing you again in the future."

"I guess so. I'm sorry, Garret."

"It's done. And you must have done something right, because she is an exceptional girl."

———

ON THE WAY TO midtown, Garret ran into a mousy woman from the *Times* who had profiled him. They chatted for three blocks, and she eventually said, "Are you all right?"

"Fine," Garret replied.

"Because you haven't stopped smiling."

They reached the corner.

"Well, I've had some news. Not fit to print just yet, however."

He leaned down and kissed her on the cheek, and she giggled in a voice Garret hadn't heard before.

"When it is, you know who to call," she said.

They parted and Garret couldn't walk fast enough. Even though his legs seemed to be keeping him above ground, he felt rooted down. From now on, there was more than him. A piece of himself out there in the world. He was a father.

part two

relatives

29

GARRET FOUND LUCY in the basement of the theater with Sheila, putting some finishing touches on the costumes.

"I'm going to borrow her for a minute," Garret told Sheila.

He led her into the hallway. A thin shaft of light from the basement window cut through the space between them. He looked at her acutely, noticing everything. The curve of her upper lip, the lovely brightness in her eyes, her slender arms.

"I spoke to your mother."

"What? How—"

"Never mind, never mind. I want you to move in."

"What?" Lucy was bewildered.

"It's silly for you to commute, and your internship will be starting soon, and—"

"Wait . . . for real?"

"For real."

Garret stepped forward and hugged her tightly but also gently, as if she were the most fragile thing on earth.

"Are you crying?" Lucy asked.

"No, allergies. See you later."

"OK, thanks so much! I promise I'll be a respectful roommate. No more redecorating!"

Garret smiled. *You'll be a little more than a roommate.*

THAT AFTERNOON, Garret sat out on his fire escape, the clouds obscuring part of the spires in the distance. His new-found happiness was coated with a thin black lining. *How could this have happened now, right after I confessed to Alan?*

He dialed England and put his cordless on speakerphone.

"Mum, are you sitting?"

"Yes, dear, what is it?"

She sounded weak, her voice not its usual timbre.

"You OK, Mum?"

"Fine. I had an MRI done. . . . It was just a routine, no need to fret."

There is no such thing as a routine MRI.

"Wait a second. What are you saying, Mum?"

"Nothing, dear. What is it? What are you so keen on telling me?"

He was so anxious to tell her that his enthusiasm eclipsed his concern.

"Well, you know the girl I'm helping . . ."

"Yes, the one you are so fond of, Liz, is it?"

"Lucy."

"Lucy, yes."

"Well, do you remember the American bird I was dating at Oxford, with the—"

"Oh my lord, yes, I have a picture of you two."

Garret looked up, closed his eyes. Bits of rain started to fall and he let the drops hit his face. Everything seemed to be filled with possibility. He thought that if he didn't keep breathing he would burst.

"You're a grandmother."

He could hear her catch her breath.

"Is this confirmed?" she asked.

"Yes, Mum. Can you bloody believe it?"

He could hear a pounding noise. *Was she jumping?*

"Garret, I have a granddaughter? What, what are you going to . . . I must come at once!"

"I . . . I want to be her father. That is, from here on out."

The rain got stronger, but he didn't care. It felt wonderful to just let the wetness sink in. He could hear kids laughing down the block and realized that they too had parents, people that brought them into the world, and that everyone was connected in some way.

"Garret, my dear . . . oh."

"Mum. You alright?"

A silence. *Was she crying?*

"Certainly, I just . . . Oh my! What does she fancy? You know, for frocks and things?"

"She's, well, sort of a hybrid of styles. You'll see when you meet her. Don't worry about frocks just yet."

"This is extraordinary. My lord."

The rain stopped and for a moment, the street looked washed clean. "It's like a dream."

"My lord," she said again, softer.

"I must go now, Mum. I'm coming back over for meetings on Friday, and I'll take the train up and see you. Pop will be on his hunting trip, correct?"

"Yes. Darling, congratulations!"

He hung up and looked at his watch.

She'll be home in minutes.

He went inside and changed out of his wet clothes. Looking in the mirror, he realized the place he needed to tell her. Better to do it in public.

His mind raced with the words: *my child, my child.*

30

AS LUCY OPENED the orange doors of the bakery and started walking south, a dirty-looking kid in a gray skullcap rushed up and followed her.

"Where have you been, Loose? You never come to the pool anymore. . . ."

"Alex. Didn't you take off for California?"

"Only got as far as Ohio. Hey, want to smoke one out?"

"No, thank you."

Alex inched closer as they walked, sharing her umbrella.

"Jeez, what crawled up your butt?"

Lucy had one of those adult moments when you look at someone from your past and cannot figure out what it was that ever attracted you. It seemed eons ago that he was in her dorm room. Her mom was right about one thing. She would keep in touch with Cora, but the Alex chapter was over. He was a remnant from another life.

"I don't know, Alex. I don't want to just sit around an empty pool partying everyday. I want to accomplish something. Don't you?"

"Sure, but like . . ."

"You shouldn't use the word 'like.' It compromises what you are saying."

"Jeez. This gay guy's really got to you, huh?"

They reached the end of the block and Lucy stepped back.

"He's not 'this gay guy.' He's my brilliant, successful friend who happens to shower a lot more than you do. Now if you'll excuse me, Alex, I must get going."

She turned the corner and strode confidently away.

OK, maybe that was bitchy. But Alex was just a stage. Next!

———

WHEN SHE REACHED Garret's place, he was nervously waiting by the door. He grabbed his keys and then Lucy's hand. He turned her right back around.

"What is it?"

"Come, let's go," he said.

"Wait, I brought—"

"No waiting, come on."

"Garret, you're freaking me out."

He grabbed the pastries she bought, put them down on the floor, and led her back out the door. On the street, he shuffled them into a cab. The rain was coming down harder now, splattering off the roofs of parked cars as people huddled under awnings waiting for it to pass.

"Garret, where are we—"

"Sshhh, trust me."

Garret told the cabbie to stop, paid him, and led Lucy up the grand steps to the museum. He paid for both of them with all he had, a hundred-dollar bill. He didn't wait for the change.

"If I wanted to see some art—"

"Lucy, enough."

Garret took her hand and led her into a giant, high-ceilinged room that was covered with an exhibition called *Clouds* by Georgia O'Keefe.

The clouds covered the ceiling and walls, puffy white on cerulean blue. The room was vast and empty of patrons aside from three old women huddled in the corner.

Lucy looked around, mesmerized, and sat down in the center of the room as if the beauty of it struck her down to the floor.

Garret sat behind her and whispered into her ear, "This is a kind of flying."

Lucy could sense something was coming. She wanted to know what it was, and had this strange feeling that Garret was going to confess feelings for her. Her own feelings for him were there, nestled like small coals in the bottom of her tummy. *Is he going to kiss me? Is he tired of being gay?*

"There is something I must tell you."

"You're pregnant," Lucy said.

Garret smiled. "Not exactly."

Just kiss me and get it over with, Lucy thought, licking her lips while turning around to face him. "What?"

"Your mother and I, we . . ."

Lucy had her eyes closed and wasn't really listening.

". . . knew each other in college."

Her face slowly paled, eventually matching the clouds all around her.

"What?"

"I'm . . ."

"Oh . . ."

". . . your father."

". . . my God."

The old women in the corner inched closer.

Lucy averted her eyes, stood up, and went to the opposite wall. She felt dwarfed against the massive backdrop of the painted sky. She turned around, looking at Garret as if for the first time. She stayed that way for a minute in the silence of that great room, unable to pinpoint what emotion she was feeling. The information was suspended in her heart, hovering like a small insect, waiting to settle.

How could this be?

She held in a breath and slowly approached him. She reached for his chin to turn his head toward her and noticed that his eyes were wet, and they quickly embraced.

"Allergies, huh?" she said into his shoulder.

She could see one of the eavesdropping ladies dab at her own eye.

"The plane," Lucy said. "I got bumped . . ."

Garret held her head in his hands and said, "Listen, let's go for a walk in the park, alright? We've got some thinking to do."

They walked away slowly, still stunned. The ladies clapped as they passed. Garret and Lucy looked at each other in disbelief, unable to help laughing a little.

"Show's over," Lucy said.

———

THE RAIN HAD STOPPED and the city seemed temporarily reborn. They walked side by side with a similar gait. Garret looked up at the gray sky, Lucy at the ground.

"I'm starving," Lucy said, and then stopped him in the middle of the sidewalk, a group of Jersey girls scoffing as they circumvented the two of them. "Hang on a sec, can we just talk about the fact that you're my fucking father? I'm British!"

Garret led her on so they weren't blocking the pedestrian flow.

"Well, yes, I suppose so. But we're going to have to work on your accent."

"This is unreal. I need food before I pass out."

The avenue was full of life—a well-oiled machine working overtime all around them. Old women with tiny dogs, people carrying large instruments and appliances, kids playing hooky with cigarettes behind their ears.

They got food and sat on a nearby stoop. Lucy could feel herself withdrawing, curling in. She went back up to the stand and bought a soda.

"You know, you should stay away from cola," Garret warned.

The fact that she had wanted to kiss him turned her stomach and choked the back of her throat. "Oh, OK . . . I see how this works," she snapped. "Walk in after seventeen years and play daddy? No, sorry. You can't tell me what to do."

"I didn't know you existed!" Garret protested.

"But you said you had a feeling."

"Yes, but—"

Lucy stood up and slammed her burger on the sidewalk. "I'm that feeling, Garret! You could have known me all along!! Don't you see that? Wake up, Garret, wake up!"

"It's more complicated than—"

"No, actually, it's real simple, Garret. It's called parents and children." She held out the palm of each hand as a visual display. "Usually they are involved in each other's lives. I mean, how am I supposed to feel about all this? And my mother avoiding the issue all these years. I know it's mostly her I should blame, but I have to be mad at someone right now. I feel like throwing something."

Garret looked at the food strewn across the sidewalk.

"You already did."

"Something else, then. Bigger."

Lucy looked around, fuming. "I have to go, Garret. I have to go. It's not your fault, but I have to go now." She stormed away, bumping into a businessman and knocking down his briefcase. She kept moving, starting into the park.

She couldn't separate the well of feelings percolating inside her. Relief. Anger. Joy. Fear. Confusion. Shame.

She found an open patch of grass and lay down on her back, staring up at the muted sky, now the color of a dirty nickel.

Garret is my father.

31

AFTER SPENDING nearly two hours at the gym, Alan ate frozen yogurt in bed while talking to his mother, who was aghast at the news.

"Behind your back?" she howled through the phone, "On the day he died? Christ, Alan, what—"

"I just can't help thinking that something more went on between them, something that made Mitchell's heart . . . I don't know, like he was so excited it pushed it over the top. . . ."

"Honey, we all know Mitchell's heart was not in tip-top shape, it was—"

"My best friend, Mother. The both of them . . . I feel so humiliated."

"Oh, sweetheart."

"I'm afraid Garret is out of my life." Alan reached for his cat, who curled in beside him and licked the excess yogurt off his spoon. "From now on, it's just me and Tramp."

He sat up after he hung up the phone and caught himself in the mirror. He lifted up his shirt. *At least I'm getting thinner.*

The phone rang again, and he let the machine get it. Garret sounded parched.

"Alan, I know you want to kill me right now, but something happened. I have to talk to you. Can you ring me, please?"

Oh sure, Alan thought. *Pass the fucking butter. What does he expect me to do, go on like everything's normal? Fat chance.*

He picked up the phone, stared at the numbers, and then put it back down.

How am I going to ever look at him the same?

He started watching bad reality TV but couldn't focus. He found a chocolate bar in the freezer and started to unwrap it. Just before he took a bite, he threw it in the trash.

Why did he tell me now? Why did he tell me at all? This will change everything.

Once again, he replayed Mitchell's last day in his head, now armed with the truth. There were so many tears already shed. He couldn't bear to get upset again; it was too tiring. He looked at the pad with the lawyer's number he still hadn't called.

He didn't love Garret that way. Did he?

———————

ALAN DECIDED TO go for a walk, and the burden that crushed his mind was momentarily lifted by the city at night: the soft amber lights in all the windows, the faint rumble of the subway underneath him, the smell of spices from all around the world. He and Mitchell had traveled a lot, and the trip that always came to mind was river rafting in Zimbabwe. Mitchell had fallen overboard and Alan jumped in to save him. As it turned out, Alan was the one in danger and had to be scooped out from under the boat by the guide. That night in their hotel room, Mitchell hired some musicians off the street to come up and play for them. They ate baguettes and black olives and drank really cheap African rum. Maybe it was the fact that it was a near-death experience or that he was forever humbled, but Alan was so glad to be alive he wanted to stretch that moment into a lifetime.

His regular coffee shop on Greenwich Avenue was hopping.

He ordered a decaf and sat down by the back and observed the room. Lots of nervous-looking Woody Allen types pecking away at their keyboards and flipping through worn journals, and a few teenagers who were so amped up on caffeine they looked as if they might explode, talking so fast he couldn't discern what they were saying.

He opened a *Voice* and happened to turn right to an ad for the play. A blond kid who looked about six years old wandered up and said, "Have you got a dime?"

Alan gave him a quarter. "Where's your mom?"

"John."

Alan didn't know if John was the boyfriend or the bathroom. The kid looked at him the way Mitchell had when they first met—clear and unconditional. Alan pointed to his own name on the page. "That's me," he said.

The boy seemed skeptical.

"I'm a director," Alan explained.

"Do you get to do the lights?" the boy asked.

"Yep," Alan said.

Presumably the mother, in low-rise jeans and a tiny halter top, came out of the bathroom and smiled at Alan.

"Honey, are you bothering this man?"

"No," Alan said. "We were discussing the usual . . . you know, economics, the war in Iraq."

She smiled again and led him away.

When he got home he went through his closet and threw out all the plaids, and several pairs of his outdated pants.

Then he sat on the couch and looked at the poster for the show, again at his name, this time larger. "I'm a director," he said again, and thought of the boy in the coffee shop. How to him, a play wasn't blocking and emotions and words. It was lights, fantasy, colors. If only everything were that simple.

32

WHILE GARRET searched the park, part of him was waiting for someone to tap him on the shoulder and tell him it was all a dream. But he couldn't help but feel that Lucy had come into his life for a reason.

He took a narrow bridge across a pond and then jogged the curvy path that led upward to some outcroppings for a better lookout. He finally noticed her on a bench that was slightly out of the way, a willow tree gracefully curling over it. She was fiddling with her crushed soda can. He walked over and quietly sat down next to her. She kept herself occupied with the can, but after a few minutes placed it at her side and said, "So what was she like then, my mom?"

Garret drew in a deep breath. "She was fiery and stubborn, like you. As a matter of fact, she painted my bathroom orange."

"Was there, you know, romance?" Lucy asked without looking at him.

"Of course. As a matter of fact, I think I know the night you were conceived. Your mum had cut her finger and had stained her dress. She came to my dorm door all bloody."

"Was she drunk?"

"No," Garret chuckled. "She had been cutting an apple. I bandaged her hand and . . ."

Lucy picked up the soda can again and looked up at him. "And?"

"And I got the stain out of her dress."

Lucy laughed. "That is fag 101."

"So, she had my T-shirt on, and as she was changing back into the dress . . . I . . ."

"OK, TMI. But how long were you together?"

"A few months, really. It was right around the time when I was still deciding who I was."

"You mean that you were gay."

"Precisely."

A woman wearing a parka in the July heat, and carrying what looked like an old blender, approached them and held out her hand. Garret gave her a quarter and she smiled, flashing yellow teeth.

"How did you know?" Lucy asked, turning with a different look, not so much admiration as respect.

"Well, I had a mate called Robbie. We did everything together. And one day it turned into something more."

Lucy rearranged herself on the bench.

"And she caught us, your mum."

Some howling kids went by on skateboards and startled the woman with the blender.

"Poor Mom. It feels weird to say that, since I'm so pissed at her right now. But that must be hard, you know? So many women fall for gay men."

"She didn't seem too invested in me. I didn't think I'd break her heart, but maybe I did. She vanished, and I never saw her again after we parted ways. I realize now that she went off to have you."

They looked at each other and the magnetic current between their locked eyes was so powerful that they had to break away from its stronghold, turn their heads at the last second.

"You're my dad," Lucy said. "That's going be a problem. I think of you . . . more as my friend."

"That is favorable, though, right? That's what parents strive for."

"This will change everything."

"It will, Lucy, it will. But hopefully only in suitable ways."

Lucy leaned her head on Garret's upper arm and he gently stroked her hair. Pollen floated around their heads and a group of joggers went by, their breaths in a clipped rhythm. They sat as they did on the Tube in London that fateful night.

After a while, Garret said, "You are a star. The world has no idea what it's in for."

Garret had a brief vision of him, Alan, and Lucy living in some castle somewhere, baking bread and eating by candle-light. He knew by now the world wasn't a fairy tale, but he was starting to believe in this, having a daughter.

"Are you mad at my mother?"

Garret thought about it. *Of course I am, but what am I going to do about it now?*

"It was an incredibly selfish thing to do," he said.

"Like you sleeping with Mitchell?"

Garret looked away from her and lit a cigarette. "Well, if you put it that way, yes, I suppose so."

Just then, Garret knew what he must do.

"I have to go see him, Goose. You alright to get home?"

"Yes."

They hugged, and Garret walked her to the train. Then he got into a cab and headed toward Alan's apartment.

33

LUCY SAT ON Garret's balcony and lit a cigarette. She rarely smoked, but the occasion warranted it, to say the least. She immediately got on the phone with Cora.

"Yes, he's my father, and no, I'm not high, Cora. I was about to kiss him when he told me, can you fucking deal? I don't know, I don't know what to think. . . ."

Lucy looked up at the sky for some sort of answer, but all she saw was more clouds. The late afternoon had brought a diminished light that hinted at mystery.

"Listen, see you at the pool in twenty?"

Lucy crawled inside, downed a glass of water, grabbed her keys, and headed out the door.

The heat on the train platform was suffocating. In the summer, it was always a relief when the train came because even if it was packed, it would be cold. The 6 train sped toward her and she got on. She found a seat and looked at the commuters with a sharp eye. A Latina doled out snacks to her toddlers. A greasy-haired man read an old copy of *Leaves of Grass*. A hipster girl wrote something on her hand.

These people are strangers to each other. Or so they think.

SHE MET UP WITH Cora on the stairs in the shallow end. Cora thought her recent news was the coolest thing ever.

"You already love the guy, and how awesome is it that you have a gay dad?"

"I know, but I feel manipulated. Like some master plan was happening that I had no control over."

"Hello?" Cora said. "It's called *life.*"

The pool had gathered trash since last time. More people had found it and were hanging out there. Pretty soon it would be off-limits.

"What has your mom said about it?" Cora asked.

"I haven't talked to her. I'm going to kill her."

It started to rain again, large drops that splattered the bottom of the pool, creating bursts of water that fanned out. Lucy and Cora got up and moved under the motel awning. They shared a candy bar as they talked.

"You're so lucky," Cora said. "I mean, my dad's a total geek. He wears boat shoes."

"Well, at least you had one growing up."

"True, but you turned out pretty well, Loose. And now you're about to intern at Heather fucking Bridges."

In all the chaos, Lucy had forgotten about her impending internship. Cora was right. She *was* lucky. "I know, right? It's like, pinch me already." Lucy let the chocolate melt on her tongue the way she used to do when she was little. "So, if I'm a famous designer someday, will you work for me?"

"If I'm not a rock star, sure."

Lucy laughed at the thought of Cora singing that Go-Go's song in their school talent show. "Don't quit your day job."

Cora made a cat noise and they got up to go back uptown.

Lucy showed her Garret's place and they ate Chinese delivery, sitting on the floor against the orange wall.

"You know, you're basically rich now," Cora said.

"Shut up."

"Seriously, look at this place!" Cora got up and walked around, touching everything, opening drawers for quick peeks, picking up vases and knickknacks and holding them to the light.

"Well, the whole point is for me to be rich myself. I mean, my whole life I thought I would just grow up and be poor like my mother but now, being in this city and especially meeting Heather Bridges, I want it for myself. I want to be my own, self-sufficient woman."

"Wow, listen to you." Cora stuck her clenched fist in the air. "Girl power."

Lucy took the extra pair of chopsticks and used them to tie up her hair.

"I just want to go to sleep every night and feel a sense of accomplishment. It's funny, all the career counselors from our school told me I wouldn't get anywhere unless I went to college. They're so jacked."

Cora picked up the framed picture of Trevor.

"Open the frame and look behind the picture," Lucy said.

"Damn," Cora said, fanning out the others. "Your dad's a ho."

"It's funny, though, I haven't really seen him with anyone. I wish he would go for Alan, but there's major history there."

Lucy looked up at the tall window and silently wished that Garret and Alan were talking at that very moment, coming to some sort of agreement. They had to. The play was about to open.

"Gay men are rabid," Cora said.

"Everyone's rabid. I just think they are more forthcoming with their desires."

"Hmm. Slightly."

They ate in silence. When it came time for the fortune cookie, Lucy passed. She'd had enough revelations for the day.

34

ALAN WAS WATCHING *American Idol* at a crucial moment when he jumped at the sound of his buzzer. He walked over to the intercom and said, "State your claim."

"It's me, Alan. Buzz me in."

Alan had an avocado mask drying on his face and a towel wrapped around his head. He was wearing only boxers and red socks. He pushed "talk" again.

"There's nothing I have to say, Garret—"

"Alan, this is important. There's something I must tell you."

Alan took the towel off and dried his hair while talking.

"You already fucked my late husband and lied to me, so what could it possibly be now? You want to shag me? Keep dreaming."

"Alan! Please."

"Fine, fine, what is it?"

"Can I come up?" Garret asked.

"Depends."

"On what?"

"On the severity of the information," Alan said.

"Right, well. Lucy . . . Lucy . . ."

"Is having your child?"

He heard Garret laugh.

"Stick a nickel in it," Alan said impatiently.

"*She's* my child."

"What?" Alan dropped the towel he was holding and stared at the shape it had made on the floor.

". . . I'm her father. Alan, I'm a father."

He hit the buzzer and immediately started to wash off the green mask. He wanted to kill Garret, but what could he say? If this was true, well, it was fucking remarkable.

The front door slowly opened and Garret entered cautiously. Alan dried his face and tightened his robe.

"Now, hold on, I am still furious with you, but let's back up a minute. This little crumb of news, is it confirmed?"

"Yes, it's real, Alan. Her mother and I were together at Oxford, before I came to the States."

"She was the one who—"

"Caught me in the shower with Robbie Sparks."

"Holy shit. I need a cigarette," Alan said.

"You don't smoke."

"I do now. Hand one over."

Alan reached out his hand and Garret gave him a cigarette. He coughed a little on his first drag.

"We found each other," Garret said.

As betrayed as he felt, after the third drag Alan started to smile. "I feel like you should go on *Jerry Springer*."

Garret walked behind Alan, hugged him lightly. Some of Alan's unwashed mask got on Garret's cheek. Alan put out the cigarette as Garret sat down in the opposite chair.

"Forget that, I need a Valium or something. A pick-me-down."

"Alan, let's not create more drama than we already have."

Alan got up and walked toward Garret. He wiped the green spot off Garret's cheek and took a deep breath. "Where's Lucy?"

"At my place. I asked her to move in."

"This is all too much."

Garret stood up and grabbed him by the shoulders. "I want to be a better person, Alan. I know I haven't had a proper start."

"I'll schedule all the talk shows. We'll make millions," Alan said with a flip of his fingers.

"Stop."

Garret got up to leave and paused at the door, turned around, tried to speak.

Alan held up his hands. "Don't say anything else, not tonight."

"Right. Bye, then."

After Garret closed the door, Alan said, "See ya, Dad," fell dramatically back on the sofa, and began to fan himself with his script.

How could he be mad at Garret now? The man just found out he was a father. Plus, he could never be mad at Garret for too long; it had always been that way. He went to his kitchen and poured himself a glass of water, downed half of it before calling his mother to fill her in. She was astounded.

"No, mother, I'm serious."

"For Christ's sake, I don't even need to watch TV with you around!"

"Or read the tabloids," Alan said.

"Do you like her?"

Alan paused for a second, then answered. "Yes. Yes, I do."

THAT NIGHT ALAN couldn't sleep and it didn't help that his air conditioner was on the fritz, so he decided to take a walk and left his apartment in a daze, not sure where he was headed. He wanted to be glad for Garret, but his mind kept reenacting the airport scene: Mitchell's face in his hands, everyone around who was trying to help becoming faceless blobs of color. He realized Mitchell was going to confess that he had slept with Garret. That was what was in his eyes. As horrible as the act was, the thought temporarily calmed him.

Eventually Alan reached midtown, which seemed creepily deserted at that hour on such a windless night. Though he hadn't known where he was going, an unknown pull had taken him to the alleyway off Fifty-fourth Street—the stage door.

Inside, the theater was completely empty and dark. He flipped on a single overhead stage light and walked into it. He stared out at the empty seats.

Thank god for this place.

The very same theater that he had met Mitchell in, on a day when a record snowfall had stranded them there. Mitchell had told him he looked good in green, but the shirt he had on was actually blue. Alan smiled at the thought and started to tap dance slowly, eventually singing a bass line along with the steps. His feet and his voice built to a crescendo and he ran up the aisle, spreading his arms out. Maybe this was his way of telling Mitchell Garret's news and forgiving them. Alan knew that of all places, Mitchell's soul was in this theater.

He jumped back onto the stage and reentered the shower of light, spun around, and collapsed.

I'm too old for this.

He heard soft clapping from the balcony and quickly stood up, tried to look out to see but was blinded.

"Encore, encore," he heard a man say.

Alan recognized the voice immediately.

"What . . . what are you doing here?"

"I couldn't sleep. I came to see you."

"How'd you know I'd be here?"

Garret lit a lighter in front of his face and said, "I did the math, dear."

Alan ran to the side of the stage and flicked the houselights on. Garret was gone. He ran out to try and find him, and Garret snuck up from behind and grabbed him. Alan shrieked like a little girl and turned around, slightly shaking.

"Sshh, sshh. Wait here."

Garret ran to the side of the stage and cut the houselights so that all that remained was the one stage light, a soft shower of milky white falling on the black stage.

Garret let his jacket drop to the floor. Alan tried to say something, but Garret put his fingers on Alan's lips.

"Sshh."

He is not going to kiss me, Alan thought. *I cannot disregard the humiliation, not now.*

The stage door, which Alan had carelessly left unlocked, burst open and a bum came in, drunk and carrying a half-eaten bagel.

Garret and Alan started to laugh. They led the man out into the alleyway and locked up. They went to an all-night diner and Garret ordered eggs. Alan had some soup. They didn't talk. There was too much to say. Instead, they felt the comfort of simply being together, in a city of millions.

When they parted on the street, their hug lasted a while.

35

LUCY WAS CRASHED on the couch when Garret came home, even though the TV was blaring an infomercial. He carried her into the bedroom, and with the weight of her in his arms, he could feel the depth of his love. He carefully placed the covers over her, and sat down on the floor of her room while she slept, the moonlight slicing an oblong shape onto the floor. He began to softly hum.

After a while, he went to his room and got into bed. He dreamed that Lucy had a baby and in the hospital it was put into his arms by Alan, who was the doctor. He couldn't tell if it was a boy or a girl, but his mum was holding a blue balloon.

He woke up groggy and made an extra-strong espresso.

It was a clear July day. Bathed in the morning sun streaming down from the skylights in the kitchen, he explained to Lucy that he had to go to London for a quick meeting and then up north to check on his mother. Two days he'd be gone.

"My grandmother!" Lucy said.

"That's right," Garret said. "She's absolutely thrilled. Be prepared for frumpy dresses."

Lucy giggled. Perhaps they were refusing to let it, but their dynamic hadn't really changed.

"You'll be OK while I'm gone?" Garret asked.

"Of course."

"No painting or wine drinking?"

"Promise."

Garret packed his small carry-on and took a car to JFK. While checking his email in the private British Airways lounge, several handsome and probably married men gave him the eye, but he ignored them, concentrating on his Blackberry.

The flight was painless due to an Ambien and a lot of sleep he had to catch up on. He went straight from customs into a cab, and when he arrived at his meeting in central London, he thankfully got a second wind. He was pitching for more investors to get on board when the play would move to the West End after its Broadway run. One of the casting agents pulled him aside as he was leaving and said, "Getting laid, are we?"

"On the contrary," Garret replied. "But I'll take that as a compliment."

He went out into Piccadilly and walked by the same chip shop he had been to with Lucy. He was still bursting with the idea that he was a father. He got on the Tube and rode to St. Pancras Station. On the train ride north he sent a text to Alan:

> Meeting a success. I think they're in.
> Now we can cast.
> Did we secure the ballroom for the opening night after-party?

It occurred to him that Alan might not want to continue working together. Their embrace the night before felt like it was the end of something. The thought physically crushed him and he sank down in his seat.

He dozed off again and was awakened by a buzz on his Blackberry.

> Ballroom secure.
> Lucy and I are having dinner.

The text was terse, but he was relieved that there was communication. When he arrived up north, the haze was so thick it blocked the view of the Millwards' driveway.

He entered his house and put down his bags. At the still distinctive smell of his father, his body shuddered.

"Dear!" Dorothy came down the stairs and took Garret in her arms.

He looked her up and down and said, "Mum, are you OK? Why did you get an MRI?"

"Oh dear, you didn't come all this way to talk about boring tests. Come with me!"

She led him out the front door and over to the shed next to the garage.

"It's a ridiculously English morning, isn't it?" Garret said while walking through the fog.

"Yes, but I'm sick of being English. Besides, I have an American granddaughter!"

With some struggle, she freed the two rickety bikes from their tangle. She spun the wheels, checked them, let her smirk become a smile, and said, "Well, let's have a go!"

They rode cautiously, imbalanced at first, but slowly got into the groove, cutting through the wispy fog down the old-hedged roads, pedaling faster. For a second, he thought it was Lucy he was following and not his mother. The roads seemed to be alive, made of promise. Was he finally moving forward?

Garret watched his mother, who started to sing an Irish ballad really loud, until the song turned to tears, and she cried as she continued riding, faster and faster.

An old man from a nearby village stopped his truck to watch them go by. He seemed mesmerized.

We probably look like ghosts in this fog.

She beat Garret to the top of a hill and as she began to

descend she took her hands off the handlebars and stretched her arms out at her sides. Her wailing turned to laughter, a pure release of joy.

This was strange behavior for Dorothy, but it didn't matter. It was no longer an English countryside, but a beginning.

THAT NIGHT, when Dorothy cooked Garret's favorite meal, he did notice something different about her. The way her head sort of jerked and she'd get lost in thought. They ate by the fire as Garret told her how meeting Lucy transpired and how he betrayed Alan. It felt good to talk freely to someone who he knew wouldn't be so quick to judge. His mother had always loved him unconditionally.

"This sounds like one of your plays," she said.

Garret sipped his wine and found himself staring at a pile of finished crossword puzzles. "Is he really coming?"

"Well, I am," Dorothy said, cutting up her meat and taking a bite. "And Lord knows he probably couldn't last a minute without me here."

His mother choked a bit and Garret patted her back.

"I'm fine. Listen, dear, you help yourself to pudding. I'm going to retire early. I want to speed up time so I can see Lucy sooner."

"Soon enough," he said, and kissed her on her forehead. "Thanks for tea."

THE NEXT MORNING the sun was out and the green hedges around the house glistened. His mother was still sleeping, so he left her a note and caught the local bus to the train station.

As Garret waited for the train he ran into his old pastor, a skinny man with kind eyes and a thin smile.

"Garret, lovely to see you," he said, squeezing his shoulder. "You know, I spoke to your father recently."

"Yes?"

The pastor tilted his head as if it was private information. "Came to my house in the middle of the night."

"Why?"

The man smiled and took Garret's hand in his.

"Well, he wanted some advice," the pastor explained.

"And?"

"Let's just say I modernized his way of thinking slightly."

The train started to enter the station, and Garret remembered loving that sound, as a kid going into the city with his father, wondering how something so powerful could even exist.

"I see. Was he responsive?" Garret asked over the noise.

"Hard to tell." The train arrived at the platform.

"Well, thank you, Pastor."

"Just trying to help. You take care now."

"Will do."

"Cheers."

On the train, Garret thought he recognized a plump woman smiling at him across the seat and smiled back.

"It's me," she said in a high, lilting tone. "Bette. I was your nurse?"

"Oh, right! Sorry, it's been—"

"Ages, I know. I must say though, this is strange, because only the other day I ran into your father in London. He barely recognized me as well. I've gained a little weight."

"Don't be silly. You look the same," Garret lied. "What was my father doing in London?"

"You know where I saw him? In a bookshop! I didn't think he read anything except the paper."

"Crosswords."

"Right. Anyway," she said with a cheeky grin, "it looks like he was brushing up on your lifestyle."

Garret's face reddened as she went on.

"He was pretending to be perusing architecture books, but really he was in the queer section."

Coming out of her mouth, the word sounded dirty. He tried to picture his father in a gay bookstore. *First Pastor John and now this?*

"Well, that is a bit surprising," Garret said.

"Anyway, don't mean to gossip, but I thought you might like to hear that."

She got off at the next stop and patted Garret's head.

"Bye now," he said.

———

ON THE PLANE home he didn't sleep. He had a lot to think about: Alan's forgiveness, a new daughter, his mum's strange behavior. He counted his hopes and blessings:

> Alan will forgive me.
> Lucy is a miracle.
> Mum will be fine.
> Maybe Pop is making an effort.

36

ZIGZAGGING HER WAY to Grand Central to meet her mother, Lucy tried not to fume. When her mom arrived, they greeted each other shyly on the platform, almost as if they didn't really know one another. Tourists and commuters shuttled around them as they walked slowly, leaving the station and heading south on Park Avenue. When Lucy could not take it anymore, she grabbed her mother and sat her down on a bench outside an office building. Role reversal.

"Why, Mom, why? Were you just not going to tell me forever?"

She saw in her mother's face a deeper shade of vulnerability—she seemed genuinely scared.

"I didn't want you to be disappointed. I knew Garret was gay, even then, and—"

"Like I care!"

A bald man who was smoking next to them walked to the end of the block to give them space.

"Well, this was a long time ago. And you're not a normal teenager."

"Oh please, Mom, wake up and smell the macchiato. We live in New York City. How could you be so ignorant?"

"I know, but—"

"No buts, Mom. It's just not fair, I don't know what to think, I'm so confused."

A woman tried to swoop up her little boy who was running

wild, waving a red popsicle. The boy screamed, not wanting to be held back.

"Maybe this was the way it was supposed to happen," Joyce said.

"Yeah, Mom. Gee, I'm not going to tell my daughter who her father is because someday she might run into him on a plane. Good logic."

Joyce snickered. "Well, I thought hard about telling you after you took to Uncle Edward so much."

"Yes, and why didn't you?"

"You always loved him," Joyce said, as if caught in the memory. The boy nearby calmed down as his mother replaced his popsicle with some goldfish in a plastic bag.

"Yes. And he's gay, mother, camp as a row of tents."

"I should have figured Garret's sexuality wouldn't have bothered you. Look, honey, I was selfish. But I did try and contact him the first time you asked, and I had no luck."

"Can't you see it's not about sexuality? It's about having a father. What bothers me is not knowing. Always has."

Joyce touched Lucy's cheek and said, "I just hope we can all get along."

How do adults just do that? Just move on, like it's nothing. As if a child's life is some passing thing, like a head cold.

"Well, we'll see about that," Lucy said.

LUCY BROUGHT her mother to Garret's place again, and this time Joyce seemed to notice everything. She studied a portrait of Garret done by a famous modern painter. She said, softly to herself, "I should've known."

"What?"

"Nothing."

"No, not nothing. You said something." Lucy wasn't going to let anything get by her, not after all this. She felt a surging power, as if she had one up on her.

"No, I didn't," Joyce said.

"Yes, you did, and it's usually the things that we say under our breath that mean the most."

"Alright. I said, well . . . I should have known before. I noticed something familiar about the painting, and the way every surface in here is gleaming. I even thought twice when you spoke his name."

Lucy felt proud. "It's beautiful, isn't it? It's been featured in *Architectural Digest*."

Her mother sat down slowly and scratched her head. "Garret, when I knew him, was obsessed with studying, becoming powerful, successful. I was just a pastime to him really; the sex wasn't even that great. But I admired his drive." She leaned back and sighed. "I feel so terrible, Lucy."

"You should, Mom."

"For not telling you, not telling Garret. For drinking it all away. But you turned out pretty great considering your mother is . . ."

Lucy watched her mother's eyes twitch and well up. She felt her own strength form a wall around her and resisted the urge to comfort her. She felt betrayed, and right now she had to stay inside her own hard shell.

"Mom . . ."

Joyce put her arms out, pleading to Lucy, who finally gave in and hugged her, but then pulled back and stood her ground.

"I'm not going anywhere. But I'm moving in with Garret." Lucy got up and lightly ran her finger along the orange wall. "And you know what? I was thinking on the subway . . . it will take me a while to forgive you, but I can't change anything up to this moment. I don't want to dwell."

After a minute, Joyce said, "I do love you, you know that?"

Lucy played with her bracelets and then looked up at her mother and sighed. "Yes, I do."

They were silent.

"I had a drink today," Joyce said.

"What?" Lucy could feel her nostrils flare and heat surge through the skin on her face. "I thought you were on the wagon, with Stanley and all."

"Just one."

Lucy stood up and turned around, enough anger inside her to break something.

"One is enough, Mom. Don't you know that? I'm not holding your head over the toilet or driving your car. I'm not bringing you aspirin and—"

"OK, OK." Joyce put her open palms in the air to stop the incoming wrath.

"No, it's not OK. Does Stanley know?"

"No."

"Well, you're going to have to own up to it. Go talk to Stanley, do whatever it is you do, but I'm finished for today. I'll see you at the play opening. And please, wear something nice and show up sober. I will not have you embarrassing me."

Joyce gathered her bag and walked with a lowered head toward the door.

37

IN GARRET'S living room, Cora helped Lucy try on the Lilly Pulitzer dress she was slated to wear on opening night. It was white with a low neck and tiny reflective buttons scattered throughout.

"Oh my god, where did you get this?" Cora asked.

"One of the PR people got it on loan. Dad says I can't keep it." Lucy turned her back to Cora. "It feels strange saying that word."

"It's all very *Twin Peaks*," Cora said, strapping her in. "But I must say, you are going to look fabulous."

She spun around. "Tops, that's what Garret says." She walked around the room, the dress trailing behind. "I have to be careful not to trip."

Cora clapped.

Lucy fell onto the couch, looking up at the ceiling. "Cor, I don't even know what to think anymore. My mom fell off the wagon, my best gay friend tells me he is my father, and I'm about to start the job of my life."

"Well, at least your life is exciting. I didn't even get into Hunter."

Lucy got up and walked over to the full-length mirror. The dress was nothing like anything she had ever worn. It shimmered and hugged her body perfectly.

"My grandmother's coming," she announced.

"I thought your grandmother died."

"On Garret's side. A little old lady from England."

"Awesome!" Cora squealed. Lucy sat down on the floor, the dress a blanket of glimmering white fanned around her.

Cora went over by the window and lit one of Garret's cigarettes. "I'm so jeal," she said. "I could so get used to this lifestyle." She took a sophisticated drag. "But isn't it weird to think that your mom slept with him and you had a crush on him?"

"Beyond," Lucy said.

"Whatever, worse things happen. I mean look at *Desperate Housewives*."

"That's a soap opera, Cora."

"True."

Lucy didn't want to ruin the dress so she got up carefully, slipped out of it, and put it back on the hanger.

"Listen," Cora said, "most conventional families are super-dysfunctional anyways. I think you're making out OK, considering."

Lucy knew she was right. Garret was the coolest father she could have wished for. But she still felt imbalanced—a faint uneasiness, a lack of control.

Cora flicked her cigarette out and they went into the kitchen and poured Diet Cokes.

"Yeah, but what's going to happen next? I feel like I'm just waiting for another emotional earthquake to happen," Lucy said, watching the bubbles in her glass.

"The only earthquake that's going to happen is when everyone falls down after they see you in that dress."

They took their drinks back into the living room and watched a *Project Runway* episode. Lucy saw herself as one of the designers, forced to be creative under strict guidelines and short time frames. One of the contestants included a hat in her design and Lucy immediately noticed its flaws.

When Cora had to go, they did their ritual handshake and kiss on the cheek.

"You're the best, Cora."

"Just don't forget about me when you're at the top."

———

WHEN GARRET CAME home, Lucy immediately did a second showing of the dress.

"Stunning, Goose. Absolutely stunning."

Lucy held out her arms, twirled around, and said, "I'm glad you approve."

She followed him into the kitchen, where he flipped through his mail. He seemed more animated than usual. Was it nervousness?

"So, be prepared to meet your grandparents," he said.

"They're both coming?"

"Yes. Apparently my father is coming around. And I have a feeling it's because of you. Mum told me he was reluctant, but he was asking questions about you. I don't know if I'm ready for all this. I'm knackered and jet-lagged and ready to collapse."

"OK," Lucy said, "but what about Alan?"

"Well, he said we should go on talk shows."

Lucy giggled. "Typical Alan response."

"I told him about Mitchell and he was not pleased, but you, my dear, have upstaged that drama. At least for now."

Lucy made Garret his favorite tea and poured him a steaming cup.

"Ta," he said.

She followed him into his bedroom, where he lay down with all his clothes still on. She sat on the foot of the bed and rubbed his feet.

"Oh, that's divine," he told her.

After the foot rub, Lucy got up to give Garret some space. "Listen, I was thinking while you were away. If I can forgive my mom and you can forgive your dad, I guess Alan will have to forgive you."

"Seems like a good plan. Goodnight, princess."

"'Night."

She kissed him on the cheek, turned out all the lights, and got into her own bed.

I have a father now. And he's perfect.

Well, mostly.

38

THE NEXT DAY and a half went by at lightning speed as Garret made all the last-minute preparations for the opening. His interaction with Alan was cordial and businesslike, more out of necessity than friendship. Putting the play on was like giving birth—they had to go in and do it, no matter what, and pray that everything transpired with flying colors. Four healthy limbs, a packed house—a new life that miraculously took shape.

Garret paced the cavernous hotel lobby, which was spotless and smelled of cigar and aftershave. It was an old-money place on Central Park South that his mother had always liked. He watched a young couple bickering near the concierge while their little boy banged his lollipop against the wall.

Dorothy peeked around the corner and spotted him.

"Pssst!" she said, startling him.

"Mum!"

They embraced, and Garret smelled her signature scent, a mixture of flowery detergent and spicy perfume. To him it was the only thing that smelled like home.

Dorothy stepped back and beamed proudly at him in his pinstripe suit with the a dark red handkerchief peeking out of his pocket.

"You look smashing as ever!"

"Oh, stop, Mum. Where is he? Is he here?"

Dorothy sheepishly pointed a finger at the ceiling. "Resting," she said.

"Grim as ever?"

"Not so bad. He's here, Garret. But more important, where is Lucy?" Dorothy's unabashed excitement made her eyes expand with a little girl's wonder. "I simply cannot wait to lay my eyes on her! Your father acts aloof, but I know he's pleased. He's just such an old bore."

Garret looked at his mum and wondered what it was about her that was unusual. Dressed a little more carelessly, she seemed loosened somehow, almost fearless.

"Listen, I cannot see him now. I'm just going to wait until tomorrow, after the bloody thing opens, then I'll be able to . . . I . . . just can't. . . ."

"It's fine, dear, just fine. But pray tell, where is the little angel?" Dorothy was shaking with anticipation.

"She's not so little. She's resting at my apartment."

"I'll bet she's . . . oh, Garret, I'll bet she's beautiful!"

"She is, inside and out." Garret's pride was uncontainable. He smiled.

Dorothy fanned herself with a brochure. "I'm sure of it!"

"So, Mum, your tickets are at the box office, and I will see you at the reception, OK?"

"Garret, one thing."

"Yes?"

Dorothy looked around to make sure no one could overhear her and said, "Does she look like me?"

"Come to think of it, she looks more like you than she does me."

When they kissed and hugged good-bye, Garret breathed in his mother's aroma for an extra few seconds. As he left, a young bellboy gave him the eye and Garret grinned but didn't turn around.

Pop is here.

Garret remembered when he was a teenager his father had made a teasing comment about one of the girls in the village, Pamela. He thought Garret was keen on her. She had red hair and worked at the little golf shop. At that point, he already knew he had feelings for boys. In fact, he had shared a wank with two of the caddies behind the shed where they washed the carts. But after his father's comment, he had desperately wanted to like her, to kiss her, to see if he could ignite a spark. He asked her to the dance and they drank too much beer and went back to her house. He ended up helping her pick out the outfit she was going to wear to her college interview. There was no physical attraction, other than a desire to style her. He should have known. But still, he went to college and dated girls, tried as best he could to please his father and his endless questions. He wanted to bring one home and show him, say, *Look, Pop, I'm hetero*. After Joyce, he realized it was a lost cause. Now, riding in the back of the cab, the summer sun orange and red through the spaces between the buildings, Garret was thankful for that one thing his father had done. Because now he had a child and it made him feel more essential, more rooted in the world.

He felt like anything was possible.

39

ALAN FELT THE usual mixture of joy and dread as the crowd gathered in a keyed-up, pre-show mood. He watched Lucy, looking angelic in her white, flowing dress, escorting the couture-laden celebrities and investors to their seats.

When she had a free moment, Alan pulled her aside. "Good smile, honey. Just don't walk too fast. Some of these people, especially the financial patrons of the arts, need a little extra time—don't want to overwork their pacemakers. By the way, welcome to the family."

Lucy smiled.

"OK, here's one." He motioned to a man in a bright green suit. "Tell him he looks dashing as a frog, but Halloween is still a couple of months away."

Lucy giggled and approached the elderly gentleman.

"Right this way," Lucy said through a smile, taking the man's arm.

Alan could see Dorothy and George sitting patiently in the producer's box, waiting for the curtain to go up. As horrid as the man seemed, Alan noticed that George was quite attractive for his age.

He received the ten-minute warning and went backstage. He fiddled with his watch and noticed his sweaty palms. He was not worried about the show, he knew everything was ready—it was Garret he was worried about. *Where was he?*

Someone handed him a large, fragrant bouquet as the curtain went up. The card read:

A—
It was a moment in time, an untimely mistake.
The man loved you more than I thought any human being was capable of.
Let's do this one for him.
G

Alan stared at the card and closed his eyes briefly. He gave the flowers to a stage tech and said, "Do something with these, please."

He assumed Garret was in the lighting booth, where he hid on most opening nights. Just as well.

The play transpired, as Alan tended to think of it, like a road. A twisting and winding story that was always alive. He loved this part, seeing all his little suggestions and ideas take shape and feeling the buzz of a captivated audience charge the atmosphere. The gasps and laughter from the house were all reactions to his baby. Despite the latest drama, he was content, thrilled even. He had lost twelve pounds, he wasn't talking to his mother so incessantly, and the crowd was eating it up.

Miss Fanny Pack, his lead, who apparently had turned down a Woody Allen film for the role, was delivering her lines effortlessly and with calculated grace. Although completely poised and calm, underneath she was on fire.

During the second act, he noticed one of the supporting players waiting in the wings next to him, shaking out his hands, his face extremely pale.

"Something wrong?" Alan asked.

"It's my debut on Broadway, and all these scouts are here."

Alan pulled the kid aside.

"Listen, this is *your* night. I've done my job, and you know your shtick, so all you have to do is go out there and shine. I've seen you do it five hundred times, so forget about the scouts. They're going to love you so much they'll probably wet their Depends."

The kid smiled.

"Now, give me your arms."

Alan took each of his arms and shook them out. Then he rubbed the back of his neck. More color had returned to the kid's face as he turned around.

"Thanks Alan," he said as the stage manager cued him to enter.

Alan watched him proudly as he played out the scene. At that moment it all seemed worth it.

When Miss Fanny Pack came off for a break, Alan dabbed at her forehead with his handkerchief.

"I just want to tell you," she said, preparing to go back on, "you're one of the best directors I've worked with."

"Thanks, dear. Now go kick some more ass." Alan pinched her butt as she walked back onstage and added, "But lose the fanny pack. They went out with pleats."

One of the angels came up behind him and said, "Easy, you need her."

"I need all of you," Alan said.

He looked up at the lighting booth and could just make out Garret's silhouette. *You bastard*, he thought. *It is so hard to hate you*.

40

IN THE LAST moments of the play, the angels were suspended above the seats, held up by invisible rigging. There was a mutual intake of breath from the audience.

Lucy looked up and was overwhelmed. She grabbed the leg of the person next to her, who looked at her as if she were a strange animal.

"Sorry," she whispered, reaching up to try and touch them.

As the actors took their bows, the standing ovation seemed to shake the building. Garret and Alan entered the stage from either side as the crowd howled even more. Onstage, Garret whispered something into Alan's ear and Alan turned bright red.

Lucy said, to no one in particular, "That's my dad."

After the houselights came up, Lucy walked with her mother and Stanley to the grand ballroom where the reception was being held. She took Stanley in for the first time.

Not bad, she thought. *Seems overly eager, a tad game show host. Better than NASCAR, like most of the other ones.*

"He looks like one of those motivational speakers," she whispered to her mom. "But aside from the general teeth-overkill, he seems sweet."

"Be nice."

Lucy smiled at him when they were back in earshot.

Though she wouldn't dare create a visual, at least her mom was getting some. It was more than she could say for herself.

She wasn't concerned with boys at present; it was all about career. *The rest will come, right?*

They walked up the long stairway lit from below and entered through the giant doors. The guests mingled underneath a high ceiling adorned with a crystal chandelier the size of a small car.

"I'll be back," she told her mother.

In the ornate ladies room, Lucy dabbed at the corners of her lips and looked herself in the eyes.

A slight older woman to her right rearranged her beige scarf three different ways and finally put it back in her purse.

"Better without the scarf," Lucy said.

The woman smiled politely, as if the comment was about the weather, and applied a touch of lipstick. As she walked by to leave, the woman's face morphed into a surprised expression in the bottom corner of Lucy's mirror.

"Is your name Lucy?"

She nodded.

"Oh dear, I'm . . . I'm Dorothy. . . ."

The woman twitched like a stunned bird.

"Garret's mother? Oh my god!"

All of a sudden Dorothy looked as if she was going to weep, but stopped, and they just stared at each other.

"You know," Lucy said while shifting her weight, "I thought this was going to be awkward and all, but you seem, I don't know, we seem . . ."

"Come now," Dorothy said, leading Lucy out of the ladies room, "we've got a lot of catching up to do." They approached George, who was fidgeting on one side of the dance floor, looking slightly out of place.

Before they reached George, Garret intercepted Lucy and picked her up, twirled her around, then put her down for their special greeting: both sides of the hand, a bump on the hip, and a blown kiss.

"What did you think, Goose?"

"I laughed, I cried, it was better than *Cats*."

Dorothy grabbed George's arm and said, "Come now."

"Alright, alright."

Lucy heard her whispering to George, "She's even more beautiful than I'd imagined." She felt her face redden as George sheepishly approached. She whispered to Garret, "He looks like more of an ankle biter than a bulldog to me."

Garret turned to look at his father, who slowly took off his hat.

Lucy walked the few steps over to him and stared at him hard in the eyes. "Hi, Grandpa. I'm Lucy."

George nodded his head, his expression as blank as a cold, starless sky.

As Lucy stared at him, his face slowly became infused with color.

"I want us to be a family. Can you help me with that?" Lucy said.

George started to shake a little, as if the once impervious walls around his heart were beginning to cave in. He reached out his arms. As they hugged, Lucy whispered into George's ear, "Now get your ass over there and greet your son."

George walked over to Garret and held his head in his hands before bringing it to his chest. He said something into Garret's hair, but Lucy only heard the words, ". . . terribly sorry."

Garret didn't say anything, but he didn't pull away.

41

AFTER GARRET AND ALAN made toasts, the reception guests slowly became more vibrant and unglued from the alcohol and the rousing sounds of the tuxedo-clad band playing Frank Sinatra and other crooners.

"Isn't that sweet," Alan said, coming up behind Dorothy, who was watching her husband dance with Lucy.

"Indeed," Dorothy said, regaining her composure.

Alan noticed she looked a little bedraggled and said, "Can I get you some coffee?"

"No, dear, but can I ask you something?"

"As long as it doesn't involve tools," Alan said.

Dorothy laughed. She put her hands on his shoulders and squeezed.

"Will you look after Garret? I mean, if he never settles down?"

Dorothy gave him an open, pleading look, and the sadness in her eyes chilled him.

———————

ON THE DANCE FLOOR, he saw Garret tap his father's shoulder to cut in on his dance with Lucy. George obliged and walked over to where Alan and Dorothy were standing.

"Well, I haven't had that much exercise in years," George

said, clearly loosened up from the alcohol. "I'll just step outside for a bit."

George stepped back out onto the veranda and Dorothy placed her damp palm on Alan's wrist and said, "Will you excuse me, dear?"

As she went outside to talk to her husband, Alan stayed within reach of the slightly opened patio doors. He knew something was up, and he couldn't help but succumb to his inner Nancy Drew.

He heard George say, "A nice girl, that Lucy."

Then Dorothy's head jolted upright and her words came out like deadweight, three apples dropped into a bucket. "I'm dying, George."

"What?" George replied.

"Nothing, dear," Dorothy said. "Nothing at all."

Alan felt his heart drop to his feet.

I must have heard wrong. Buying? Flying?

For the rest of the evening Alan watched Dorothy. She looked like a frail bird with a terrified expression—as if at any moment some large thing could swoop down and crush her.

Please god, not another death.

He decided to dance with her. She was light on her feet at first, but then began to sink against him so that he was partially holding her up.

"The play was lovely," Dorothy said.

"Thanks." Alan felt tongue-tied. "You . . . you look beautiful tonight."

Dorothy looked directly into his eyes and said, "You really think so?"

"Oh, I see," Alan said. "You just want to hear it twice."

Dorothy smiled and started to dance more steadily.

Alan's light-headed buzz lost its shine. He suddenly felt clouded over.

"Let's get you a drink!" he said, taking her elbow and leading her over to the bar. It was really him that wanted the drink. And he deserved it.

The food table was strewn with debris. Alan always thought there was something melancholic about the remains of a festive atmosphere. But this was opening night; there was no room for sadness. Nevertheless, the look in Dorothy's eyes reminded him that sadness was not something you could turn off—like Mitchell's that day, the fear in her eyes was palpable.

42

AFTER DOING SHOTS with the band and closing down the place, Garret and Lucy took a cab back to Garret's apartment. Alan had beaten them there and was passed out on the couch—he looked sated, almost smiling. There was a half-finished bottle of scotch next to him.

Strange, he doesn't drink scotch, Garret thought. *And why is he over here?*

"Look how cute he is!" Lucy said.

He is cute. He didn't deserve to lose Mitchell.

"Goose, would you be a pet and get me the blanket from the hall closet?" Garret asked. "He must be here because his mother's staying at his place."

Lucy obeyed, coming back in a flash.

"Thanks for a great night," Lucy said.

"If I say 'Sleep tight,' is that too fatherly?"

"You've got a lot of years to catch up on."

"Right, then. Sleep tight."

Garret covered Alan with the blanket and gently kissed his forehead. He sat by his side for a while and watched him. He noticed the muscles starting to show on his arms, and that his face had lost some of its roundness.

Alan woke up as Garret started turning the lights off.

"Oh, I'm sorry. . . . I'll just . . ."

"It's okay, Alan, just sleep here. I thought you left with . . ."

"I was with your mother," Alan said sleepily. "Did she seem normal to you?"

"What do you mean?"

Alan turned and pulled the covers up to his head.

"She was . . . she was . . . she's beautiful."

Garret went to get Alan some water. Clearly he was out of it. After Alan took a large sip, he said, "Thanks, Garret."

In all the chaos of the last few weeks, Garret had forgotten to ask Alan if he had called the lawyer about Mitchell's estate. "You know, I talked to your mother, she said this lawyer can get—"

"I know, but I thought twice about it. It's so morbid, me going after his estate."

"Alan, he left it to you!"

"Garret, it's not in my nature," Alan said, slurring his words.

"Listen, just rest now."

"OK. But tell me, Garret, was he . . . was it good?"

Garret couldn't get into this now. He couldn't lie anymore, but he was not about to tell him that it was amazing. That he let Mitchell fuck him and it felt like flying. That he tasted every curve of his body, that they were greedy and drunk with lust. He couldn't tell him that it was more than sex, it was a deeper plane. That they were transported to another place. But the truth was, if Mitchell hadn't died, it wouldn't have happened again. Garret knew that. It was this tiny balloon of sexual tension that had finally gotten high enough into the atmosphere to pop. Mitchell loved Alan only. It didn't mean he wasn't flawed. Flaws are what beauty is made of.

"I don't really remember," Garret said.

Alan made a noise. "Yeah, right."

"Did you get my flowers?"

"Oh, shit! Yes. Someday you'll tell me. Or maybe not. Fuck, it's so hard. . . ."

"Alan, thanks for toasting Lucy, that was tops."

"You are the last person in the world who should be a dad," Alan said, and was snoring ten seconds later.

When Garret got into his bed, he thought about what Alan said. Maybe Alan was right. But Lucy was doing so well now, and Garret liked to think he had a hand in it. He believed in her, which was a good start.

43

LUCY DRESSED understated for her first day in low-rider jeans and a frilly, warm-toned top, taking the cue from some of the girls she had seen when she had gone in for the interview. She pushed through the large glass doors and took a deep breath. She didn't know where she was going, but she walked with confidence.

A pale, angular woman with long scissor legs stopped right in front of her, blocking her path.

"Are you Lucy?"

"Yes."

She barely nodded.

"Gina. Come with me."

Nice to meet you too, Lucy thought.

Gina, whose face looked void of pores, led her through a bunch of cubicles into another part of the building that was industrial and almost futuristic—pristine white walls leading up to impossibly high ceilings with exposed silver beams and diffused light coming from long, rectangular, frosted windows at the long end of the room. They walked right through a fashion shoot, where a striking girl with purple-black skin was holding a giant blue-swirl lollipop over half her face. Her bikini matched the lollipop. The director was prancing around with a Miniature Pinscher in his arms.

"He never puts the dog down," Gina said, as she led her behind the large off-white curtains. "It's kind of scary."

They entered another large room, lined with clothing racks and vanities and women with names like Jay and Sari wearing measuring strips as scarves while sneaking cigarettes.

She was told to steam the clothes on the racks that needed it. Gina was more pleasant after she learned of Lucy's hat collection.

"Millinery work is cool," Gina said, while applying lip gloss. "Headwear is sort of a dead market, though."

"Well, maybe I can revive it."

At break time, she called her grandmother, who was supposed to take her shopping in Soho that afternoon. Coming back from the coffee shop across the street, she looked both ways three times before crossing. Life seemed unbearably precious. She had done reckless already. Her whole thirteenth year was basically spent shoplifting, tagging, and raiding her mother's cabinet of pharmaceutical friends. Then she met Cora and was impressed by her handbags and her cute, Ivy League brothers—not to mention the biggest swimming pool she had ever seen. Cora had given her an application for a scholarship at the boarding school and she got it. Her mother cried when she told her. Ever since then it was drawing, designing, and occasionally getting stoned with Alex. Now here she was, steaming clothes at a Heather Bridges shoot.

Gina seemed to spend most of the day walking around being willowy. She carried a pad with nothing written on it and a bottle of SmartWater that she never opened. She eventually put them down and studied her nails. Then she really seemed to look at Lucy for the first time.

"How old are you?"

"Almost eighteen," Lucy said casually.

"Do you model?"

She shook her head and hung up the top she had been steaming. She was starting to sweat a little from the heat.

"That girl's fifteen," Gina said, pointing to the model that was being shot.

"I want to be a designer," Lucy said, reinforcing what she had said earlier. One of the seamstresses raised her eyebrow. "I know—I'm a seventeen-year-old intern. But there it is."

The seamstress laughed.

"OK, dreamer," Gina said, "before you leave, please take Heather's garbage out. The girl who usually does it called in bulimic."

When Lucy entered Heather's office, almost everyone was gone. Apparently Heather didn't want the cleaning people taking out her personal garbage. Lucy was instructed to take it to a Dumpster three blocks away. She had thought Gina was joking, but here she was carrying a small plastic bag down Seventh Avenue, then east on Forty-eighth. When she got to the bin she couldn't help but to peek in and see what all the fuss was about. There were three plum seeds, about fifty shredded Equal packets, an unopened box of truffles, and an empty prescription bottle with a ripped label.

Lucy threw it in and said, "Whoopee."

As she walked across town to her grandmother's hotel, she thought to herself, *Do what you have to do. People would KILL to take out Heather Bridge's trash.*

44

GARRET SNUCK INTO Alan's apartment and located the lawyer's card. This had gone on too long, and maybe all Alan needed to carry it through was a little help. He took a cab to the law offices and sauntered up to the big-haired secretary.

"Yes, James Steele, please."

"Do you have an appointment?"

"Yes," Garret lied. "It's in regard to Alan Roth."

"I don't see . . ."

"If you could please just let him know I'm here; it's rather important. Cheers."

He sat down and felt a buzz in his pocket. A text from Lucy:

Had to take out Heather's personal trash
Do you know about this?
Going shopping with your mum!

Garret smiled and was called in. He put away his phone and was suddenly face-to-face with the lawyer.

"I know you don't know me, but I am very close with Alan Roth, the gentleman you were trying to—"

"Yes."

"This sister of his, who, by the way, was never even civil to Mitchell unless she wanted money, has not only taken the apartment but has frozen a lot of Mitchell's assets."

"Yes, I spoke with Alan regarding that, and he wasn't sure

whether he wanted to bring her to trial, even though he clearly has a case."

"Well, he does. And as soon as possible."

Sympathy registered in the lawyer's eyes as he leaned back in his chair.

"I see. Well, what I can do is have my assistant update the papers and you can bring them to Alan to sign. Can you wait here for a while?"

"As long as it takes."

"Great. Oh, and I will need . . ."

Garret reached into his pocket. "I can take care of that now as well."

"Fine."

———

AFTER GARRET got the papers he went by Alan's gym and waited for him outside. He ran into an ex-shag and had an awkward cigarette with him.

He sat on the stoop and typed a text back to Lucy:

Tampons?

Summer in New York was miserably hot and humid, but on days like today, when there was a significant breeze and the dusk light made the city take on a glow that seemed even more peaceful contrasted to the usual chaos, it was lovely. A small kid walked by, followed by his humming mother, then three young men walking two French Bulldogs who sniffed him briefly before moving on.

"What are you doing here?" Alan asked when he saw Garret, who got up and did that little shake of his head.

"I need to talk to you about a few things."

"Where are your parents?" Alan asked.

"They're leaving tomorrow. We're having dinner."

He could see thin shadow lines on Alan's triceps as he slid his bag up and over his shoulder.

"You're looking quite buff, Alan. This gym thing is working, no?"

Alan's face got redder than it already was. As they started walking, Garret stared up at the rectangle of darkening sky.

"I never thought I'd say this, but I like it," Alan said. "Even though the place is brimming with fairy muscle gods—which I never understood. These giant, muscled, hairy men who look like they can lift an eighteen-wheeler and when they open their mouths this squeaky voice comes out of them, saying something like, "Bruce! Cute thumb ring!""

Garret laughed.

"But a couple people recognized me," Alan said, sighing and motioning for Garret to sit next to him on a bus bench. "One even asked me about Mitchell, as if he was around the corner or something."

"Oh my, what did you say?"

"Nothing, I just stared at him."

Garret fiddled with the folder he was carrying.

"That was one of the things I needed to talk to you about."

"Ugh, Garret, what's done is done. I'm not going to be a drama queen about it. I feel like shit, but time will change that. I know that neither of you did it to intentionally hurt me."

"Of course not."

An ambulance went by, disrupting the glow of the afternoon with a pang of reality. Garret pulled out the papers for Alan to sign.

"Well, this brings me to my next issue."

"What? You went to the lawyer?"

"And I will drag you to the hearing if need be. Let's go."

THEY MADE THEIR WAY over to Alan's apartment and Tramp's excitement over Garret seemed to make Alan jealous. They sat in silence with the papers between them.

"What about all the fees?" Alan asked.

"Done."

Garret used the empty folder to fan himself, as Alan's air conditioning was still not working. Alan got them both ice water and put his own glass against his forehead.

"I just want you to get what you deserve. And don't worry about Jane."

"She's a mollusk."

Garret loved the words Alan used to describe people.

"She doesn't have a leg to stand on. You were his partner, Alan. It's all on paper, and he left half to you. As a matter of fact, I'll arrange it so that you barely have to see her."

Alan looked at him with what Garret hoped was a newfound respect.

"Thanks."

Garret walked over to the window and his eyes followed a flock of tiny birds in the distance, flying in formation, seemingly lost without each other. Group or die.

45

LUCY GRABBED her grandmother's hand when she saw her in the lobby and rushed her outside the hotel.

"OK, so I know it's only been my first day, but I heard that Heather mentioned my hats!"

"Oh dear! That's splendid!!"

They couldn't find a cab, so they decided to take the bus downtown. On the way, Lucy showed her designs to Dorothy, who seemed to be concentrating on her breathing to fight off the welling emotion inside her. "These are magnificent!"

"Well, when I have my first runway show, maybe you can model one of them."

Dorothy turned and stared out the window. "Oh, don't be silly. I'm an old lady." She said softly, "I don't even buy green bananas."

"No, you don't be silly. You look tight!"

Dorothy laughed and then stared with a forthrightness that Lucy could feel, as if she was physically shaken.

Lucy took her smooth hand and held on to it as the bus continued downtown.

IN THE FIRST store, Lucy made her try on a low-backed red dress and Dorothy looked like she had seen herself for the first time.

"You are *so* getting that," Lucy said.

In the next store Lucy scored some New Religion jeans and a sleek pair of black Jimmy Choo's.

She explained to Dorothy that in the fashion world, having Jimmy Choo's was like breathing—absolutely necessary.

A few thousand dollars later, they sat down for coffee.

"Shopping is exhausting," Dorothy said.

"Are you kidding? I could've gone on forever. That dress we got you is so . . ."

Dorothy eyes suddenly receded into their sockets and her head dipped.

Lucy ran up to the counter and asked for a cold towel. Her heart pounded as she dabbed at Dorothy's forehead until she came to.

It must be a hot flash, Lucy thought. She put her arm around Dorothy and passed her some water.

"Jeez, what was in that espresso?" Lucy asked.

"Oh dear, I think we've had enough excitement for the day. Why don't we get a cab back to the hotel and I'll squeeze in a bit of a nap before dinner."

"Sounds good. Are you sure you're OK?"

"Oh, I'm fine," Dorothy said, as Lucy led her to the street and into a cab.

On the way back to the hotel, Dorothy said quietly, "Do you really think the red dress suits me?"

Lucy smiled. "It looks super-chic on you."

"What does that mean?" Dorothy asked, confused.

"It's a good thing," Lucy said, and took her hand again. "And I'm thinking you should wear some heels with it. Do you have any?"

"Well, they're only one-inch, I'm afraid."

"Those will do," Lucy said.

"Oh dear, I feel like I've known you all along. . . ."

Lucy noticed Dorothy still had the towel from the coffee shop. She looked out the window as if she was searching for something.

"What are you looking for?"

"What, dear?"

"You look like you are searching for something," Lucy clarified.

Dorothy blinked and raised her shoulders. "Just looking. You know I haven't been to New York since the eighties."

"When it was cool," Lucy said.

"Well, I believe it's still cool—especially now that you've come on the scene."

The cabbie stopped in front of the hotel and Dorothy gave Lucy a twenty-pound note.

"What am I supposed to do with this?"

"Oh, sorry." She switched to an American twenty. "See you tonight?"

"Yes, and thank you thank you thank you!"

Dorothy grabbed the bag with the red dress and held it up, saying, "I'll wear it."

Lucy made sure Dorothy was inside and safe, and then told the cabbie to take her back to Garret's apartment. She was devising what to wear with her new shoes and remembered Garret's text. She replied:

No tampons.
But is she snorting Equal?

46

ALAN SIGNED THE PAPERS because he knew Garret was right—he did deserve what was left him. Mitchell's assets had totaled close to nine million dollars and the checks he was receiving from Jane didn't quantify, not to mention the apartment he was forced to move out of. The truth was, vacating the place had helped. In the days after he died Alan kept finding reminders—a credit card receipt, the almonds he ate, a hidden toothbrush in the shower—and realized there was so much history in those walls that he couldn't live within them anymore. Alan put down the pen and didn't look at Garret. He walked into his room and lay on his bed.

Garret came in and started pacing. "I'm glad Pop came and all. I just don't know what to say to him."

"It's not a casserole," Alan said.

"What?"

"It's not going to happen overnight."

Garret looked like a child when he stood that way, eyes wide and head slightly cocked, his arms dangling free. He popped a mint into his mouth and said, "What am I supposed to say, 'Hi, Pop, how've you been the last twelve years?'"

"How about starting with something like, 'Hi, Pop, did you know I'm wearing a cock ring?'"

"Alan!"

"Sorry. You are though, right?"

Garret waved his hand. It wasn't a yes or a no.

"I'm still so angry at him, but part of me wants to just crawl into his arms. It's odd."

"Sounds familiar," Alan said under his breath.

"And Mum, she seems so peculiar. I can't grasp what is going on."

Alan couldn't bring himself to tell Garret what he overheard Dorothy say. She could have simply meant she was tired. Although there was something in the quick flash of her eyes that screamed with fear. But it wasn't his place to get involved.

"Well, all I know is you're coming," Garret said.

Alan sat up. "To dinner? I wasn't invited!"

"You are now. So get grooming. You can show off that new hot body of yours."

Alan blushed. How could Garret play with his heart like that? He surely knew that Alan had feelings for him. Wasn't it obvious? Or maybe when you are friends with someone for so long you cannot see beyond that. "Be at the hotel at eight," Garret ordered.

"If you insist."

Garret stood up and brought his head inches from Alan, who could smell the mint on his breath.

"I more than insist," he said, and turned around, letting himself out.

Alan lay in the pleasant glow of Garret's aftermath. He thought of Dorothy on the patio of the ballroom, the gray wispy hairs that framed her delicate face. *Dying? She can't be; the woman is so young at heart. What would Mr. Good Heavens do?* He decided to go on as if he'd never heard the words. He had his own dramas to deal with.

He picked up Tramp and went into the bathroom, noticing the picture above the towel rack of Mitchell standing under the marquee for *Jesus Christ Superstar.* He remembered they had eaten two dozen oysters that night, in the restaurant with the floating rose petals. Mitchell was a romantic but wouldn't easily admit it. Alan was a romantic but hid behind sarcasm. When Mitchell first told Alan he loved him, he traced the words onto his back with his finger.

He got under the water in the shower and tried to think of it as washing things away, like what he always told his actors: *Get out of your head.*

He shaved as Tramp watched him with a dull look. Alan resisted the urge to talk to the cat in case Consuela would suddenly appear and chastise him.

After he finished dressing he caught his reflection in the full-length mirror and thought, *I do look different.* He pictured himself on one of those cheesy commercials where they show the before and after.

All I did was snort diet pills and drink Crystal Light!

He walked to the restaurant so he could experience the city. It had cooled a little, and all the patio tables outside were overflowing with open bottles of wine and half-eaten dishes, patrons talking and texting and smiling. Alan couldn't imagine a city with better restaurants. Even the tiny pizza joints were worthy of kings.

When he arrived at the hotel, he took a big breath and straightened his bow tie.

Here I come.

47

THE HOTEL RESTAURANT had deep red walls with black trim and lilacs on the tables that left a pungent sweetness in the air. Lucy deliberately sat next to George. When the rolls came, she noticed he picked off the top and only ate the bottom part.

"I do that too," Lucy said.

He looked at her as if to say, *So?*

She glanced over at Garret and Alan, who looked handsome sitting together in their pressed shirts and blazers, freshly showered and alert.

Dorothy seemed renewed after her nap. Throughout the meal, Lucy noticed her looking around at each face. Midway, she proposed a toast, her head swaying a little as she clinked the glass with her fork.

"We finally are a family," she said. "And even though Alan's not flesh and blood, I know you have been family to Garret, which makes you my family."

She took up her wine glass.

"Mum," Garret said.

"I am so happy just sitting here, I can barely talk. . . ."

She glanced over at George, who was looking at her peculiarly.

"The family of misfit toys!" Lucy said, breaking a somewhat tense moment.

Alan hollered and everyone finally drank. Except George.

The waiter brought them two more bottles of pinot noir. Garret explained to his father about the grapes, how they are thin-skinned due to the geography of the region they are grown in.

"Thin skin, huh?" he grunted.

Alan showed Lucy how to eat a mussel with another empty mussel shell. Lucy thought it was weird, but Alan wasn't exactly Mr. Normal, and that was what she liked about him.

"Lucy, tell everyone the news," Dorothy said, adjusting her new red dress.

"Well," Lucy said, looking mostly at Garret, "I know I've only been there one day, but someone overheard Heather mention my designs."

Garret's smile flooded the room.

George raised his glass, trying desperately to be the patriarch. "Here's to Lucy."

Everyone took another sip from their glass, except Garret.

"I can't remember the last time George made a toast," Dorothy whispered to Lucy.

"A super-original one too," Lucy said and Dorothy lightly slapped her hand.

"Child abuse!"

Dorothy laughed nervously. When Alan had to rush off to a press meeting for the play, he made his way around the table and kissed Dorothy last.

"That dress is stunning," Alan said to her.

"See?" Lucy said.

"Look, dear," Dorothy said, pointing at Garret and his father sharing a cheesecake.

"Be careful sharing that with Garret," Lucy said to him. "You may get cooties."

George scoffed at her and kept eating. Garret looked at his father with barely concealed disdain.

Toward the end of the meal Lucy rested her head on her grandfather's shoulder. He petted her hair tentatively.

After the check was paid and they said their good-byes, Lucy and Garret walked quietly home, sated and calm.

"I don't know, Goose," Garret said. "Maybe he's finally getting over it."

"Maybe he just needed to see you in your element."

"Doubtful."

When they reached the stoop, Lucy pulled out a review of the play and said, "I almost forgot, I saved this for you."

The headline read: *WINSOME DRAMA ENLIGHTENS BROADWAY*.

"I usually don't read them, but thanks."

"It's super-complimentary. It says the show is refreshingly real in the age of the 'Disnification' of Broadway."

"Indeed," Garret said. "I just ran into one of the most remarkable actors that Alan went to Julliard with, and he's playing a fish in *The Little Mermaid*."

"Tragic," Lucy said.

"Beyond," Garret said. "Listen, you go in, I'm just going to walk over and check on Alan real quick."

Lucy smiled and said, "You do that."

Perhaps due to her newfound English heritage, Lucy now had a taste for tea. She picked out some of Garret's special Earl Grey and put the kettle on. She hung up her dress and washed her face with Garret's foaming face cleanser. She fixed her tea and settled in to watch *Project Runway*. She loved how the challenges were so unique. In that episode, they had to design for their mothers. She dozed off on the couch and dreamed she was on the show but had to design something for Dorothy. The cameras were all around her and Garret and Alan cheered from off the set. When Dorothy went down the runway in a beautiful cream-colored hat with lace and a single blue flower, she just kept walking. As if the runway ended in thin air.

She woke at 3 a.m. and walked sleepily toward her room. She peeked into Garret's door on the way and saw that he hadn't returned.

48

HER GRANDPARENTS left the following day, and for the next few weeks Lucy didn't see much of Garret, as they kept different hours. But they kept in contact via text and e-mail, which seemed to be the way everyone did it these days.

The internship was going swimmingly. Gina warmed up to her even more, especially since the word around the office was that Heather liked Lucy's designs. She continued to have trash duty, as the girl who called in bulimic was apparently now anorexic. The trash still contained mysterious items, but nothing concrete aside from a receipt from a plastic surgeon's office. Heather appeared so flawless; what did she have done? The procedure was blacked out with a pen, but the price was twelve grand. Lucy kept it for ammo, maybe because she had watched too many movies.

The New York summer got more suffocating and sticky, but a hint of fall was now in the air—especially at sundown when the wind came in from the Hudson River, carrying with it a promise of dropping temperatures and falling leaves.

In addition to steaming clothes, Lucy had more responsibility now. She handled some of Heather's travel arrangements and appointments and was the only other person besides Gina who had Heather's cell phone number. Apparently the digits were actually worth money. She worked as hard as she could and the staff noticed. Her free time was spent perfecting her designs—three of which she snuck into Heather's box. What did she have to lose?

Since Garret had helped Alan gain possession of Mitchell's East Hampton place, the two of them were spending a lot of time renovating it and reading scripts.

It was a wet Friday when Lucy came home and could sense right away that something was off. The wind had blown papers all over the apartment and she walked over to the wide-open window.

Garret was on the balcony. Even though it had started to mist, she could tell he had been crying.

"What is it?"

Garret looked at her with a seriousness she had never seen before and said, "Mum."

"No." She flashed to Dorothy's face on the bus, drained of color. "Is she . . . ?"

Garret just nodded slowly. He looked so vulnerable, so help-less, that Lucy felt like she was looking at a completely differ-ent person.

"Apparently she's been sick since before the opening. Did you know this?" Garret asked.

"She fainted when we went shopping. I thought it was menopause," Lucy said.

"When I look back on it, it was strange, her behavior. I should have known."

"Yes. Come inside though, will you?" Lucy said.

They sat on the couch for a while in silence and Alan came over. No one said a word. They each just sat still, thinking.

"What will George do?" Lucy finally asked.

"Yes, what will he do," Garret said in a mocking tone.

Shockingly, Alan said nothing, just rested his hand on Gar-ret's forearm.

"He'll need help," Lucy said.

Garret got up and left the room, and Alan quietly poured a

drink. He drank half of it and put it down, then went after Garret.

Lucy finished the drink Alan had started and in her head began devising a plan. It may have been stupid, but something told her it was right.

Before she went to bed she looked in on Alan and Garret.

Garret was curled on the bed in a fetal position, staring at the wall. Alan was sitting next to him, running his hand through his hair. As sad as the day was, Lucy was touched by the scene. No one could comfort you as well as someone you've known forever. Although she was slightly jealous, she let the door silently close and climbed into her own bed.

Could I have done something? Should I have told Garret about her spell in the coffee shop?

She got up and looked out the window. A small yellow leaf fell on the sill, stayed there for a moment, and then slipped away.

THE DAY BEFORE the funeral, Lucy got called into Heather Bridges' office. She was hoping it wasn't to be scolded, as Heather rarely called people in to be praised.

"Have I done something wrong?" she asked right away.

Heather was poised and perfect as usual. Lucy could not tell from her expression whether she was going to chastise or promote.

"You are off to England in a few hours, no?"

"Yes," Lucy said, trying to mask her sadness. "I never even knew she was sick. I mean, a little, but I didn't think . . ."

"How is Garret taking this?"

"Well, he and Alan now have Mitchell's old place in East-hampton and . . ."

"So he's in denial."

Heather was so blunt sometimes, but that's how it was in the ruthless game of corporate fashion. Lucy could play it, but she refused to let it overtake her. A tear tried to push out of her eye.

"We all are, I guess," Lucy said.

Heather checked her teeth in a gold-plated mirror the size of a chocolate bar and smiled. "Well, this isn't necessarily opportune, Lucy, but most great things in life aren't, you'll see. There's never a right time. But . . . "

Is she firing me?

"I have some good news for you. Frances Bean, do you know her?"

"No, sorry."

"Lucy, what have I always told you?"

"Don't apologize; it weakens your edge," Lucy answered.

Actually, you only told me that once.

"Right. Now, Frances is a big figure in Milan and other fashion Meccas. She is on the tip of a lot of people's tongues, mainly because she is filthy rich and likes to throw piles of money at new designers."

Lucy felt her palms gathering moisture, her leg start to shake.

What is she getting at?

"Well, now that you've had quite an effect on our staff here, I have given your hat collection a second look. In fact, I received a personal call from Miss Bean after sending digital renderings to her. She actually dialed my number herself—unheard of. She wants to fund your line, under my umbrella of course . . . which means you will have to hire staff and oversee design, manufacturing, and marketing. She loved your catch-phrase, by the way, what was it?"

"Glorified Housewives."

"Whatever. The point is, you need a lawyer. I will take twenty percent across the board, and you will need my facility, name, and contacts to launch the line. Here are all the documents; you have five days to accept or decline. I suggest you have someone look at these ASAP."

Lucy couldn't believe what she was hearing. Her own line?

She wanted to call Garret, but weren't he and Alan already on the plane? And she only had two hours to get to Newark for her own flight.

"What is wrong, dear? You're barely eighteen years old and just got offered your own line," Heather said.

Lucy searched her brain for a catch. There had to be one.

"Whose name will be on the label?" Lucy asked.

"Mine, naturally, but you will be the chief designer, and you will move from unpaid intern to making six figures. Math problem?"

"No, Heather, this, this is incredible. It's just, I have to go—"

"I know, the funeral. Listen, just take your weekend and call me on Monday. Find a lawyer in England or somewhere fast. Miss Bean cannot be delayed; she drops deals as fast as her Hermès bags."

Lucy briefly wondered if it wasn't Heather Bridges who was really making the deal here. She smiled politely and took the documents.

"I don't know what to say."

"Let's start with 'Thank you.'"

"Thank you," Lucy said, more as a question than a statement.

On her way out, everyone in the office looked at her expectantly, asking with their eyes, *What went down in there?* They sensed Lucy was bound for something greater, and they wanted to get close enough that it would rub off.

She couldn't talk to anyone. Not now. She grabbed her packed suitcase from the coat check and ran down the steps and out the door, got in a cab. She was comatose, holding the documents in her hand as if they were some hidden treasure, some key that would unlock the rest of her life. She stared at the pages but couldn't read the words.

Dreams happen?

49

GARRET SAT SMOKING on the airport curb next to Alan, their packed bags beside them. He felt angry and tired. "She didn't tell me," he said. "I get a message from my father with the funeral location . . . for fuck's sake!"

"You wouldn't have wanted to see her, that's what he told me," Alan said.

"What? You talked to him? When?" Garret stood up fast as his phone rang. It was Lucy. He flicked out his cigarette and answered it.

"Dad, you are not going to believe . . ."

"Listen, Goose, I can't talk. I'll see you in England, OK?"

"No, no, wait!"

Garret hung up as Alan answered the question.

"Yesterday," he said.

"Since when do you have private conversations with my father?"

"Garret, please calm down. He called asking about the flight info. They didn't tell you because they probably wanted you to have a last memory of her looking well. It was her choice, not his. Breathe."

Garret closed his eyes and searched his mind for pictures. There she was, giggling with Lucy at the theater, clumsily dancing with Alan. Sitting proudly and talking loudly at the restaurant in the red dress. That was how he'd remember her. But fury still boiled in the bottom of his belly. "I still feel cheated, and I'm sure Lucy does too. How am I going to do this? I haven't even really cried yet."

"Don't worry," Alan said. "I'll be there."

Garret looked at Alan, who was wearing his sympathy face. It was sweet, but he didn't want sympathy. He wanted to have tea with his mother.

Alan straightened Garret's tie and said, "Just don't die on me at the gate."

Although overwhelmed, Garret was grateful Alan was coming with him, that he didn't have to face all of it alone.

When Alan had gotten on the stand to fight for what was rightfully his—what Mitchell had left him—he simply said, "He liked me better." The judge had smiled. Since she had already taken the apartment in New York, Alan was made sole proprietor of the Easthampton house. When they first went out there, Alan cried a little, and as they walked along the beach at twilight, a band of seagulls seemed to follow them. The clouds that hugged the horizon were fiery red.

"When we were in the theater that night, were you going to kiss me?" Alan had asked, dodging a wave to avoid getting his feet wet.

Garret didn't answer but put his arm around him, and they walked in silence, both of them knowing that something was happening but afraid to actually say the words.

That night they watched movies and ate pizza. Then they got into bed and slept in each other's arms, holding tight, grasping for the power of something beyond themselves.

In the last few weeks, Garret had felt as if his heart was opening, getting wider and stronger, but now he felt so small and alone, even with Alan next to him. It was as if someone had cut the string of a kite and he was floating away. The woman who had grounded him to the earth was gone.

———

WHILE WAITING to board, Alan tried to distract Garret by reading him snippets from *US Weekly*. He was barely listening, still cut off and suspended.

"Soldiers dying in Iraq and the whole world's worried about Paris Hilton in jail," Alan said. "Did you know it was a leading story on CNN? The scary thing is, I actually *care*. The media is so manipulative."

When their row numbers were called, Alan had to practically pull the dazed Garret out of his seat.

After the plane took off, Garret put on his iPod that Lucy had loaded up for him. A remake of a Joni Mitchell song came on that seemed especially fitting. *You don't know what you got till it's gone.*

Alan was eating grapes and staring out at the clouds. Every once in a while, he would put his hand on Garret's thigh or brush his shoulder with his own. Garret stayed lost in the music: Starsailor, Beck, Cat Power. He loved Lucy's taste— each song seemed to hold him captive and tell a story, and he was grateful for the escape.

After landing, they went directly from the airport to the train station and up north. When they arrived at the house it looked as if no one was there. It was already chilly for August, and the birds were screaming.

They entered cautiously and put down their bags. "I'm famished," Alan announced, starting toward the kitchen. Garret slowly went upstairs. His parents' bedroom door was shut, and he just stood there. How many times had he stood outside that door as a boy? He put his ear up to it. He couldn't hear anything.

He came downstairs and Alan brought out some slices of ham and a block of cheese. They ate in silence, until Garret motioned around the room and said, "All her things. What do people's things become? I mean, they become other people's things, but at what point do they just fizzle out, with no trace that the person existed?"

Alan stopped eating but didn't say anything.

"I want to keep her things, Alan."

50

LUCY'S FLIGHT was chaotic—in addition to the usual summer-travel madness, a million thoughts swirled around her head in a delirious dance. Thankfully, Gina had slipped her a Xanax and she was out for the second half. Even though she was quite groggy when she arrived, she managed to find the Gatwick express and then transferred trains in central London. When she arrived up north, Alan was the one who picked her up and they almost got into an accident driving to the house.

"I can never adjust to the driving-on-the-left thing," Alan said. "It's such a nightmare. How was your flight?"

"Fine. How is Garret doing?"

"He's in avoidance mode. He spent all morning toasting bread to make sure it was browned just right. Wasted about a loaf."

Lucy stared at the hedges out the window and realized she was about to attend her first funeral ever. She told Alan and he said, "In my experience, people tend to get drunk."

Before she could confide her news, the car was already pulling into the pebbled driveway.

"I'm afraid you'll have to drop your stuff off and we'll go right to the church—they're all already there."

"OK," Lucy said.

LUCY STOOD OUTSIDE the church and told Alan she'd be right in. The day was gray and bleak, but a few thin rays of light streamed through the thick layers of clouds.

Maybe that's her, Lucy thought.

It was quiet, save for the sound of a stout woman in what looked like a bonnet, sucking on a cigarette and blowing it out in quick bursts.

"You're gonna miss it, love."

"Can I have one?" Lucy asked.

"You smoke?"

"In dire circumstances."

"Buggers'll kill ya," the woman said.

"Who are you?"

"Bette. I was her nurse. Known George and Dorothy for quite some time."

Bette lit Lucy's cigarette, and they stood apart, looking at the ground.

"Was she in pain?" Lucy asked.

"Not too bad. George was there every step of the way. For the last week he slept in the chair by her bed."

The thought of this usually insensitive man waiting by her grandmother through the night, coupled with a brisk wind, made the hairs on Lucy's arm stand at attention.

Bette and Lucy smoked in silence until she grabbed Lucy's arm and said, "Come, love," and led her in to the last pew to the left. She could see her father stepping up to the podium. He wiped his mouth and stood up straight.

"I'd be lying if I said this wasn't a shock for me, or if I said I'm not angry. I'm very angry, for a lot of reasons. I don't know why the world takes people away, but I do know this: I wouldn't be here today, proud of who I am, had I not been brought into this world by my mother, my friend, and the grandmother of my beautiful . . ." The words were unintelligible. Someone handed him a tissue, and he dabbed at his eyes. Lucy was next. She whispered, "Wish me luck" to Bette as she got up and approached the podium. The aisle went on and on.

Like a runway, she thought. *Will my hats be on a runway?*

She took a sip of the water on the podium and started talking.

"I was just walking up here, and I was thinking about, well, about, myself . . ."

A few people chuckled.

". . . about my own human drama . . . the drama of the living . . ."

She hadn't planned what she was going to say.

"I spent a wonderful afternoon with my grandmother in New York, and I foolishly thought there would be more of those to come. I am just happy to have had the chance to meet her because I didn't even know I had a father until I met this fabulous gay guy on a plane."

A few of the gray hairs started to mumble and the younger people laughed, including Garret himself. Alan gave her the neck slice.

"Anyway, this is not my story. This is a story of a courageous woman who nurtured a son who didn't always fit into the boxes drawn for us by society. This was a woman who was at times alone in the world, alone in her battle, like we all are . . ." Lucy stopped all of a sudden, grabbed her bracelets and went on. "There was one thing that she said to me, when we were in a slightly . . . drunken embrace. The words got lost in my hair, but I still heard them. She said, 'I can die now.'"

Lucy walked down from the pulpit.

A few other people, including Bette and the pastor, read passages and spoke. George didn't say anything, but he greeted everyone cordially as they left the church.

On the way out, Alan whispered to Lucy, "Nice speech."

They hugged. She loved hugging Alan because aside from always having a soft fabric on, he smelled nice. A simple, manly smell that she had always missed growing up. Garret always smelled of fancy cologne, but Alan had a scent that reminded her of home—what she knew of it, anyway.

51

GARRET WALKED with Alan along the stone path to the reception hall. Some small children screeched and ran after each other as if it were just another day, except they had to dress up. From the look on his face, Garret knew what Alan was thinking: *Mitchell.*

In the last few weeks, the Mitchell topic had disappeared, but Garret could sense that it had returned, and he was not surprised, being that death was in the air.

"Today was the day I met Mitchell, you know," Alan said.

Garret fought back a wave of contempt. *Did this day have to be about Mitchell?*

"Alan, this is my mother, for fuck's sake."

"You're right. I'm sorry."

One of the kids splashed mud on Garret's cashmere pants.

"Fucking hell!" Garret yelled.

The kid started to cry. Alan grabbed Garret by the arm and whisked him along faster. "This better be open bar," he said.

———

GARRET SMOKED next to Lucy outside the reception hall. Now that she was his daughter, he felt more protective.

"I don't want you to start smoking all the time," Garret said.

"I won't, don't worry . . . it's just, listen. Do you know a lawyer here? I need one ASAP," she said, mimicking Heather Bridges.

Garret's face twisted up. "Are you mad?"

"Look, I know this is inopportune, and I shouldn't even be thinking about myself, but Heather Bridges got funding for my collection. She offered me a six-figure salary."

What?

"Goose, that's all splendid, but it is the day of your grandmother's—"

"A grandmother I was cheated away from!"

"Look—"

"No, you look, Dad. Look around you. This isn't exactly functional, is it? Look, I'm sad all right? Mainly for you, I'm sad. It's just, I only have one week and need to—"

"Just stop. I'll give you the info tomorrow. And put out that cigarette. Can we just wait until tomorrow?" Garret looked at her expectantly.

"OK, OK, sorry," she said.

They hugged and Garret asked quietly, "Did Mum really say that? 'I can die now'?"

"Yes."

Garret sighed and put out his own cigarette. "She always wanted me to have children. So did Pop, though he'd never admit it. It's weird to call him that again, Pop, but I suppose I had better get used to it. He's all I have."

"Um, hello? You have a daughter?"

Lucy looked hurt but beautiful in the fading light, the fields stretching behind her in brilliant green.

"These hills, this weather, this country . . . she belonged here. She used to take me for long walks to the village, and on the way we'd stop and feed the ducks day-old biscuits and leave pence on the train tracks. She made you feel like she was discovering everything with you, and that the world was filled with unimaginable things."

Lucy sat down and looked out at the landscape, resting her chin in her hands. Garret sat next to her and poked at her bracelets. He had never gotten the chance to hold Lucy's hand and walk her through the forest, feed the animals. But a thought came into his head and seemed to carry with it a quick flash of warmth: someday maybe he could do that with a granddaughter. He looked at Lucy, who seemed to be producing tears, although it could have been the moisture in the air.

"I'm proud of you. I am."

"You sure have a strange way of showing it," Lucy said.

"Cut me some slack, as you say."

"Right, as *you* say."

He could hear people laughing behind the reception hall doors. "Alan's probably doing some shtick," Garret said.

"Scaring the villagers," Lucy added.

Some people hugged Garret as they left. They smiled at Lucy, and one of them said she looked like Dorothy. Garret realized she really did. The pert nose and the small ears, the long delicate neck.

He took her hand and then turned to go inside.

"Six figures?" Garret asked as they walked up to the bar.

"Yeah, can you even deal?"

"Unbelievable."

Sure enough, Alan was holding court with some of Dorothy's friends. He was imitating his own mother. Garret was glad that people were having fun, as his mum would have wanted it that way. His eyes searched the room for his father and finally saw him sitting alone by the window, an uneaten plate of food next to him.

52

THE OLD DRAFTY reception hall looked more like a barn. There were cucumber sandwiches and lots of beer and champagne. Lucy understood why people got drunk at funerals. Forget about the loss and celebrate the future. Still, it looked wrong—all these ladies laughing and tipping glasses up to their little lips. Lucy kept telling herself to relax, but it was hard to stop thinking about Heather's proposition.

After the reception, they made their way back to the house and George seemed to hit a brick wall. He went upstairs and fell asleep on top of the covers with all his clothes on and didn't wake up until the following evening. Lucy went in a few times to make sure he was breathing. His face was so soft as he slept, such an extreme juxtaposition from his tight, stern expression during waking hours.

In the roomy kitchen Lucy thought of Dorothy cutting toast points in the shapes that Garret made. She could feel her presence, and it was at once soothing and eerie.

There was food everywhere, brought by all the people in town. Lucy stared out the window and tried to calm her restless mind. George eventually came in and piled up a large plate, starting to eat ravenously as she watched him. After Lucy laughed a little, he said, "What?"

"Shouldn't talk with your mouth full," Lucy said.

He smirked, put the plate down, and started a fire. It was strange to build a fire in the summer, but it was northern England. She also assumed it was more out of ritual and comfort than necessity. Lucy watched his weathered hands crumpling the crosswords he had already finished. The words burned with barely a sound.

George stood up to admire his work, then filled his pipe and sat down. He stared at the flames, seemingly in concentrated thought.

Alan and Garret came in from their walk. They said hello, but George didn't respond. After Garret asked if he'd eaten anything, he slowly nodded his head.

The four of them drank tea in a silence that was eventually broken by the sound of Lucy's cell phone. She looked at the caller. *Heather's private line.* She excused herself as Garret rolled his eyes.

She heard Alan say, "We're supposed to be grieving and your daughter is taking calls from fashion icons."

She figured Garret must have filled Alan in. She made her way outside and answered on the last possible ring. "Hello?"

"Lucy, I'm so sorry to bother you at this time, but Frances wants you to meet her in Milan on Wednesday. I need your address because I'm sending you the ticket."

"Milan."

"Yes, in Italy. Her villa," Heather said.

"My god."

"Do you know the address where you are now?" Heather asked.

"Yes."

"Fine, text it to me within the hour."

"Fine," Lucy said automatically.

"And please give Garret my regards."

Regards, Lucy thought, *how informal.* She'd heard from one of the PR people that Heather had made out with Garret on a dare at some after-hours club.

She stared at the deserted road that led away from the house, perfectly trimmed hedges on each side and a lonely bird circling. She fantasized about her hats going down a runway, worn by tall, glamorous models. She put the phone in her pocket and turned back toward the house.

When she got inside, George spoke his first full sentence since the funeral. "Wear a jumper when you go out there."

Lucy stood there, stunned by the presence of him, his eyes resting softly on her, and she felt a sinking, hollow emptiness that went further than sadness. She wanted to touch him, but she didn't, she just nodded and gently sat down.

For most of the evening, George didn't speak again, until Lucy, the last one to head upstairs, folded the blanket she was using, and George's voice jolted her.

"Do that again," he said.

Lucy unfolded and refolded the blanket, patted it with her left hand as if giving it a peck of affection.

"The triangular shape," he said, "and the way you tap it. Dorothy does that . . ." then, with a sharp humility, "did that, rather."

She looked at him and for a moment his face started to give way to the beginnings of a smile. She went to the kitchen and got a brownie, placed it as a diamond in the middle of a green napkin. She put it in front of him and straightened the edges of the napkin. Without speaking, George started to eat it. Halfway up the stairs she heard that voice again, simple but somehow haunting.

"Good night."

She turned around and nodded, headed up to the attic room.

She stood outside of Garret and Alan's door and debated disturbing them. She knew this was not a time to be thinking about herself, but Milan now? The whole thing was snowballing and she needed a sounding board.

She sat outside the doorway and thought about Italy, what she was going to wear, and how in the world she was going to pull all this off.

53

GARRET AND ALAN lay still in what used to be Garret's bedroom, a crack between them from the two single beds pushed together.

He heard someone in the hallway and whispered, "I cannot believe I'm sleeping in my childhood home with a man."

"Oh, live a little, call me a boy, look!" Alan showed Garret his hard-on.

"Jesus! Put that away!"

"Yeah, that's what he said."

"Who?" Garret was confused.

"Never mind. Would you rather I just masturbated in the bathroom?"

"What? Heavens no."

"Garret, your father's gotta get over it. You're all he has."

Lucy knocked lightly and peeked her head through the door to say goodnight.

Garret tilted his head at her and said to Alan, "Not all he has."

"Well, thank the lord she's not a dyke," Alan said, rearranging his pillow. "Lucy, promise me now that you won't gain twenty pounds, adopt a cat, and grow a mullet. OK? Thanks, honey."

"Goose," Garret interjected, clearly used to Alan's antics, "who is this person that's backing your line?"

"Someone named Bean," Lucy answered.

"Frances Bean?"

"Yes."

Garret and Alan turned to each other, smiled, and said simultaneously, "Lesbian."

"I'm not going to Milan to have sex with her!"

"What? You're going to Milan?" Alan was now out of the bed with the sheet wrapped around him like a toga. "This is incredible!" He looked at Garret. "This girl . . . and you are still a girl in our eyes, honey, is going to Milan to have tea with Frances fucking Bean? Not to—"

Garret cut Alan off.

"Listen Goose, you're not going anywhere until we talk about this. Alan and I have a meeting tomorrow night in London. I suggest you come down with us so I can introduce you to Oliver."

Alan rolled his eyes. "Oliver now?"

"She needs a lawyer, Alan, this is big stuff."

Lucy ran up and kissed Garret on the cheek. "Thanks, Dad."

Alan put out his cheek dramatically for his own kiss and she blew it into her hand and touched his cheek.

"Jesus, I don't have scabies," Alan said.

"'Night!"

"Why Oliver?" Alan asked Garret after Lucy left the room.

"Alan, I slept with him once years ago, and jealousy is so not sexy."

"I'm not jealous, just concerned. He's sketchy."

"What lawyer isn't?" Garret asked.

"Good point."

They settled in to the bed and lay in silence. Garret liked to listen to Alan's breathing; it comforted him more than he cared to admit. What was happening to Lucy? It had been so disorienting to find out that he had a daughter and then immediately turn her loose. He loved having her at the house and was glad she had the internship, but things were moving so fast.

Alan made his little puffing sound and Garret smiled. He got up and went to the little bathroom in the hallway to get a pill. He lingered outside the closed door of his parents' bedroom again. Even though he still had pent-up anger toward his father, he secretly hoped he was OK—the man had just lost his wife of over forty years.

He got back into bed and sighed. Alan mumbled and ruffled his sheet and promptly continued to softly snore. Garret thought of the time his mother took him for a ride on those bikes, the joy in her voice and the unexpected tears. That was his last strong memory of her, and he realized she must have known then. She was just trying to live.

He didn't want to ever know that feeling. Like most everyone, he simply wanted to get old and die in his sleep. It must have taken courage for Dorothy to keep it all inside, and not crumble or crave sympathy. She was *dying*.

Garret felt alive, but scared. Life seemed delicate.

He curled up against Alan and felt his warmth, like he was nine years old again, running into his parents' bed during a violent thunderstorm. That room, that bed, was always a haven where everything would be all right. Now, he barely knew the man who was sleeping in there.

He held on to Alan, a buoy in a vast rough sea.

54

FROM THE MAKESHIFT attic room, Lucy could hear Alan and Garret talking softly, and she found herself smiling. She had known it was meant to be from the night she made them dinner. Then a couple of weeks afterward she had come home and seen Alan's clothes on the floor through Garret's slightly open door.

The next day, she had asked Garret how it finally happened.

"Something clicked, Goose."

He was smiling easily, his eyes glossy with warmth and a touch of mischief.

"We slept together but didn't do anything sexual, for a while. Last night he took me to our old favorite restaurant, which isn't even around anymore. He made them open it for one night, and tracked down the old chef, flew him in from San Francisco. The place was filled with candles and flowers *everywhere*. They made us a special meal and . . . at one point I looked over at him and thought, *This is it*. Not cute boys in dark alleys and meaningless sex; this is real love."

"That's it?"

"Well, I can't tell you about the sex part now that I know you're my daughter."

"True, but you can tell me this. Who made the first move?" Lucy asked.

"It was mutual, really. We were looking at each other in the cab and our faces got closer and closer, and then we were kissing."

"And?"

"The rest is history."

Lucy smiled at the memory as she pulled the covers up to her neck.

———

THE NEXT MORNING Bette came by to look after George while Lucy and her "two dads" embarked on their jaunt to London.

On the train, Lucy stared out at the window and was momentarily calmed. The hills looked like the backsides of sleeping giants. She thought about George and how he asked her to fold the blanket again. His raw vulnerability, the childlike sorrow in his eyes.

Alan was twirling the train schedule pamphlet into a tight cone. "I thought Oliver was a legal aide," he said.

Garret answered without looking at him. "He was, but now he has his own practice."

Alan rolled his eyes. "The only thing I remember Oliver practicing was being on his knees."

"Please," Garret interjected, "my daughter's in our presence."

"I'm almost eighteen," Lucy said, "and—newsflash—I know what a blow job is."

"Well," Alan added, "just be careful of him—he certainly had his little claws around Garret."

"Alan, must we always dwell in the past? This is now. I'm rebirthed or however you said it, remember? I'm with you."

Lucy smiled out the window. Out of all the things she had imagined for her life, sitting on a train with her gay dad and his bitchy boyfriend, about to fly to Milan to discuss her own hat line with an eccentric billionaire, was probably the furthest possibility.

OLIVER WASN'T THERE, but his assistant said he had been expecting the documents and would look them over first thing in the morning.

Alan told them he would take the meeting alone, leaving Lucy and Garret to themselves. They walked around Regent Park among various dogs and their owners, nannies with small children, and kids in school uniforms. It was a beautiful, crisp day and the trees always looked better in England. In spite of the peaceful park, Lucy felt conflicted, a battle being fought inside her. She kept fumbling with her bracelets.

"What is it, Goose?" Garret asked her.

"I'm scared shitless. Maybe this is too early . . . what do you really know about Heather Bridges?"

"You know more than I, sweetheart. We share the same hairstylist is all."

"Didn't you kiss her?" Lucy asked.

"Well, yes. Briefly."

"So it is true. Anyway, the girls chat around the office, saying she is *oily*, that she's screwed people over in the past. And one time, I caught her crying in the bathroom in this strange, whimpering way. Not to mention the whole trash thing. I don't really trust her, like I do you or Alan. And it's her name, on the product, it's—"

"It's six figures, Lucy. Don't suppose there are a lot of eigh-teen-year-olds making that, do you?"

"The models do."

"Yeah, and they spend it all on coke," Garret said.

"And diet pills," Lucy added.

He was right, but for some reason she kept seeing the look on George's face, one of deep love tainted by desperation.

"There's one thing," Lucy said.

"What?"

"Who's going to be there for George?"

Garret stopped her on the pathway and faced her. A few jog-gers circumvented them. Two dogs had a brief spat in the dis-tance.

"He'll be fine. He'll grieve, and he'll move on."

"What about you?" Lucy asked.

"I'll do the same," Garret said flatly.

"Look, I know you have a lot of resentment for him and that it's rightful, but I don't have that with him. He's been nothing but nice to me, and he's my grandfather. Someone's going to have to be there with him, even if it's for just a while."

"There's Bette and—"

"You told me he hates Bette!"

"No one is going to be my mother," Garret said.

They started walking again, and Lucy felt like she was form-ing her ideas as she spoke them.

"I'm not saying someone has to replace her. I'm saying that someone should be with him, and maybe that someone should be me."

Garret threw up his arms. "Lucy, you are on the verge of a career . . . and now your debating to give it all up for a bloke who abandoned his own son for ten-plus years?"

He started walking faster and she caught up to him. She had to make two strides for every one of his. A few passersby looked at them oddly.

"Yes, I have a great opportunity," Lucy said. "But I'm young, Dad, and my talent is not going anywhere. Maybe I could have my own line without Heather's name on it. I just don't want to jump right into the first thing—"

"Lucy, you're acting mad."

"Well, all I'm saying is, your pop, as you call him, he looked at me with such desperate eyes . . . like I was someone that could really understand him."

"Do you?"

Lucy sat down on a wooden bench next to a giant tree and Garret followed suit.

"I don't know."

A group of girls passed them, smoking and laughing. As the sun dipped behind a cloud, Lucy said, "I wanted to know her more, Dad, I really did."

"Well, there are pieces of her still living in you." Garret looked up as if humbled by the towering tree, the expansive sky, all the beauty around him. "If you hadn't come into my life, I don't know what I would've done."

They embraced, the way they had on the Tube when they first met, except this time it was Garret who was in tears.

55

ALAN KNEW THAT something heavy was going on with Garret and Lucy, so he didn't say much on the train back up north. Bette was still at the house at midnight when they returned. She informed them, out on the porch, that George had not eaten much and was unresponsive.

"Well, thanks for your help. Cheers," Garret said and headed in with Lucy, leaving Alan alone with Bette, who lit a cigarette.

"He never really liked me," she said.

"Yeah, his own son either. Go figure."

Bette said her next words casually, as if commenting on the weather. "I kissed her once, you know. Dorothy."

Alan had to rattle his ear with his finger. Just when he thought things couldn't get more dysfunctional . . .

"It was only once, ages ago when we first moved here, but George caught us, and hasn't much cared for me since. It wasn't like I was a lesbian," she laughed when she said it, as if being a lesbian were a silly thing. "But you know, we got into the sherry and we were just kids really—"

"Listen, this has been real and thanks for sharing, but I have a boyfriend I have to go sleep with."

"A good-looking one at that," Bette offered.

"Keep your lips away from him," Alan said.

He went inside to find Garret and his father not talking to each other—shocker. They had hugged at the premiere, and apparently George had said he was sorry, but that was it. *Yeah, sorry for completely abandoning you, my only son.*

Alan noticed George stealing looks at Lucy from behind his crossword. All of a sudden, he just wanted to go home. He was glad to be there for Garret, but he missed his cat, the gym, and their steady lives. It had been so easy, pairing up with Garret— logical yet still, for Alan, unexpected. Recently they had gone to a party and Alan had watched Garret, completely uninterested in all the guys hitting on him. He was amazed. And since he'd gotten thinner, his own jealousy had been ameliorated, and he remembered someone telling him, "You guys seem so happy." He wanted that feeling back.

At the trial, when Alan had come out of the courtroom, Garret was standing there with three dozen roses. He could barely see Garret's face. When they got to the beach house they put the roses in every room and opened all the windows. As they made love to the sound of the rushing ocean, Alan kept waiting for someone to wake him up. Tramp was so jealous he barely stepped off his little cushion.

"The cat's going to die of heartache," Garret had said.

They didn't leave the house for days, having scripts delivered and holding conference calls from the landline. Alan had wanted that week to last forever. Unfortunately, life happened outside those saltwater-stained walls and now they were dealing with the real, hard edges of reality. Alan put his hand on Garret's shoulder and he gently pushed it away. He clearly was distracted by something and Alan was too tired to care. Covering the pitch meeting alone turned out to be exhausting, but he felt noble in his efforts. He knew whatever brooding was going on in Garret's head had to run its course.

He went upstairs and got into the bed with the crack down the middle. He thought of that scary woman kissing Dorothy.

Eew. He secretly hoped that Garret's mood had nothing to do with him. He had done all he could. He pulled the pillow up to his chest. No Garret, no Tramp, no ocean, just a pillow.

Later, when Garret crawled into bed, Alan stirred.

"You OK?" Garret asked.

"Fine, you?"

"Fine. But take your underwear off. I want to do it just to spite him."

I'll take it when I can get it, Alan thought.

Garret slowly kissed Alan's collarbone and shoulders. Alan started to make noise, but Garret put his hand on Alan's mouth and pressed lightly. He lost track of time, could only concentrate on Garret's fingers, and the way his lips skimmed the surface of his skin. Even when he was ripped, Alan never thought of himself as sexy, but somehow Garret allowed him to own his body, to unfold his coil of self-consciousness so all that was left was bareness. He arched his back and turned his head into the pillow, his voice still muffled by Garret's palm.

He said *Stop* but what he meant was *Don't stop, ever.*

Garret entered him slowly and carefully, never letting his lips leave Alan's skin. This was not an escapade. This was love, and Alan kept the knowledge like a secret in his own clipped breath, still underneath the gentle weight of Garret's hand. A passing car's headlights briefly illuminated them through the window, and then fell away.

56

IN THE MORNING when Lucy grabbed George to lead him outside for a walk, he didn't say yes or no, just put on his cap and followed her.

As they walked down the road in the fresh country air, Lucy took his hand. He seemed content, as if he had finally gotten out of his head for a moment.

"I wish I could have spent more time with her," Lucy said.

"Well, she couldn't stop talking about you when we returned from New York. Her last months were filled with Lucy, Lucy, Lucy."

She wondered if he was just saying that to be nice. "Can I ask you something?"

"Why not," George said, the slight wind ruffling his white hair.

"Do you really think being gay is wrong?"

He didn't answer, and Lucy didn't push it.

They went by the little market, and George stayed outside while Lucy went in and got them coffee.

"So, I overheard you're off to Italy," he said when she returned.

"Yes. Later today. I'm not quite sure I want to go through with it, though. It seems rushed, and at the wrong time." She blew on her coffee and took a small sip. "I know this might sound strange, but I thought about staying here with you for a while."

For the first time since the funeral, George's face seemed to come alive. Then his eyes went cold again. "Don't be silly."

"Well, what will you do with none of us here?"

"Get on, I suppose," he said, sipping from his own cup.

"Well, we know that Dorothy did—"

"Everything?"

For a second, Lucy saw Garret in his face. He started to walk a little slower, as if he might be losing his balance.

"What's wrong?" Lucy asked.

"Would you mind if we sat down a minute?"

They found a bench by a bus stop, carved with names and hearts and promises of other people's lives.

"The bus hasn't stopped here in years," George said. "But they never took the bench away."

They watched a tiny red car buzz by.

"I suppose that's what it will be like for me," George said through a sigh. "Dorothy has passed by, and I'll just be waiting here on this bench. But she'll never come."

———

WHEN THEY GOT BACK home, they stopped on the porch and looked at each other with clear, searching eyes. During the next hour George did his crosswords and Lucy perfected her designs. She wondered where Garret and Alan had gone for so long.

"You know, George, you have to be nicer to him."

"What do you want me to do?"

"I don't know, engage him in something," Lucy said.

"Actually, I was going to order some wine and he knows so much—"

"There you go! Perfect."

George gave her a quick smile and they went back to their work.

———

LATER THAT AFTERNOON, as Lucy was about to take off for Heathrow Airport, Alan and Garret were still not back, but she found a note Garret had written.

> Goose—
> Be careful and don't sign anything until you talk to Oliver.
> And please don't throw this away,
> Dad

As her car pulled away, she saw her grandfather watching from his bedroom window. She blew him a kiss.

On the trip down south she wondered what the hell she was doing but forced herself to think rationally. Garret was right; she wouldn't sign anything yet—she was simply going to meet the woman. No harm in that.

During the flight she was distracted by images of George. Staring at the fire, writing in the words, looking at her with that unanswered question in his eyes.

When she arrived in Milan, it looked like a city dipped in dirty water, but she immediately noticed the heightened sense of fashion. Ladies sporting Gucci sunglasses and cropped skirts, the men looking classy in cufflinks and freshly polished shoes. She loved hearing the Italian language out loud—it was rhythmic and melodic, and spoken with such unbridled passion sometimes it jolted her when she passed people's conversations.

In the square, the teenagers had strong Roman noses and exaggerated features like some of the models she had worked with back in New York. *Maybe this is where they find them*, she thought. The taxi driver hummed along to the radio, and Lucy couldn't understand the words but knew it was a song about longing, a melody of love.

When she arrived at the towering gates of Frances Bean's estate outside the city, she felt like a real adult. A lithe man with an angular face and a white uniform gathered her things and walked her down the long stone drive. Every rock in the drive-way seemed placed by hand, and she could hear the sound of fountains and violins.

She sensed that the man's body was lean and smooth under-neath his pressed uniform and crisp shirt. Before he led her into Frances Bean's boudoir, he brushed his face close enough so that she could smell him: soap, fresh lemon, and smoke.

Screw the hat line, she thought. *I need Mr. Butler's clothes off.*

He introduced her hostess.

Frances Bean was nothing like Lucy expected. She was huge, in fact, large enough that the chair she sat in was most likely designed for her. Her voice was surprisingly high and her accented words—a strange, European hybrid—seemed to chortle out of her mouth. She was draped in opulent, colorful fabrics, but the elegance was lost somehow—the outfit seemed over-planned.

"You've got on well with Adolpho, I see."

Lucy hadn't gotten his name. "Yes. Frances, it's such an honor to meet you!"

"Well, since I'm going to be at the helm of this fashion ship that Heather plans to feature in her shipyard, I wanted to meet you in person. Dinner will be served in the east wing; Adolpho will show you. Here, this rings him." She handed her a small beeper device that said "A" on it.

"Wow," Lucy said, "hottie-on-demand."

"What?"

Lucy just smiled. Thankfully, one of the staff handed Frances a phone, and she softly said, "Excuse me."

After being shown to her room, Lucy took a bath in the massive tub and got into a large white robe that had been laid on her bed by one of Frances's female staff. The room emanated a sense of gluttony—rich reds and gold and crushed velvet, vases sprouting with fresh-cut tulips. The old portraits were beautiful, but if you looked closely, the faces were sad. Most likely painted during wartime.

Lucy ran her finger over the button on the beeper, not quite pushing it. *Fuck it*, she thought, *I'll make up a reason.*

She started pacing and looked into the gilded mirror. She ran her hand through her hair, which was a little longer now and shaped by Garret's stylist. She had long since taken out the nose ring, and the tiny hole looked like a period to a forgotten sentence.

Sure enough, three minutes later, he was there, white gloves and all. He came over and walked toward the bed. From where she was lying, she could see where his pants protruded at the crotch. *Oh my god*, she thought, *this is like a fucking porn movie.*

"Miss Walker, what can I do?"

Maybe it was the bath, or the hat line, or being on her own in Italy, but Lucy couldn't fathom ever feeling this uninhibited.

"Give me your gloves," she said, her tone not unlike Heather's.

He smiled as if it was a pleasant joke, but Lucy didn't laugh, so after a minute he took off the gloves finger by finger, keeping serious eyes. His hands were slender and clean, almost hairless. He placed the gloves neatly on the chair by the bed and said, "You are very pretty."

"Thank you. Now, show me your hands."

He smiled again. Perhaps he had been through this before.

Lucy remembered she still had a condom that Alan had given her in New York.

He held them out, and she kissed the left one. His buzzer went off, and Lucy yelped as he pulled his hand back.

"Excuse me," she said, laughing a little.

"No, excuse me. I will go to Miss Bean. Be back?"

"Hope so."

57

THOUGH THE DINNER was elaborate and scrump-
tious, Lucy had no idea what she was eating half the time. Even
Garret would have been impressed. Lucy found the other
guests to be slightly neurotic, though very fashionable and
amusing. Luckily, almost everyone spoke English. She felt
swooped into such a different, complex world, though it became clear there was really no reason for her to be there.
Frances wouldn't ask her about her designs; she would simply
fund them. And to do that she needed to get a "vibe." Even
though Lucy was half everyone's age, her youth was on her
side—she had heard Heather mention it would get the line lots
of "ink."

Around the third course, Lucy started keeping an eye out for
Adolpho. His uniform was white, while all the others servers
wore brown.

She remembered a text from Heather ordering her to
"charm the fuck out of her," but it was hard to concentrate. *Is
my father rubbing off on me?*

After dessert Lucy told Frances that her house was simply
divine, and that she would certainly design a hat solely for her.

"That would be lovely. Something a little more understated.
I don't want anything that will take away from my face."

Honey, you need to take away from that face as much as you can,
came Alan's voice inside her head. She was giddy from the

meaty Cabernet, which the servers never let fall below the apex of the antique crystal goblets.

"Of course. Well, it was an amazing dinner. Good night," Lucy said with a smile, then added underneath her breath, "I've got to go fuck your butler madly."

"What?"

Oh my god. Get a hold of yourself.

"Oh, nothing. I'm looking forward to seeing my daddy."

Frances looked at her strangely but was quickly distracted by a brown jacket filling her coffee.

Lucy excused herself and stepped into a library, took out the international phone Garret had given her, and placed a long-overdue call to her mother. She answered on the first ring and Lucy said, "Hey! I'm in Italy!"

"What?"

"Yes, Milan."

"Well, Lucy, nothing shocks me anymore with you. I got your message—you are starting your own fashion line?"

"I think so. I'm not sure. I'm having one of Garret's lawyer friends look over the contract."

"That's so exciting!"

"I know, I'm freaking. But how are you, Mom?"

"Well, I'm good. I still want a drink or a pill every day but it's been over three months now. You have a sober mom. Whoopee."

"You can't know how good that makes me feel. And Stanley?"

"He's in the other room. He's fine. How is Mr. Millward taking it?"

Lucy thought of George's normally cool and distant eyes, how they softened in front of her, as if she generated a heat that melted him from within. She gently touched the binding of some old plays that lined the library shelves.

"Not very well. Someone is going to have to stay with him for a while, and I'm afraid it's not going to be Garret. The chasm between them is too wide. He likes me, though, I can tell. And it feels nice to have a grandfather, you know?"

"Yes, of course, I'm glad. Well, please send him my best, if he remembers me."

Lucy checked to see if she still had the beeper.

"I will, Mom. Take care, love you."

"OK, you too. Be safe!"

Lucy hung up and thought: *I think she's letting me go.*

She placed one more call to Oliver's assistant and arranged to meet with him in the morning back in London. Then she snuck back upstairs to her room and immediately buzzed Adolpho. He arrived in minutes and whispered through the cracked door.

"I will be finished in about one hour. Can you wait for me?"

"Sure. But why are you whispering?" she asked.

"I don't know!"

Lucy spread all her designs out on the quilted bedspread. She couldn't even imagine them actualized yet. She dozed off and Adolpho woke her when he came back. His gloves were already off.

"Now, here I am. What can I do for you, Miss Walker?"

"Take it all off," Lucy said groggily.

"The pleasure is mine."

He locked the door and stepped back over to the bed. She watched him remove his uniform, folding each item and placing it on the chair. Then he crawled next to Lucy on the bed, his socks still on. Her heart gained speed.

She touched Adolpho's taut skin and buried her face into his thick black hair. She kissed random places until she reached his big lips. Time became suspended.

Adolpho started with her arms, then her knees and everything in between. Lucy did not think of her dead grandmother, her gay father, her impending fashion deal, her troubled grandfather, or her recovering mother. She was simply taken on an ethereal, jaw-dropping ride.

When she came, he grabbed her head and kissed her, the whole time staring intensely into her eyes. As they lay still, catching their breath, Lucy was trying not to smile. *This will be something I'll remember forever.*

As if planned, his buzzer went off and he popped up and frantically put his uniform back on, giggling the whole time.

Even in her state of euphoria, she once again saw a flash of George's face, a cold animal waiting to come inside. Right then, something clicked inside Lucy's brain.

"What am I doing here?" she said to no one in particular.

"Looking sweaty," Adolpho said, smiling.

"I can't do this . . . I can't do this hat line. It's the wrong timing. He needs me. George needs me. He's my grandfather. Besides, I don't want Heather's name on my hats, they're my hats. . . . I've been working on them for two years. Something is sketchy with her anyway; I just don't know what. And Frances, she's, well, she's kind of freaky."

Adolpho giggled again.

Lucy got up on her elbows. "My mother will probably never forgive me and neither will Garret, especially because Garret still hates George, but that's not my story, that's not my pain. I think what I need to do is help this poor man, he has nothing really, except me."

Lucy looked up at Adolpho standing over her, the tiny black trail of hair leading down from his belly glistening with moisture.

"You don't understand me, do you?" She asked.

"In more ways than you know," he answered, buttoning his shirt. He kissed her lightly on the forehead and snuck out of the room like a mischievous child, still putting on his coat.

———

LUCY SAID GOOD-BYE to Frances the next morning as if everything was in order, but she was still unsure. One thing she knew was that she wanted Adolpho's number, which was actually the home of his mother—figured.

Frances was clueless; thankfully their romance seemed to slip by her unnoticed. "I am so glad to have met you," she said, fanning herself with a Sotheby's brochure. "Although there is something, dare I say, *green* about you, I can tell you have a great spirit. I like to meet every designer I fund face to face, you see."

"Yes, of course," Lucy replied. "I look forward to both of us attaining greatness."

Where did that come from?

58

GARRET SAT ACROSS from his father, watching him methodically fill in the crosswords. As long as he could remember, his father had been lost in those puzzles. Focusing on words that he supposed were different than the ones he wanted to say, the ones in his heart. Garret wanted to use the words that were in his own heart, but where would he begin? Probably with a *fuck you*, but that wasn't a good start, considering.

He was halfway up the stairs when he heard his father's voice.

"You ready to let her go?"

Garret turned around and looked at him, his mind a swirl of sharp thoughts, ammunition ready to be hurled at him. But all he could say was, "Who? Mum?"

"No, Lucy."

"I'll never let her go, that's the thing. Not like you did." He shook his head and started back up the stairs. There was something about parents that no matter how old you were, they still made you feel like a child.

George stood up and put down his beloved crossword, started pacing a little. "Garret. I wondered if you could help me order some wine. I've got the catalogue, but well, your mum used to do it. And I know you're quite knowledgeable."

This is how it happens? All of a sudden we just start talking to each other?

He stared at his father and realized he was sincere—he really wanted the help. In the way he paced and swung his arms a little, Garret saw himself. He had an impulse to run into his arms, but instead he just smiled and said, "I'll look at it in the morning."

George nodded his head slightly as he sat back down.

Garret sat outside the door to his old room and thought about Mitchell, wondered if this was all some sort of payback. His mother was gone. How long would his father last? And why was Lucy talking so crazy in London?

He crept inside and got into bed. Alan sleepily turned and cradled Garret's body against his own. Garret was turned on, but not by Alan. He was thinking about Oliver, and the bike messengers, and countless others. Sex with Alan was lovely, but in a nurturing, tender way. The others held a more carnal attraction. Becoming a father was one thing, but going into a monogamous relationship? Yes, being with Alan at the beach house was splendid and felt comfortable and right. But now, suddenly, he wasn't sure if he could really pull it off. On top of that, he felt ashamed to be thinking about promiscuous sex at a time like this. But it was common to feel prurient in times of death—as devious as his acts may have seemed, they provided a chance to connect with another person in the world, in arguably the most intimate and fearless manner. He remembered after 9/11 in New York, he kept hearing moans and passionate cries in his building, and how in general people held onto each other, stood closer, had sex more. Human contact seemed crucial to survival. Garret felt like that all the time, and it didn't matter if he knew the person—it was just a moment in time that screamed *you are not alone.*

He slowly got up to go to the bathroom, shut the door and turned on the water, put his hand under his boxer briefs, and let out his already grown erection. He thought twice about going in and waking up Alan, but it was too late. His mind became a fast-cutting montage of his previous escapades and he stroked himself until he released into the sink and washed it down the drain.

———

THE NEXT DAY Alan and Garret took a long walk to the same cliff that Garret had walked with his father on that cold day in December years ago. He loathed it when people used the word, but he needed *closure*.

"As much as she annoys me, I don't know what I'd do if my mother died," Alan said, waving a stick he had picked up.

When they arrived, the fog looked ominous but beautiful. There was a heightened sense of danger in the air, with the crashing waves fifty feet below and no fence to hold anyone back.

Garret lit a cigarette as Alan fixed his scarf. He loved the way Alan looked after him, but hated it right now. He wanted space.

"I have to know something, dear," Alan said. "And now is as good a time as it's ever going to be to ask you."

Garret took a drag and slowly let the smoke out.

"I love you, Garret, I always have, but what I had with Mitchell was a lifetime, and I hope that we'll have a lifetime together, too, and fuck, what am I saying?"

Garret felt his stomach rumble. "What is it?"

Alan's face started to get all red and patchy. "Did he say any-thing?"

"Who?"

"Mitchell. That morning. I know you said he was in a rush, but did you talk? What was the last thing he said?"

At that moment, smoking in the fog, Garret didn't care. The

truth was all that mattered. "I have replayed that morning over and over in my head."

"I'll bet you have."

"Alan, this is not a time for a bloody joke. Not the sex. I have tried to find the reason why, the catalyst, what the fuck in bloody hell we were thinking."

"He always had a crush on you."

"Alan, he was mad about you. Everyone knew it. We flirted with each other, as did you and I, let us not forget."

"You're getting off the subject. What did he say?" Alan prodded.

"He said that he couldn't wait to get to Paris with you."

"Garret, I'm not a half-wit." Alan started walking closer to the edge of the cliff. The fog sporadically blocked Garret's view of him. Alan threw the stick off and Garret ran up to him.

"OK, he said something about his lack of hygiene. That you'd be able to tell."

"What?" Alan asked.

"You know how he was always very hygienic."

"His teeth were blinding."

They laughed nervously. Garret felt himself sinking, losing strength. He briefly wondered how much time it would take to reach the sea, if the ride would be suspended like in the movies. "Will you ever forgive me? I mean, really?"

"I think that I will, Garret. I may already have, but don't push it."

They stood in silence, the white mist enveloping them, and eventually moved closer to keep warm.

59

OVER PEANUTS and a ginger ale on the flight back to London, Lucy wrote down the pros and the cons of going through with the deal. They were about even, but slightly weighted by the pros due to Lucy having a salary that would enable her to travel more and buy all the things that tempted her from the glossy windows of Manhattan's finest boutiques. She tried to calculate what that kind of salary would mean on a weekly basis, and the numbers were more than she could have imagined. Maybe someday she could even buy her mother a new car.

She landed and took a taxi to Oliver's office in the fashionable part of London's East End. It was like parts of Brooklyn—once industrial and barren and now dotted with hip cafés and artistic youth.

The office was in a converted loft. The assistant brought her water and sat her down on a leather couch opposite Oliver, who was sexy and sly with dark brown spiky hair and a small cleft on his chin. She could immediately see why her father "shagged" him. He thumbed through the pages of the contract, then put it down and rested his hand under his chin. Lucy desperately wanted him to say the deal was bad. It would be so much easier to blame someone else for passing it up.

"The deal is solid," Oliver said. "I have a few requests, but—"

"Like?"

"Well, she has you locked in for five years. I'd cut it to three with some sort of option clause. And you should have final approval on the product. I'll fax the requests directly to her."

"Thank you very much," she said and took the contract back from him. "I have to go up north to see my grandfather now."

"Mr. Good Heavens?"

How did he know about that?

"Yes." Lucy realized that her hands were shaking.

"Are you alright?" Oliver asked.

"Not really."

They stood up and Oliver took his large hand and placed it on the small of her back and led her out into a greenhouse attached to his office. It was bright and verdant and smelled of fertility, of beginnings. Oliver started to water the plants.

"When I have to make a big decision, I usually come out here. It's a bit soothing isn't it?"

"Yes." It was so cute to see such a hot guy caring for the plants. She could see why her mom, and countless others, had fallen for gay guys. She was determined, however, not to let it happen to her.

"You're young, Lucy. This decision is not going to make or break you."

Lucy touched the soft pedal of an orange flower. "Well, that's not what a lot of people think."

Oliver put down his water pitcher and said, "What do you think?"

Lucy closed her eyes. She thought of Adolpho's lips on her collarbone, Frances's intense face, Heather's pushy voice, Garret crying in Regent Park. "I don't know, Oliver. I really don't know."

He walked over and gave her a hug. They agreed to sleep on it, and Oliver had his driver take her to the train station.

———

WHEN LUCY ARRIVED at the house up north, no one was there, except George, still in his spot on the couch. She heated some soup, ladled two bowls, and set one in front of him. He ate it with vigor.

"I'm going to stay here for a while," Lucy said, "if that's OK with you."

George froze mid-bite, and then slowly put his spoon down.

"Honestly?" he asked quietly.

"Honestly. I think it would be good for you to have me around . . . at least for the next few months."

George did something Lucy had never seen him do, or even knew he was capable of doing. He didn't make a sound, but tears gathered and fell.

Lucy got up and stood behind him, hesitated, then awkwardly put her arms around him. He stopped, inhaled a deep breath, and picked the spoon back up. Lucy handed him his handkerchief from his own pocket and sat back down.

He took another spoonful. "Good soup. I'm keen on it."

Lucy's phone beeped. Heather Bridges had called five times and she had not returned her call.

"Popular girl," George said.

Lucy turned off her cell phone and got up to stretch. George finished his soup and carefully put the bowl down.

"You're going to have to move from there, you know," Lucy said.

George grunted.

"And where the hell are Dad and Alan?" She asked.

"Walk."

"Well, if I'm going to stay here, you're also going to have to do more than one-word answers."

"They've gone for a walk."

"That's better. Now, let's get you upstairs."

Lucy led her grandfather up the stairs and into the bathroom.

"You've probably got days' worth in there, so take your time."

Lucy went downstairs and onto the porch, looking for Garret and Alan. After she didn't hear anything for a while she went back upstairs and saw that the bathroom door was slightly open. George was on the floor in a crouched position, crying with no sound again. Lucy gathered him up to his knees, smoothed her hand up and down his back.

"It's OK. Don't cry." Lucy felt inept. *Why do people say that? It never helps.*

She got him up and into his bed and kissed his forehead.

As she left, he said, "Lucy."

"Yes?"

"Ta."

WHEN LUCY CAME downstairs, Alan and Garret had returned, looking like they were in shock.

"Where is he?" Garret asked.

"In bed. Peed like a racehorse too."

Alan pointed at the empty soup bowls and said, "How did you get him to eat?"

"He likes me, you know," Lucy said.

"We didn't know you were home, Goose. How was Frances Bean?" Garret asked while giving her a hug.

"Kind of strange."

"You think?" Alan said, plopping himself down on the couch.

"I could hear your commentary in my head, actually," Lucy said to Alan. "She likes my designs, and the trip was completely exciting, but I . . . I don't think I'm even going through with it."

"What?" they both said in unison.

Lucy gathered the bowls to take them into the kitchen. "I don't think I'm going to do it right now. I think I'm going to stay here with George."

Garret sat down and let his head fall into his hands. "You're not serious, Lucy."

Alan's eyes widened in horror.

Lucy looked at the both of them. "I've never been more serious in my life."

"What about your hats, Lucy, your big break?" Alan pleaded.

"They're not even putting my name on them. I think I can do it myself later. I don't want to rush into anything." She put the bowls into the sink and returned to the living room. Just like in Regent Park, by saying the words she was convincing herself. "If this opportunity came to me so fast, there is no reason why I can't find my own funding and do it my way." She folded the crossword and placed the pencil beside it. "Besides, George needs me."

"What about your life, with us in New York?" Garret's voice seemed up an octave.

"Jesus, you guys, it will only be for a while. Besides, after Mitchell's estate was settled, you've been at the beach house a lot."

Garret stood and threw up his arms, made an exasperated

noise, and left briskly through the front door, letting it slam behind him.

Alan patted the couch next to him so Lucy would sit down. "Please, please say you'll give this a little more thought. Your collection—"

"My hats will always be there; George will not—and he's my family, don't you get it? I'm not going to leave him here alone like Garret will do."

"That is so not fair."

"Yeah, well, guess what? Life's not fair."

Alan gave up and went out after Garret.

Dusk had descended. From the window, she could see Garret venting at Alan in the diffused light of the front walkway. Lucy went back up to check on George, who had been looking out the window as well. Without turning around, he knew she was there.

"They're not too keen on you staying," George said, still looking out at them.

Lucy walked over to him, gently took his wrist, and guided him back into bed.

"It's not their choice."

"Right," George said. "You're a woman now?"

"Well, yes, I guess." She pulled the covers up to his neck.

"You know, Garret's heart has already been broken once," George said.

"Yes, thanks to your extraordinary sensitivity," Lucy reminded him.

"I'm talking about the sixth grade."

George turned on his side and Lucy cut the light.

"Would you mind just sitting in that chair for a few moments?" he asked quietly.

"Not at all. But once you start snoring, I'm gone."

THE NEXT MORNING was bright and cloudless, and Lucy went out for a walk before anyone was up. She made it to the cliff, wondering how in the world her cell phone worked up there in the middle of nowhere. She finally checked Heather's messages. She closed her eyes and let the sun warm her, gathering the fortitude to return the call.

Thankfully, she got voicemail.

"Hi, Heather, it's Lucy. Sorry it's taken me a while to return your call . . . the cell phones are crazy up here. I'm afraid I'm going to have to wait on the offer for a while. I appreciate everything you've done for me, but I need to stay with my grandfather until he gets through this. It could be weeks or it could be months. . . ."

She couldn't believe she was saying this.

Is this going to be a decision that will haunt me forever?

". . . but I'd be willing to talk again at that time, whenever it may be. I really hope you understand. Call me. Bye."

She hung up and spun around. She started running back to the house, and saw Alan outside on the porch, smoking.

"You're smoking?"

"Well, your father's gone a bit cold on me so I need some oral fixation," Alan said.

"I know you guys think I'm crazy, Alan, but it's something I feel. This is where I need to be right now."

"Well, I do admire your courage, always have. Your father—that's another story."

"I'm going in."

Garret was on the couch drinking coffee. Lucy came in and

took a sip of it, then said, "You're going to talk to him, right? You're leaving in an hour. Please."

"It's not him I'm worried about. It's you, Lucy."

"We all need to be forgiven. You, too. Just be behind me on this. I need you to."

Garret moaned a little. "I'll try. But I still want you to think about it. It's not too late."

"OK. But go upstairs. Please?"

Lucy smiled as she watched her father slowly ascend the stairs.

60

GARRET ENTERED his parents' bedroom and could still smell his mother. He felt hot around his neck. His father was reading, and didn't close the book until Garret sat down. He knew it was time, and he let the words out in a clear, steady tone.

"For all those years that you didn't speak to me, I never told people that I had a father. So, in a way, I shut you out of my life as well. Maybe there was something I could have done, but I didn't. I felt so rejected. And for years I acted in ways that erased that rejection . . . and I succeeded, for quite a long time. But then I found Lucy, you see, and everything changed. And I love her with a heart I never even knew I had. I just want you to know that she has just been offered a chance of a lifetime and she is giving it up to be with you. I lost Mum, too, Pop, and now I'm about to lose Lucy to the same person that shunned me because I—"

"Alright!" George threw the book down. "That's enough. Just . . . just leave me alone now."

Garret grunted.

Typical.

He got up to leave, but his father's shaky voice stopped him in his tracks.

"She doesn't have to stay. None of you do."

Garret looked at his father.

"Well, at least you're talking to me now," Garret said.

"It's a start."

"Yes, it certainly is."

He had always known it, but now he really felt it. It was George's problem, not his. His throat seemed to open and the hotness around his neck disappeared. It occurred to him that he didn't really need his father. Why should he have to make the effort? He started to leave again, and George sat up.

"Wait. Now that she's gone, I . . . sit down, please. . . ."

Garret sat down and stared out the window. The neighbor's dog was sleeping in the shade, oblivious to the world.

"Isn't there something you did that you'll always regret?" George asked.

Mitchell, Garret thought, but didn't say it, just nodded his head.

"Maybe you're just like me," George concluded, as if the notion had just entered his brain.

"As scary as that is to me right now, I just may be." Garret drew a circle with his finger on the dusty window. "I ordered the wine for you." He stood once again and made his way toward the stairs. "Good-bye, Pop."

"She loved you more than me," George said.

Garret turned around. "If that's supposed to invoke pity—"

"No, no. She didn't want you to know. I almost called you. I dialed even. It was her only request not to tell you she was sick. I had to, I couldn't . . ."

Suddenly Garret wanted to wrap him in his arms. Instead, he put up his hands. "It's OK, it's OK."

"You know, everywhere we went she would talk about you," George said, looking through the circle Garret had drawn on the window.

"Yeah? And what would you do, cringe?"

"Well, sometimes, yes. And I'm angry about that now. Angry at the world too, at whatever it was that made you—"

"Nothing made me gay, Pop, don't you get it? I just am!" Garret had never raised his voice to his father, and the following silence was bone chilling.

Eventually, Garret walked over to the bed and placed his hand on his George's chest. It was the first time he had touched him in years. His father's heart was going double-time.

"I'm not sorry anymore," Garret said.

"Don't be."

George stared at his son with a look that Garret remembered from a long time ago. He tried to soak it in. He wanted to carry it with him.

After a minute, George patted the bed next to him and Garret sat there. Words seemed like adhesives not strong enough to cover the holes or hold together the broken pieces. For now it was about letting warmth in. Garret's shoulder was two inches from his father's and that was enough. Silence, and warmth.

A little while later Garret spoke without turning toward his father. "Don't let her stay, Pop. It's not about me and it's not about you. For her sake, don't let her stay."

61

AFTER SEEING GARRET and Alan off, Lucy went inside and probed around the house. Everything was so quaint and perfectly placed, as if it had been there forever. She went over to Dorothy's knitting table and opened up a drawer, and there, sitting on top of a pile like an exposed secret, was a picture of Garret and her mother. In the picture, Joyce looked like she was about to explode with happiness. Garret looked cool and collected as always. *I was probably in her stomach then*, she thought with a shudder. She slipped the picture into her jacket pocket.

George descended the stairs looking groomed—his hair was slicked back and he was freshly shaven.

Lucy got out a pad and pencil. "OK, you're going to have to tell me what you eat. I'm going to the store."

"The market?"

"Yeah, the market."

George rattled off some ingredients while he sat down with the new crossword that Lucy had set out for him. He moved as if there was more heat in his bones.

"OK, I'm off," Lucy said.

Halfway down the driveway, she realized she had forgotten her cell phone. When she returned to get it, she could see through the cracked door that George was using it. She watched him walk back and forth, his body in what seemed like a state of anxiety. He turned toward the door and Lucy ducked so he wouldn't see her.

She scooted off the porch and headed toward the market. An

older woman who was walking her dog gave Lucy a big smile, and she noticed the hat she was wearing—it was eggplant-colored and adorned with small white beads. She imagined it being a hat that she designed.

The market was empty except for a small boy who played with a jar of lollipops, rearranging them as if they were a vase of flowers. Lucy found almost everything that George had requested and paid the shopkeeper, a man with a long beard. The boy looked up at her and said, "You from around these parts?"

"Can I get back to you on that one?" Lucy asked.

The boy unwrapped one of the lollipops and said, "I suppose so," and stuck it into his mouth.

On the walk home she saw a flock of small birds circling above the old schoolhouse. She stopped and stared at them, thinking that she could actually stay there for a while—even though she had barely known Garret a year, she realized that this was where her roots were. Part of her had been growing here the whole time.

AFTER LUCY UNPACKED the groceries she took a long shower. While drying herself, she heard someone humming and realized it had to be her grandfather. She put on a robe and started to look through some of Dorothy's summer clothes that were stored in the attic. For the most part they were outdated and too big for her, but she found one item she loved: a thin, pale green sweater with one pink rose embroidered at the point of the V on the collar.

Lucy went downstairs and made a big salad and some baked beans, and she and George ate on the couch, watching *The Office*.

"Dorothy never liked to eat on the couch," George said.

"Well, I'm not Dorothy, am I?"

"No, but you're wearing her sweater."

"Very observant," Lucy said.

"It suits you."

"Thanks." When the show went to a commercial, Lucy asked him why he was using her cell phone.

He got up and turned the TV off and sat facing her, straddling the foot cushion. It seemed an odd choice for such an old man. His face was twitching, and his eyes were blinking fast.

"What is it, Grandpa?"

"I tried to call your . . . your boss. But I couldn't get the bloody phone to work." A flash of embarrassment passed through his face.

"What?"

"So I called Garret instead. He's going to sort it out. Listen," he said, looking up at the ceiling as if trying to gain strength, "I am so very flattered you want to stay here, but I won't have it. I can't . . ."

"George, it's not the end of the world."

"No, it's the beginning. For you."

"Did Garret put you up—"

"Shh. We're going to watch the rest of this show, and then we're going to do the washing up, and tomorrow will be a new day."

———

THE NEXT MORNING Lucy went downstairs and the house was eerily quiet. She looked outside and saw a gentleman standing next to a taxi.

God, he really was serious. Now?

Lucy walked outside, where George was paying the driver.

"Grandpa, what are you doing?"

"It's all arranged; you're going to New York. You'd better hurry," George said.

"Are you on crack?"

"Good heavens, no, haven't even had a scotch. Let's go, young lady."

"Grandpa, I told—"

"Listen," George said. "Garret arranged it all. You are still going to your meeting and taking the offer, and I'm going to come in a few days. I spoke to Alan this morning."

"But your life is here," Lucy said.

"Was, dear, was here."

Something about George's face made Lucy jump into his arms. It seemed like a perfect plan. The taxi driver smiled.

"Whoa, hold on there, child. Don't disable me before I get there!"

Lucy dashed inside, threw her stuff in her bag, slipped on the green sweater, muttered a "good-bye" to the attic, grabbed her hat renderings, and leaped down the stairs.

62

AFTER THEIR PLANE landed in New York, Garret lost Alan in the terminal for a bit and they reunited in baggage claim. The belt wasn't moving so they took a seat and Alan flipped through the paper.

Alan put the paper on his lap and tilted his head. "I spoke to your father."

"What?" Garret asked. "I'm thrilled he came around about Lucy, but now he's calling my boyfriend?"

"I had your Blackberry. I was thinking, since I own the beach house, and we have your place in the city, my apartment is empty. The lease isn't up for a few months. Why don't we put him there? Then Lucy can still visit him. Best of both worlds."

As much as he wanted to agree, Garret was skeptical. "Well, aren't you just full of bright ideas."

"Garret, it's just a thought," Alan said, getting back to his paper.

"Well, let's get Lucy on track first."

The buzzer went off and they stepped toward the belt. Alan put his hand on Garret's shoulder and for a brief instant, Garret felt claustrophobic.

When their bags flopped down at the same time, Alan said, "Look! His and his!"

ON THE CURB, Garret announced that he was going into the city and not to the beach house as they had planned.

Alan started to object but just nodded his head instead. "You need space, I get it."

Garret kissed Alan and they got into separate taxis.

On the ride into the city, Garret thought of his mum in the red dress at the restaurant, laughing on the old bike on the country road. He felt the urge to sob like a newborn, but he felt numb. Seeing the skyline from Queens, he could feel the sexual draw of New York—his former habits beckoning him to escape it all.

He dropped his stuff off at the apartment and, against his better judgment, went for a drink at one of his old stomping grounds in Chelsea. The young men, mostly ethnic types in tight T-shirts and the latest jeans, looked him over. Their dark eyes and sly faces seemed so hungry. He sat down and ordered a double.

"Hey, sexy, where've you been?"

It was Joshua, the stagehand. He looked high on something.

"Going mad. Wanna come?" Garret said.

"Sure."

To the soundtrack of uninspired house music, Garret swilled his drink while Joshua just stared. He threw a bill on the bar and led Joshua into the back room and started kissing him, the alcohol surging into his bloodstream. His cock pressed against his jeans as he burrowed Joshua's head into the curve of his neck. *Kiss me. Wipe it away. Hurry.*

Joshua started to bite Garret's ear and he liked it. He wanted anything to deaden the pain. He tried to kiss Joshua again but kept seeing Alan's face, and Mitchell's, and his father's . . .

"Fuck!" he yelled and pushed Joshua away and streamlined

his way out of the bar. He managed to yell back "Sorry" over the cheesy beat.

He ran all the way back to his apartment and called a car service. He took off his sweaty clothes and quickly showered. When the driver arrived, he told him, "East Hampton, as fast as you can."

The driver asked if everything was all right.

"Oh, just dandy," Garret said, and then laughed in spite of it all.

Two hours later they pulled into the driveway. The house looked like it had always been there, nestled in a large dune. The moon's light was strong and the waves stirred in the distance. Garret paid the driver and crept inside. Alan was asleep on the couch with Tramp and some melted ice cream at his side.

"I love you," he said to a sleeping Alan. "I hate your cat, and I want you to lose some more weight, and I almost just cheated on you, but I love you. I really, really do. And I want my mum back . . ."

The tears were silent, like his father's. After a while, he got Alan up and led him into the bedroom. The ocean's lap over the dune felt like the soothing words of a friend.

"The city?" Alan said sleepily.

"I belong here," Garret said softly. "With you."

He pulled the covers over him.

"I'm glad," Alan said, "that you came."

63

LUCY WAS SO ANXIOUS on the flight back that she took a pill Alan had given her. When she arrived, she got a frappuccino to wake herself up and took a cab directly to Heather's building. It was after hours, so Gina and the crew were gone— just cleaning people and a few of her staff pulling all-nighters. In the conference room, Heather sat with three board members. Lucy couldn't believe they were all assembled because of her. She sat down and gently fingered the rose on Dorothy's sweater.

She looked each person in the eye as she spoke.

"This is all very exciting to me, obviously, but I was thinking in the cab over here. . . . I have . . . reservations about my name being excluded from the product. After all, they are my hats."

One of Heather's board members smiled; another gave nothing away. Heather waited for her to continue.

"So this is what I have devised. After a year, if my line does well, we incorporate my name into the label. How does 'Bridgewalk' sound to you all?"

A representative of Frances Bean perked up from the corner. "Actually, it's very fitting for a hat line."

All the board members looked at Lucy as if they wanted some of her balls. To the slight rolling of Heather's eyes, they agreed to Lucy's stipulation.

GEORGE FLEW IN the next day, and after settling him in Alan's apartment, Lucy took him to the City Grill to celebrate. They shared a martini.

"Are you sure you'll be OK here?" Lucy asked him.

"Listen, I wanted a way out of that house too. At least for now. I may be able to go back but . . . how could I live among all those memories?"

"What about your friends?" Lucy asked.

"What friends? Dorothy was all I had, aside from a few hunting mates." George sipped the martini. "Ooh, strong."

"Well, now you have Jose, Consuela's nephew. I saw you talking soccer with him."

"Football. Nice chap, that one."

Two cute guys sat down at the table next to them. They hid behind the menu and kissed each other. George squinted and Lucy put her hand on his arm. "Hey, you're in Manhattan now . . . in some neighborhoods you'll be the minority."

George looked over at the two guys with what seemed like pity.

"Maybe you can get a job?" Lucy asked.

"You don't worry about me. You get ready for your new career." George smiled and handed her the glass. "Besides, the *New York Times* crossword is something else entirely. I'll have my hands full."

Lucy noticed George had been carrying a small bag with him and asked him what was in it.

"It's just something I want you to have."

Lucy opened the package and there, folded neatly, was the red dress she had picked out for Dorothy.

———

AFTER DINNER, they walked uptown. The smell of curry wafted out of the windows, and someone was practicing scales on a sax. They passed a beautiful woman whose skin was the color of the night, with a bright green parrot on her shoulder.

"New York is like nowhere on earth," Lucy said.

"Yes," George agreed. "And from what I remember you can always get a decent Reuben sandwich, even in the middle of the night."

Lucy said good-bye to him on Alan's stoop. "My cell phone number is on the counter. And the bakery over there has killer bread."

"You mean it's fatal?"

"No, we've had enough death for a while."

George's eyes glazed over. "You sure you can get back to Garret's on your own?"

"It's a mind-set. I'm fine. You just walk like you're meant to be here and no one bothers you," Lucy said.

"OK, well, call me when you get there."

"You won't be asleep by then?"

George wiped his forehead and sighed.

"I tell you what, just let it ring twice, then I'll know it's you."

"You got it."

Lucy kissed him on the cheek and made her way back into the night. She held the dress against her chest, as if protecting it.

64

FALL CAME QUICKLY. The air was suddenly crisp and the once green leaves started to become infused with reds and yellows. Garret and Alan went into the city to see a new play by a writer they had previously worked with, and afterward they walked to Orso, where the chef brought out special courses in between the ones they had ordered. Alan passed on the fried oysters. As they were leaving, Garret did a little dance to Justin Timberlake's "Sexy Back," which was playing in the bar area.

"Doesn't he know that sexy never left?" Alan said.

"Apparently not," Garret said, kissing Alan's neck.

Instead of heading back to the Hamptons, they decided to crash at Garret's place and check up on Lucy. As they ascended the stairs, they heard music and laughter. Garret's face drained of color. *Who was in there with Lucy?*

They opened the door and Lucy jumped on him and said, "Dad!"

Garret peeked around and saw George in a T-shirt and boxers.

"Pop?" Garret said, putting Lucy down.

Alan looked at Garret. "I was meaning to tell you. Lucy set him up at my place; Consuela let them in."

"Moving fast, aren't we?" Garret said. It was peculiar to see his father in his apartment, but nothing was really shocking anymore. Life had leveled.

They all looked at each other, not quite sure how they got

there, but somehow knowing they were in the right place. Garret thought of the time he had played the princess in the school play and after the performance, the teacher gave him an extra basket of goodies for being a good sport. On the way home, he had given one of the goodie baskets to the bus driver's daughter, who was a little slow. The girl's face expanded into a smile and the bus driver went a special way to drop Garret off first. That was the first time Garret realized there wasn't always a way to figure out why things happened in the world. Sometimes it was just about following an instinct. And though he had spent a lot of time dwelling on why he was a certain way or how things transpired in the fashion they did, he knew it would sort itself out. He looked at Alan's soft eyes, at Lucy's dangling feet, at his father's skinny legs, and thought, *We are all a part of each other.*

ALAN WENT TO THE BAR and opened a bottle of champagne and poured everyone a little. "Mitchell used to say that champagne was the nectar of the gods."

They all raised their glasses and sipped. Garret walked over to the picture frame with Trevor still inside it and turned it face down. He looked up at the orange wall and grinned.

Alan walked over to Garret and rested his head on his shoulder, cupped his hand around his waist.

George winced.

"What?" Lucy asked.

Garret and Alan separated.

"I'm . . . I'm sorry . . ." George said.

"For what?" Alan asked.

"You're a good man, Alan; you both are." George took a

long gulp and continued. "And the truth is, I'm still not okay with it. But I'm going to try."

A silence fell over the room and everyone stared at their bubbles.

"And if you don't mind, I'll be around—at least for a bit," George said.

Garret sat down, leaned his head back, and closed his eyes.

Lucy hugged her knees to her chest.

Alan smiled and walked over to George. He started to put his hand on George's shoulder, but pulled it back and just stood close behind him.

At that moment, they were all a part of something much, much bigger.

Acknowledgments

I MUST FIRST THANK Simon Lupini (the little wolf) for a wonderful evening on Freedom Street in Battersea, where my love affair with England began. Michael Aisner for introducing me to Tyler Gatchell and Mark Shannon, who are both gone but as proof in this book, not forgotten; Amos and George for putting me up in Darbyshire; and Tony and Vaughan for a most memorable weekend in Brighton Beach.

For help with early drafts: Kate Gibson, Joseph Pittman, Mitchell Waters. To my publishing guru, Christopher Schelling—you rock my world. To my dear friend and mentor Stephen McCauley, I am so lucky to know you.

Mike Boone for "talking story" with me in Laguna Beach when the idea had just begun. Bill Candiloros for letting me nest in his flawless oceanside apartment in Ft. Lauderdale to work on what I thought at the time was my final draft. Yeah, right.

Augusten Burroughs and Robert Rodi for their encouragement and inspiration.

Katrina Van Pelt for her unwavering support of my artistic endeavors and for giving me the greatest gift in the world.

To my Mom, for being crazy in a good way and encouraging my dreams, and to Steve Swenson for being so kind, generous, and grounding.